J. J. Connington and ....

>>> This title is part of The Murder Room, our series dedicated to making available out-of-print or hard-to-find titles by classic crime writers.

Crime fiction has always held up a mirror to society. The Victorians were fascinated by sensational murder and the emerging science of detection; now we are obsessed with the forensic detail of violent death. And no other genre has so captivated and enthralled readers.

Vast troves of classic crime writing have for a long time been unavailable to all but the most dedicated frequenters of second-hand bookshops. The advent of digital publishing means that we are now able to bring you the backlists of a huge range of titles by classic and contemporary crime writers, some of which have been out of print for decades.

From the genteel amateur private eyes of the Golden Age and the femmes fatales of pulp fiction, to the morally ambiguous hard-boiled detectives of mid twentieth-century America and their descendants who walk our twenty-first century streets, The Murder Room has it all. **>>>**

The Murder Room
Where Criminal Minds Meet

themurderroom.com

J. J. Connington (1880–1947)

Alfred Walter Stewart, who wrote under the pen name J. J. Connington, was born in Glasgow, the youngest of three sons of Reverend Dr Stewart. He graduated from Glasgow University and pursued an academic career as a chemistry professor, working for the Admiralty during the First World War. Known for his ingenious and carefully worked-out puzzles and in-depth character development, he was admired by a host of his better-known contemporaries, including Dorothy L. Sayers and John Dickson Carr, who both paid tribute to his influence on their work. He married Jessie Lily Courts in 1916 and they had one daughter.

By J. J. Connington

**Sir Clinton Driffield
Mysteries**
Murder in the Maze
Tragedy at Ravensthorpe
The Case with Nine
    Solutions
Mystery at Lynden Sands
Nemesis at Raynham Parva
The Boathouse Riddle
The Sweepstake Murders
The Castleford Conundrum
The Ha-Ha Case
In Whose Dim Shadow
A Minor Operation
Murder Will Speak
Truth Comes Limping

The Twenty-One Clues
No Past is Dead
Jack-in-the-Box
Common Sense is All You
    Need

Supt Ross Mysteries
The Eye in the Museum
The Two Tickets Puzzle

Novels
Death at Swaythling Court
The Dangerfield Talisman
Tom Tiddler's Island
The Counsellor
The Four Defences

The Two Tickets Puzzle

J. J. Connington

An Orion book

This edition published by
The Orion Publishing Group Ltd
Orion House
5 Upper St Martin's Lane
London WC2H 9EA

An Hachette UK company
A CIP catalogue record for this book is available from the British Library

ISBN 978 1 4719 0629 9

www.orionbooks.co.uk

Printed and bound by CPI Group (UK) Ltd, Croydon, CR0 4YY

CONTENTS

Introduction by Curtis Evans   i

Chapter

    I. Romance and the 10.35   *page*   1

    II. The Prize Ram   12

    III. The Bullets   24

    IV. The Lens   41

    V. In Search of a Motive   53

    VI. The Lawyer's Evidence   77

    VII. The Bank   95

    VIII. The Passengers   103

    IX. The Doctor's Evidence   121

    X. The Marked Notes   136

    XI. Madge Winslow's Evidence   162

    XII. The Telegram   173

    XIII. The Car Snatchers   192

    XIV. The Two Tickets   208

    XV. The Keystone   219

    XVI. The Chink in the Armour   236

    XVII. The Pieces of the Puzzle   254

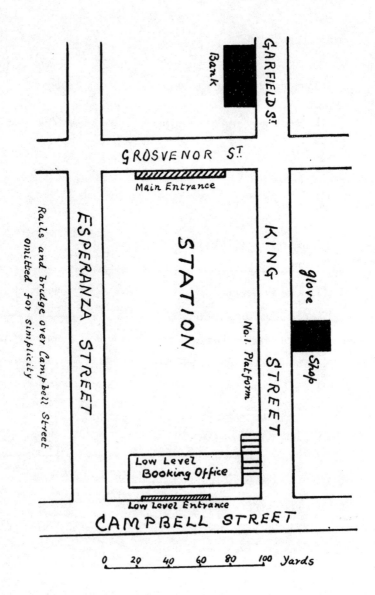

Introduction
by
Curtis Evans

During the Golden Age of the detective novel, in the 1920s and 1930s, J. J. Connington stood with fellow crime writers R. Austin Freeman, Cecil John Charles Street and Freeman Wills Crofts as the foremost practitioner in British mystery fiction of the science of pure detection. I use the word 'science' advisedly, for the man behind J. J. Connington, Alfred Walter Stewart, was an esteemed Scottish-born scientist. A 'small, unassuming, moustached polymath', Stewart was 'a strikingly effective lecturer with an excellent sense of humour, fertile imagination and fantastically retentive memory', qualities that also served him well in his fiction. He held the Chair of Chemistry at Queens University, Belfast for twenty-five years, from 1919 until his retirement in 1944.

During roughly this period, the busy Professor Stewart found time to author a remarkable apocalyptic science fiction tale, *Nordenholt's Million* (1923), a mainstream novel, *Almighty Gold* (1924), a collection of essays, *Alias J. J. Connington* (1947), and, between 1926 and 1947, twenty-four mysteries (all but one tales of detection), many of them sterling examples of the Golden Age puzzle-oriented detective novel at its considerable best. 'For those who ask first of all in a detective story for exact and mathematical accuracy in the construction of the plot', avowed a contemporary *London Daily Mail* reviewer, 'there is no author to equal the distinguished scientist who writes under the name of J. J. Connington.'[1]

Alfred Stewart's background as a man of science is reflected in his fiction, not only in the impressive puzzle plot mechanics he devised for his mysteries but in his choices of themes and depictions of characters. Along with Stanley Nordenholt of *Nordenholt's Million*, a novel about a plutocrat's pitiless efforts to preserve a ruthlessly remolded remnant of human life after a global environmental calamity, Stewart's most notable character is Chief Constable Sir Clinton Driffield, the detective in seventeen of the twenty-four Connington crime novels. Driffield is one of crime fiction's most highhanded investigators, occasionally taking on the functions of judge and jury as well as chief of police.

Absent from Stewart's fiction is the hail-fellow-well-met quality found in John Street's works or the religious ethos suffusing those of Freeman Wills Crofts, not to mention the effervescent novel-of-manners style of the British Golden Age Crime Queens Dorothy L. Sayers, Margery Allingham and Ngaio Marsh. Instead we see an often disdainful cynicism about the human animal and a marked admiration for detached supermen with superior intellects. For this reason, reading a Connington novel can be a challenging experience for modern readers inculcated in gentler social beliefs. Yet Alfred Stewart produced a classic apocalyptic science fiction tale in *Nordenholt's Million* (justly dubbed 'exciting and terrifying reading' by the *Spectator*) as well as superb detective novels boasting well-wrought puzzles, bracing characterization and an occasional leavening of dry humour. Not long after Stewart's death in 1947, the Connington novels fell entirely out of print. The recent embrace of Stewart's fiction by Orion's Murder Room imprint is a welcome event indeed, correcting as it does over sixty years of underserved neglect of an accomplished genre writer.

Born in Glasgow on 5 September 1880, Alfred Stewart had significant exposure to religion in his earlier life. His father was William Stewart, longtime Professor of Divinity and Biblical Criticism at Glasgow University, and he married Lily Coats, a daughter of the Reverend Jervis Coats and member of one of Scotland's preeminent Baptist families. Religious sensibility is entirely absent from the Connington corpus, however. A confirmed secularist, Stewart once referred to one of his wife's brothers, the Reverend William Holms Coats (1881–1954), principal of the Scottish Baptist College, as his 'mental and spiritual antithesis', bemusedly adding: 'It's quite an education to see what one would look like if one were turned into one's mirror-image.'

Stewart's J. J. Connington pseudonym was derived from a nineteenth-century Oxford Professor of Latin and translator of Horace, indicating that Stewart's literary interests lay not in pietistic writing but rather in the pre-Christian classics ('I prefer the *Odyssey* to *Paradise Lost*,' the author once avowed). Possessing an inquisitive and expansive mind, Stewart was in fact an uncommonly well-read individual, freely ranging over a variety of literary genres. His deep immersion in French literature and supernatural horror fiction, for example, is documented in his lively correspondence with the noted horologist Rupert Thomas Gould.[2]

iii

It thus is not surprising that in the 1920s the intellectually restless Stewart, having achieved a distinguished middle age as a highly regarded man of science, decided to apply his creative energy to a new endeavour, the writing of fiction. After several years he settled, like other gifted men and women of his generation, on the wildly popular mystery genre. Stewart was modest about his accomplishments in this particular field of light fiction, telling Rupert Gould later in life that 'I write these things [what Stewart called tec yarns] because they amuse me in parts when I am putting them together and because they are the only writings of mine that the public will look at. Also, in a minor degree, because I like to think some people get pleasure out of them.' No doubt Stewart's single most impressive literary accomplishment is *Nordenholt's Million*, yet in their time the two dozen J. J. Connington mysteries did indeed give readers in Great Britain, the United States and other countries much diversionary reading pleasure. Today these works constitute an estimable addition to British crime fiction.

After his 'prentice pastiche mystery, *Death at Swaythling Court* (1926), a rural English country-house tale set in the highly traditional village of Fernhurst Parva, Stewart published another, superior country-house affair, *The Dangerfield Talisman* (1926), a novel about the baffling theft of a precious family heirloom, an ancient, jewel-encrusted armlet. This clever, murderless tale, which likely is the one that the author told Rupert Gould he wrote in under six weeks, was praised in *The Bookman* as 'continuously exciting and interesting' and in the *New York*

Times Book Review as 'ingeniously fitted together and, what is more, written with a deal of real literary charm'. Despite its virtues, however, *The Dangerfield Talisman* is not fully characteristic of mature Connington detective fiction. The author needed a memorable series sleuth, more representative of his own forceful personality.

It was the next year, 1927, that saw J. J. Connington make his break to the front of the murdermongerer's pack with a third country-house mystery, *Murder in the Maze*, wherein debuted as the author's great series detective the assertive and acerbic Sir Clinton Driffield, along with Sir Clinton's neighbour and 'Watson', the more genial (if much less astute) Squire Wendover. In this much-praised novel, Stewart's detective duo confronts some truly diabolical doings, including slayings by means of curare-tipped darts in the double-centered hedge maze at a country estate, Whistlefield. No less a fan of the genre than T. S. Eliot praised *Murder in the Maze* for its construction ('we are provided early in the story with all the clues which guide the detective') and its liveliness ('The very idea of murder in a box-hedge labyrinth does the author great credit, and he makes full use of its possibilities'). The delighted Eliot concluded that *Murder in the Maze* was 'a really first-rate detective story'. For his part, the critic H. C. Harwood declared in *The Outlook* that with the publication of *Murder in the Maze* Connington demanded and deserved 'comparison with the masters'. 'Buy, borrow, or – anyhow – get hold of it', he amusingly advised. Two decades later, in his 1946 critical essay 'The Grandest Game in the World', the great locked-room detective novelist John Dickson Carr echoed Eliot's assessment of the novel's virtuoso setting, writing: 'These 1920s [. . .] thronged with sheer brains. What would be one of the best possible settings for violent death? J. J. Connington found the answer, with *Murder in the Maze*.' Certainly in retrospect *Murder in the Maze* stands as one of the finest English country-house mysteries of the 1920s, cleverly yet fairly clued, imaginatively detailed and often grimly suspenseful. As the great American true-crime writer Edmund Lester Pearson noted in his review of *Murder in the Maze* in *The Outlook*, this Connington novel had everything that one could desire in a detective story: 'A shrubbery maze, a hot day, and somebody potting at you with an air gun loaded with darts covered with a deadly South-American arrow-poison – *there* is a situation to wheedle two dollars out of anybody's pocket.'[3]

Staying with what had worked so well for him to date, Stewart the same year produced yet another country-house mystery, *Tragedy at Ravensthorpe*, an ingenious tale of murders and thefts at the ancestral home of the Chacewaters, old family friends of Sir Clinton Driffield. There is much clever matter in *Ravensthorpe*. Especially fascinating is the author's inspired integration of faerie folklore into his plot. Stewart, who had a lifelong – though skeptical – interest in paranormal phenomena, probably was inspired in this instance by the recent hubbub over the Cottingly Faeries photographs that in the early 1920s had famously duped, among other individuals, Arthur Conan Doyle.[4] As with *Murder in the Maze*, critics raved about this new Connington mystery. In the *Spectator*, for example, a reviewer hailed *Tragedy at Ravensthorpe* in the strongest terms, declaring of the novel: 'This is more than a good detective tale. Alike in plot, characterization, and literary style, it is a work of art.'

In 1928 there appeared two additional Sir Clinton Driffield detective novels, *Mystery at Lynden Sands* and *The Case with Nine Solutions*. Once again there was great praise for the latest Conningtons. H. C. Harwood, the critic who had so much admired *Murder in the Maze*, opined of *Mystery at Lynden Sands* that it 'may just fail of being the detective story of the century', while in the United States author and book reviewer Frederic F. Van de Water expressed nearly as high an opinion of *The Case with Nine Solutions*. 'This book is a thoroughbred of a distinguished lineage that runs back to "The Gold Bug" of [Edgar Allan] Poe,' he avowed. 'It represents the highest type of detective fiction.' In both of these Connington novels, Stewart moved away from his customary country-house milieu, setting *Lynden Sands* at a fashionable beach resort and *Nine Solutions* at a scientific research institute. *Nine Solutions* is of particular interest today, I think, for its relatively frank sexual subject matter and its modern urban setting among science professionals, which rather resembles the locales found in P. D. James' classic detective novels *A Mind to Murder* (1963) and *Shroud for a Nightingale* (1971).

By the end of the 1920s, J. J. Connington's critical reputation had achieved enviable heights indeed. At this time Stewart became one of the charter members of the Detection

Club, an assemblage of the finest writers of British detective fiction that included, among other distinguished individuals, Agatha Christie, Dorothy L. Sayers and G. K. Chesterton. Certainly Victor Gollancz, the British publisher of the J. J. Connington mysteries, did not stint praise for the author, informing readers that 'J. J. Connington is now established as, in the opinion of many, the greatest living master of the story of pure detection. He is one of those who, discarding all the superfluities, has made of deductive fiction a genuine minor art, with its own laws and its own conventions.'

Such warm praise for J. J. Connington makes it all the more surprising that at this juncture the esteemed author tinkered with his successful formula by dispensing with his original series detective. In the fifth Clinton Driffield detective novel, *Nemesis at Raynham Parva* (1929), Alfred Walter Stewart, rather like Arthur Conan Doyle before him, seemed with a dramatic dénouement to have devised his popular series detective's permanent exit from the fictional stage (read it and see for yourself). The next two Connington detective novels, *The Eye in the Museum* (1929) and *The Two Tickets Puzzle* (1930), have a different series detective, Superintendent Ross, a rather dull dog of a policeman. While both these mysteries are competently done – the railway material in *The Two Tickets Puzzle* is particularly effective and should have appeal today – the presence of Sir Clinton Driffield (no superfluity he!) is missed.

Probably Stewart detected that the public minded the absence of the brilliant and biting Sir Clinton, for the Chief Constable – accompanied, naturally, by his friend Squire

Wendover – triumphantly returned in 1931 in *The Boathouse Riddle*, another well-constructed criminous country-house affair. Later in the year came *The Sweepstake Murders*, which boasts the perennially popular tontine multiple-murder plot, in this case a rapid succession of puzzling suspicious deaths afflicting the members of a sweepstake syndicate that has just won nearly £250,000.[5] Adding piquancy to this plot is the fact that Wendover is one of the imperiled syndicate members. Altogether the novel is, as the late Jacques Barzun and his colleague Wendell Hertig Taylor put it in *A Catalogue of Crime* (1971, 1989), their magisterial survey of detective fiction, 'one of Connington's best conceptions'.

Stewart's productivity as a fiction writer slowed in the 1930s, so that, barring the year 1938, at most only one new Connington appeared annually. However, in 1932 Stewart produced one of the best Connington mysteries, *The Castleford Conundrum*. A classic country-house detective novel, Castleford introduces to readers Stewart's most delightfully unpleasant set of greedy relations and one of his most deserving murderees, Winifred Castleford. Stewart also fashions a wonderfully rich puzzle plot, full of meaty material clues for the reader's delectation. *Castleford* presented critics with no conundrum over its quality. 'In *The Castleford Conundrum* Mr Connington goes to work like an accomplished chess player. The moves in the games his detectives are called on to play are a delight to watch,' raved the reviewer for the *Sunday Times*, adding that 'the clues would have rejoiced Mr. Holmes' heart.' For its part, the *Spectator* concurred in the *Sunday Times*' assessment of the novel's masterfully constructed plot: 'Few detective stories show such sound reasoning as that by which the Chief Constable brings the crime home to the culprit.' Additionally, E. C. Bentley, much admired himself as the author of the landmark detective novel *Trent's Last Case*, took time to praise Connington's purely literary virtues, noting: 'Mr Connington has never written better, or drawn characters more full of life.'

With *Tom Tiddler's Island* in 1933 Stewart produced a different sort of Connington, a criminal-gang mystery in the rather more breathless style of such hugely popular English thriller writers as Sapper, Sax Rohmer, John Buchan and Edgar Wallace (in violation of the strict detective fiction rules of Ronald Knox, there is even a secret passage in the novel). Detailing the startling discoveries made by a newlywed couple honeymooning on a remote Scottish island, *Tom Tiddler's Island* is an atmospheric and entertaining tale, though it is not as mentally stimulating for armchair sleuths as Stewart's true detective novels. The title, incidentally, refers to an ancient British children's game, 'Tom Tiddler's Ground', in which one child tries to hold a height against other children.

After his fictional Scottish excursion into thrillerdom, Stewart returned the next year to his English country-house roots with *The Ha-Ha Case* (1934), his last masterwork in this classic mystery setting (for elucidation of non-British readers, a ha-ha is a sunken wall, placed so as to delineate property boundaries while not obstructing views). Although

The Ha-Ha Case is not set in Scotland, Stewart drew inspiration for the novel from a notorious Scottish true crime, the 1893 Ardlamont murder case. From the facts of the Ardlamont affair Stewart drew several of the key characters in *The Ha-Ha Case*, as well as the circumstances of the novel's murder (a shooting 'accident' while hunting), though he added complications that take the tale in a new direction.[6]

In newspaper reviews both Dorothy L. Sayers and 'Francis Iles' (crime novelist Anthony Berkeley Cox) highly praised this latest mystery by 'The Clever Mr Connington', as he was now dubbed on book jackets by his new English publisher, Hodder & Stoughton. Sayers particularly noted the effective characterisation in *The Ha-Ha Case*: 'There is no need to say that Mr Connington has given us a sound and interesting plot, very carefully and ingeniously worked out. In addition, there are the three portraits of the three brothers, cleverly and rather subtly characterised, of the [governess], and of Inspector Hinton, whose admirable qualities are counteracted by that besetting sin of the man who has made his own way: a jealousy of delegating responsibility.' The reviewer for the *Times Literary Supplement* detected signs that the sardonic Sir Clinton Driffield had begun mellowing with age: 'Those who have never really liked Sir Clinton's perhaps excessively soldierly manner will be surprised to find that he makes his discovery not only by the pure light of intelligence, but partly as a reward for amiability and tact, qualities in which the Inspector [Hinton] was strikingly deficient.' This is true enough, although the classic Sir Clinton emerges a number of times in the novel, as in his subtly sarcastic recurrent backhanded praise of Inspector Hinton: 'He writes a first class report.'

Clinton Driffield returned the next year in the detective novel *In Whose Dim Shadow* (1935), a tale set in a recently erected English suburb, the denizens of which seem to have committed an impressive number of indiscretions, including sexual ones. The intriguing title of the British edition of the novel is drawn from a poem by the British historian Thomas Babington Macaulay: 'Those trees in whose dim shadow/The ghastly priest doth reign/The priest who slew the slayer/And shall himself be slain.' Stewart's puzzle plot in *In Whose Dim Shadow* is well clued and compelling, the kicker of a closing paragraph is a classic of its kind and, additionally, the author paints some excellent character portraits. I fully concur with the *Sunday Times'* assessment of the tale: 'Quiet domestic murder, full of the neatest detective points [. . .] These are not the detective's stock figures, but fully realised human beings.'[7]

Uncharacteristically for Stewart, nearly twenty months elapsed between the publication of *In Whose Dim Shadow* and his next book, *A Minor Operation* (1937). The reason for the author's delay in production was the onset in 1935–36 of the afflictions of cataracts and heart disease (Stewart ultimately succumbed to heart disease in 1947). Despite these grave health complications, Stewart in late 1936 was able to complete *A Minor Operation*, a first-rate Clinton Driffield story of murder and a most baffling disappearance.

A *Times Literary Supplement* reviewer found that *A Minor Operation* treated the reader 'to exactly the right mixture of mystification and clue' and that, in addition to its impressive construction, the novel boasted 'character-drawing above the average' for a detective novel.

Alfred Stewart's final eight mysteries, which appeared between 1938 and 1947, the year of the author's death, are, on the whole, a somewhat weaker group of tales than the sixteen that appeared between 1926 and 1937, yet they are not without interest. In 1938 Stewart for the last time managed to publish two detective novels, *Truth Comes Limping* and *For Murder Will Speak* (also published as *Murder Will Speak*). The latter tale is much the superior of the two, having an interesting suburban setting and a bevy of female characters found to have motives when a contemptible philandering businessman meets with foul play. Sexual neurosis plays a major role in *For Murder Will Speak*, the ever-thorough Stewart obviously having made a study of the subject when writing the novel. The somewhat squeamish reviewer for *Scribner's Magazine* considered the subject matter of *For Murder Will Speak* 'rather unsavoury at times', yet this individual conceded that the novel nevertheless made 'first-class reading for those who enjoy a good puzzle intricately worked out'. 'Judge Lynch' in the *Saturday Review* apparently had no such moral reservations about the latest Clinton Driffield murder case, avowing simply of the novel: 'They don't come any better'.

Over the next couple of years Stewart again sent Sir

Clinton Driffield temporarily packing, replacing him with a new series detective, a brash radio personality named Mark Brand, in *The Counsellor* (1939) and *The Four Defences* (1940). The better of these two novels is *The Four Defences*, which Stewart based on another notorious British true-crime case, the Alfred Rouse blazing-car murder. (Rouse is believed to have fabricated his death by murdering an unknown man, placing the dead man's body in his car and setting the car on fire, in the hope that the murdered man's body would be taken for his.) Though admittedly a thinly characterised academic exercise in ratiocination, Stewart's *Four Defences* surely is also one of the most complexly plotted Golden Age detective novels and should delight devotees of classical detection. Taking the Rouse blazing-car affair as his theme, Stewart composes from it a stunning set of diabolically ingenious criminal variations. 'This is in the cold-blooded category which [. . .] excites a crossword puzzle kind of interest,' the reviewer for the *Times Literary Supplement* acutely noted of the novel. 'Nothing in the Rouse case would prepare you for these complications upon complications [. . .] What they prove is that Mr Connington has the power of penetrating into the puzzle-corner of the brain. He leaves it dazedly wondering whether in the records of actual crime there can be any dark deed to equal this in its planned convolutions.'

Sir Clinton Driffield returned to action in the remaining four detective novels in the Connington oeuvre, *The Twenty-One Clues* (1941), *No Past is Dead* (1942), *Jack-in-the-Box* (1944) and *Commonsense is All You Need* (1947), all of which were written as Stewart's heart disease steadily worsened and reflect to some extent his diminishing physical and mental energy. Although *The Twenty-One Clues* was inspired by the notorious Hall-Mills double murder case – probably the most publicised murder case in the United States in the 1920s – and the American critic and novelist Anthony Boucher commended *Jack-in-the-Box*, I believe the best of these later mysteries is *No Past Is Dead*, which Stewart partly based on a bizarre French true-crime affair, the 1891 Achet-Lepine murder case.[8] Besides providing an interesting background for the tale, the ailing author managed some virtuoso plot twists, of the sort most associated today with that ingenious Golden Age Queen of Crime, Agatha Christie.

What Stewart with characteristic bluntness referred to as 'my complete crack-up' forced his retirement from Queen's University in 1944. 'I am afraid,' Stewart wrote a friend, the chemist and forensic scientist F. Gerald Tryhorn, in August 1946, eleven months before his death, 'that I shall never be much use again. Very stupidly, I tried for a session to combine a full course of lecturing with angina pectoris; and ended up by establishing that the two are immiscible.' He added that since retiring in 1944, he had been physically 'limited to my house, since even a fifty-yard crawl brings on the usual cramps'. Stewart completed his essay collection and a final novel before he died at his study desk in his Belfast home on 1 July 1947, at the age of sixty-six. When death came to the author he was busy at work, writing.

More than six decades after Alfred Walter Stewart's death, his J. J. Connington fiction is again available to a wider audience of classic-mystery fans, rather than strictly limited to a select company of rare-book collectors with deep pockets. This is fitting for an individual who was one of the finest writers of British genre fiction between the two world wars. 'Heaven forfend that you should imagine I take myself for anything out of the common in the tec yarn stuff,' Stewart once self-deprecatingly declared in a letter to Rupert Gould. Yet, as contemporary critics recognised, as a writer of detective and science fiction Stewart indeed was something out of the common. Now more modern readers can find this out for themselves. They have much good sleuthing in store.

1. For more on Street, Crofts and particularly Stewart, see Curtis Evans, *Masters of the 'Humdrum' Mystery: Cecil John Charles Street, Freeman Wills Crofts, Alfred Walter Stewart and the British Detective Novel, 1920–1961* (Jefferson, NC: McFarland, 2012). On the academic career of Alfred Walter Stewart, see his entry in *Oxford Dictionary of National Biography* (London and New York: Oxford University Press, 2004), vol. 52, 627–628.
2. The Gould–Stewart correspondence is discussed in considerable detail in *Masters of the 'Humdrum' Mystery*. For more on the life of the fascinating Rupert Thomas Gould, see Jonathan Betts, *Time Restored: The Harrison Timekeepers and R. T. Gould, the Man Who Knew (Almost) Everything* (London and New York: Oxford University Press, 2006) and *Longitude,* the 2000 British film adaptation of Dava Sobel's book *Longitude: The True Story of a Lone Genius Who Solved the Greatest Scientific Problem of His Time* (London: Harper Collins, 1995), which details Gould's restoration of the marine chronometers built by in the eighteenth century by the clockmaker John Harrison.
3. Potential purchasers of *Murder in the Maze* should keep in mind that $2 in 1927 is worth over $26 today.

4. In a 1920 article in *The Strand Magazine,* Arthur Conan Doyle endorsed as real prank photographs of purported fairies taken by two English girls in the garden of a house in the village of Cottingley. In the aftermath of the Great War Doyle had become a fervent believer in Spiritualism and other paranormal phenomena. Especially embarrassing to Doyle's admirers today, he also published *The Coming of the Faeries* (1922), wherein he argued that these mystical creatures genuinely existed. 'When the spirits came in, the common sense oozed out,' Stewart once wrote bluntly to his friend Rupert Gould of the creator of Sherlock Holmes. Like Gould, however, Stewart had an intense interest in the subject of the Loch Ness Monster, believing that he, his wife and daughter had sighted a large marine creature of some sort in Loch Ness in 1935. A year earlier Gould had authored *The Loch Ness Monster and Others*, and it was this book that led Stewart, after he made his 'Nessie' sighting, to initiate correspondence with Gould.

5. A tontine is a financial arrangement wherein shareowners in a common fund receive annuities that increase in value with the death of each participant, with the entire amount of the fund going to the last survivor. The impetus that the tontine provided to the deadly creative imaginations of Golden Age mystery writers should be sufficiently obvious.

6. At Ardlamont, a large country estate in Argyll, Cecil Hambrough died from a gunshot wound while hunting. Cecil's tutor, Alfred John Monson, and another man, both of whom were out hunting with Cecil, claimed that Cecil had accidentally shot himself, but Monson was arrested and tried for Cecil's murder. The verdict delivered was 'not proven', but Monson was then – and is today – considered almost certain to have been guilty of the murder. On the Ardlamont case, see William Roughead, *Classic Crimes* (1951; repr., New York: New York Review Books Classics, 2000), 378–464.

7. For the genesis of the title, see Macaulay's 'The Battle of the Lake Regillus', from his narrative poem collection *Lays of Ancient Rome*. In this poem Macaulay alludes to the ancient cult of Diana Nemorensis, which elevated its priests through trial by

combat. Study of the practices of the Diana Nemorensis cult influenced Sir James George Frazer's cultural interpretation of religion in his most renowned work, *The Golden Bough: A Study in Magic and Religion*. As with *Tom Tiddler's Island* and *The Ha-Ha Case* the title *In Whose Dim Shadow* proved too esoteric for Connington's American publishers, Little, Brown and Co., who altered it to the more prosaic *The Tau Cross Mystery*.

8. Stewart analysed the Achet-Lepine case in detail in 'The Mystery of Chantelle', one of the best essays in his 1947 collection *Alias J. J. Connington*.

CHAPTER I

ROMANCE AND THE 10.35

No luggage had come by the midday local ; and George Mossley, foreman porter at Kempsford Junction, watched the passengers straggle past the ticket-collector and off the platform. When the last of them had gone, he sauntered up to the gate to continue an interrupted conversation.

" This Kipling we was talkin' about," he resumed. " I've got another book o' his out o' the Free Library."

The ticket-collector showed no enthusiasm at the news. George's new-born fervour for Kipling and his habit of quotation had, willy nilly, imprinted most of " *If*——" on his mate's resisting mind ; and Ketton shrank from the further tuition which he suspected was in store. He contented himself with an absent-minded gesture by way of response.

" 'E mentions railways in this 'un," George hurried on, lest the conversation should peter out. " 'E says—listen, Ketton !—'e says : ' *And all unseen, Romance brought up the 9.15.*' "

" No 9.15 ever come to this junction," pointed out Ketton, who was a literalist by nature. " Not in my day nor in yours either, George. You ought to 'ave known that time-table of ours better nor that."

George, with difficulty, restrained a movement of impatience.

" You don't get the idea, Ketton," he explained laboriously. " You're just one o' the sort o' people Kipling's writin' about. What 'e means is that things may be right in front o' you, and yet you never see 'em at all."

As Ketton digested this, his glance travelled up the platform and was caught by the figure of the stationmaster, who was standing with his back to them, peering into the mist which veiled the farther parts of the junction. Ketton seemed to derive inspiration from the sight.

" I get you," he admitted at last. " What you mean is something like old Boyson's shirt-tail. It's there, right in front of you ; but you can't see it, nohow. I don't see much in that to make a song about, George."

Much to Ketton's annoyance, George treated this with contempt and refused to discuss it. Instead, he approached the point from a fresh direction.

" Look at this last train-load o' passengers, Ketton, and just think of what may be happenin' to them. I seen you havin' a good look at that pretty girl that lost 'er ticket. Engaged she is—I seen 'er ring when she took off 'er glove for to hunt in 'er bag. Dressed up so fine ; probably off to meet the bloke she's engaged to, when 'e gets out of 'is office. There's romance a-starin' you in the face, you blind bat. And perhaps the cove alongside her is off after a job that'll bring him in ten pound a week. That would be romance too. And the bloke I helped out o' the front carriage—I know him by sight. He lost his peepers at St. Hubert. Romance, again. And those two kiddies runnin' up the platform to meet their daddy. Why, the whole train may have been packed with romance and you'd never see it. F'r instance, just ask yourself : the last man what give up his ticket. Where was 'e goin' ? "

" To the bar," declared the literalist triumphantly. " I seen him make a bee-line for it as soon as he got through the gate. I'd be there myself if I wasn't on duty, to get something for to take the taste o' this fog out o' my throat."

He paused to let this information sink in, then continued :

" You're addlin' your brains with all this poetry-stuff, George. I'm sayin' that seriously, and I'm sayin' it for your good. *Romance brought up the 9.15,* did 'e ? Well, it must ha' been an express that didn't stop at this here junction. All the romance you get, George, is walkin' up and down the train singin' out, 'Kempsford Junction . . . Kempsford Junction' . . . and varyin' that on the bay platforms to 'Kempsford Junction—all change ! ' There ain't no romance in that, not that I can see. And this '*If——*', that's just the same. 'Ow does it go ? ' *If you can talk with crowds and keep your virtue, or walk with Kings—nor lose the common touch.*' When are you likely to talk with crowds, George, I ask you ? The only crowds you ever see are at football matches, and they wouldn't listen to you if you did talk to them. And the nearest

3

you ever come to Kings was once when the Royal Special went through here at fifty miles an hour, and nobody so much as looked out of the window to see you standin' with your cap off on the platform. '*If you can keep your head when all about you are losing theirs and blaming it on you.*' That would be last week, like enough, when you pulled that silly old woman out o' the wrong train just when the whistle went. She'd lost 'er 'ead right enough, and she blamed it on you quite accordin' to the book, for I 'eard 'er from 'alf-way along the platform. But I don't see much romance in that. It might 'ave 'appened to anyone."

George's powers of repartee were feeble ; and, as he gave up the contest and turned away, all he could think of was :

" Well, some of it seems to 'ave stuck in your mind, for all that, Ketton."

Ketton's uncompromising rejection of Kipling was more of a disappointment than an annoyance. George regarded " *If*——" as a most valuable moral tonic, although, as Ketton had pointed out, few opportunities of practising its gospel seemed to come his way ; and, being of the type which wants to share good things with fellow-creatures, he had done his best to make a convert of Ketton.

The engine had been detached from the empty train and had gone over the points to take in water outside the station, so that only a block of deserted carriages faced George as he walked up the platform, brooding over his failure as a missionary of culture.

He opened the doors of the forward third-class compartments one after another ; glanced inside to see if anything had been left behind ; and all the time he felt Ketton's sardonic glance in his back. " Found any o' that romance o' yours, this time ? " Ketton would be sure to inquire when he had finished his inspection. " No ? Why, then, I suppose they must ha' took an' throwed it out o' the window on the road 'ere." He knew Ketton's heavy-handed kind of humour.

The middle section of the train was made up of a first-class carriage ; and, as he came to it, George's interest increased. The first-class people often left newspapers behind them ; and George had to do his reading on the cheap, if possible. The first compartment yielded nothing ; but, from the floor of the next, George rescued a copy of *The Times*. Then again he drew blank ; and at last he put his hand on the handle of the rearmost first-class compartment, and swung the door open.

His routine was to glance first at the luggage-racks. Finding them empty, he lowered his gaze and caught sight of a man's hat on the floor. Then, *Times* in hand, he involuntarily stepped back a pace on the platform. Two streams of blood flowed from under the seat and soaked into the carpet of the compartment.

George's nature had always inclined him to keep out of fights if possible ; and he had a physical aversion to blood. At the sight of these ominous rivulets, he suddenly gulped and felt sick. His first

5

inclination was to hurry off and put the responsibility of further proceedings on someone else's shoulders.

But, just as he opened his mouth to shout, the message of " *If——*" floated up in his mind almost without his being conscious of the call. Here was the emergency. Now was the time to keep his head. He turned back towards the gruesome compartment, swallowed hastily once or twice, and forced himself to peer under the seat. One glimpse of the huddled-up figure there was enough for him. He stepped back off the footboard and glanced round for assistance. The stationmaster had gone to his office ; the guard of the train was nowhere visible ; but Ketton still lingered beyond the gate, talking to the boy at the bookstall.

" Here ! Ketton ! There's a dead man under the seat o' this compartment 'ere. Get the p'lice, quick ! 'E's been shot or somethin'—blood all over the place. 'Urry, now ; 'urry, man ! Get a move on you, do, for 'eaven's sake, 'stead o' wastin' time over silly questions ! "

This final sentence was a comment on Ketton's first reaction to the news. In George's excited condition, time seemed to have changed its quality ; he watched Ketton's rush to the exit from the station with the feelings of a spectator examining a slow-motion film, and he felt exasperated at what seemed deliberate sluggishness on the part of his mate. Ketton vanished through the door ; and his disappearance freed George's mind for the consideration of other things.

" *If you can keep your head* . . . " George suddenly realised that he had much to do himself. What was the first thing ? Keep the place clear ? The bookstall boy, with fewer qualms than George, had left his papers and was running up the platform to conduct an investigation on his own account. George set off at a lumbering trot, still clinging to *The Times* ; intercepted the boy ; hustled him off the platform ; and slammed the gates in his face.

" Outside, you ! " he growled as he closed the barrier.

So that was done. What next ? It occurred to George that his initial inspection had been over-cursory, and that possibly the man under the seat was still alive and in need of assistance. His memory assured him that he was mistaken ; his physical feelings fought against any return to the ugly scene ; but that unvocal inward message bade him keep his head and carry the thing through. In response to its summons, he set off again at a trot, back to the fatal compartment.

George was no expert in matters of life and death ; but the limpness and the attitude of the silent figure were enough to persuade him that his first conclusion had been right. The body had been thrust under the seat, face downwards ; and the blood was flowing from the head. As the porter withdrew from the compartment, his eye was caught by a glitter of light from something on the floor. He made a movement as though to pick it up, then he bethought himself that the police would want things left untouched.

As he stepped off the footboard, he realised with relief that his responsibility was at an end. The stationmaster, at the first call, had run from his office, let himself through the barrier with his key, and was hurrying up the platform towards the train.

At the gate, a rapidly increasing group of people had formed, and George could see their white faces turned in his direction. As he looked, Ketton and a policeman forced their way to the front, opened the gate, and came on to the platform. The constable said something to Ketton, who remained on guard at the barrier whilst the uniformed man hurried forward. " *If*——" spurred George to one last effort in efficiency. He glanced up at the white dial of the great clock and made a note of the exact time. Then, as the policeman joined the stationmaster, George handed over his responsibility with a gesture towards the compartment.

" I feel sick," he said simply. " I'll go over there and sit down for a minute."

He walked across to one of the benches on the platform, sat down, and watched the proceedings with a wholly unfamiliar sensation of curiosity and detachment. He wanted to see what they would find to do ; and at the same time his personal interest in the affair had completely evaporated. What he most desired was to be left alone for a while until he had recovered control of himself ; but something occurred to him, and he called across to the constable.

" Mind that bit o' glass on the floor, will you ? It might be a clue or somethin'."

The constable nodded curtly, knelt on the footboard and made a careful inspection of the interior of the compartment ; while the stationmaster craned over his shoulder to see anything he could. Evidently they had stronger nerves than George. After a few moments the policeman, yielding his place to the stationmaster, withdrew and pulled out his notebook.

" Nothing much to be seen yet," he mused aloud, as he jotted down the essentials. " Body of man thrust under forward seat of first-class compartment. Last first compartment in carriage . . ."

" Last in the train," the stationmaster amplified. " There's only thirds beyond this down to the van."

" I'll draw a picture of it," the constable assured him. " What train's this ? Where does it come from ? "

" It's the 10.35 local from Horston," Boyson explained. " It stops at every station on the road and gets in here at 12.04 by the time-table. Shade late to-day, of course, owing to the fog."

The constable nodded and continued his note-taking.

" Brown felt hat on floor of compartment. Looks as if it had been knocked off in a struggle. Part of footmark in dust on the brim and hat battered rather out of shape. Bit of glass on floor. Looks like spectacle lens. That ought to be a clue of sorts, for there's no sign of a gold frame or anything like that. Must have come from the murderer's glasses ; or it looks like that, anyway. No bag. No umbrella. H'm ! "

9

He reflected for a moment before continuing.

" Body dressed in dark blue tweed with thin, whitey stripe. Hair beginning to go grey. Wounds —two at least—in head. No blood from anywhere else that I can see. You don't recognise him, do you ? "

The stationmaster shook his head.

" Can't be sure till I see his face, of course ; but I don't think it's likely. I don't place him."

" Cushions," pursued the constable. " A hole torn in the covers. Looks like a bullet-hole. We'll leave it alone just now. Windows, both shut. Glass frosted over so that no one can see into the carriage very well from outside, except at one small bit, here on the platform-side window next the engine. Nothing else that I can see just now. By the way, what's the name of the man who found the body ? "

" George Mossley."

The constable made a jotting, then closed his notebook.

" No firearms that I can see. Now I'll need to go off and ring up someone to look into the matter thoroughly. You'll see that no one gets on to this platform, and that this Mossley waits on the premises till the Superintendent comes along ? He'll be wanted then."

" What do you make of it ? " the stationmaster demanded, as the constable turned away.

" Much the same as you do, I expect. If I was committing suicide, I don't believe I'd tuck myself away under the seat to do it ; and I'm pretty sure my dead body wouldn't get up and chuck the pistol out of the window afterwards. Somebody murdered the poor beggar, right enough, whoever he was."

The stationmaster nodded his agreement.

" Whoever did it, he must have had a good nerve," he commented. " The longest clear run between stations that that train makes isn't more than seven minutes anywhere ; and he must have done his job in that time, complete. Gosh ! That's quick work, that is ! "

" Well, I'll be off to the 'phone," the constable concluded.

With a final glance round the compartment, he turned away and passed George, still clutching the copy of *The Times* as he followed the constable's figure with an incurious eye.

CHAPTER II

THE PRIZE RAM

" That's the best we can do for you," said Superintendent Ross. " It should be enough, along with what you have already, I think. And, if I were in your shoes, I'd be inclined to pull him in now, without waiting for anything else. You'll get a conviction. And, if you wait much longer, he may clear out ; and then you'll have a lot of bother in picking him up again."

As though to mark the close of the discussion, he rose from his chair, crossed over to the fire, and bent down to warm his hands. Superintendent Campden blotted his last note and stowed away his papers in a drawer of the desk at which he was sitting.

" I think we'll risk it," he concurred.

The matter on which they were engaged was a minor one ; but it had been tricky ; and Campden was relieved to find that his colleague's view reinforced his own. Ross's judgment had seldom been at fault. He seemed to have an uncanny knack of gauging exactly how evidence would look from the standpoint of the jury-box ; and, when he was prepared to take a case into court, it generally meant that a conviction was as nearly certain as it could be made with the facts available. The Superintendent

12

from Horston never overlooked the human factor in the final arbitrament. " Don't forget," he used to point out to his subordinates, " don't forget that it's no good proving a case to your own satisfaction. That cuts no ice. What you've got to do is to prove it so that it will convince a jury ; and jurymen are neither fools nor geniuses, usually, so far as my experience goes."

Superintendent Campden closed the drawer of his desk and turned to the hearth.

" Thanks for coming down," he said. " Beastly cold morning for the journey. I suppose the fog's made all the trains late. You came down on the express, didn't you ? "

Superintendent Ross nodded as he straightened his big figure and turned his back to the fire.

" The express was late at Horston," he explained, " and after that we got held up once or twice. The fog-signals were going off every minute or two ; it's pretty thick here and there on the line. We passed the local between Seven Sisters and Hammersleigh, so it was just as well I took the express."

Campden glanced at his watch.

" Want to catch the 1.22 back to Horston ? " he inquired. " You might just manage it. Or will you have lunch first and take the 2.55 ? "

Before Ross could answer, a constable knocked at the door of the office and gave Campden a message in an undertone.

" Oh, show him in," the Superintendent ordered in a tone which betrayed a certain weariness.

13

He turned to Ross.

" This is Mr. Chepstow, come to see me about some trouble over a ram, Ross. It's really not in our district, and I've stirred your people up about it ; but he lives close by here—he's a farmer in a biggish way—and he looks on me as his information-office instead of going to your people direct. I've been pestered out of my life with him lately. He's continually wanting to know what's being done in the matter ; and when he drops in twice a day it gets a bit difficult to invent progress enough to satisfy him—specially when there's been no progress made at all in the affair. Let him get his wind out to you, will you, if you don't mind ? I'm getting sick of it. Perhaps you'll be able to soothe him down a bit and take him off my hands."

He dropped his voice just in time as the door opened, and a big man was ushered into the room. A well-meaning friend had once described Chepstow as " a face like a full moon with a smile on it, and some curly hair on top." The description was accurate enough up to a point, though it had not altogether pleased the farmer. Ross, glancing up as Chepstow entered the office, thought he had never seen anyone who came so close to the typical John Bull. Only the clothes differed from the model. A big, likeable, hearty, open-air sort of man, with honesty written broad on his face : that was the impression Chepstow conveyed at the first glance.

" 'Morning, Superintendent," he said to Campden, with a glance at Ross, who was still standing with his

THE TWO TICKETS PUZZLE

back to the fire. " I've just dropped in again about that ram of mine, just to see if you've got any further forward. He's in a bad way, poor beast, a very bad way indeed, I'm sorry to say. The vet. takes a very serious view of it ; thinks he's done for, in fact, I can see, though he won't say so in just so many words. Now, have you got on the track of the scoundrel who did it yet ? Or can you make out what's at the back of it all? Phew ! This room of yours is hot when one comes into it from the cold."

He pulled out a coloured silk handkerchief and mopped his brow with it. Campden pushed forward a chair and Chepstow sat down, restoring his handkerchief to his pocket. Campden seized the opportunity which the pause gave him, and, instead of answering the questions, he diverted the farmer's attention to his colleague.

" This is Superintendent Ross, Mr. Chepstow."

The farmer swung round a little in his chair and inspected Ross's big, clean-shaven face with an obvious mixture of interest and approval.

" I've heard of you, sir," he said, with evident respect. " You're the man that hanged that scoundrel Hyndford, aren't you ? Now, that was a good bit of work, if you'll let me say so. It was, indeed. And I'm sure if I could get you interested in this ram of mine, you'd soon get to the bottom of the affair. Not but what the Superintendent here's doing his very best, I'm sure," he added unfortunately, though clearly with the intention of being complimentary to Campden.

15

"You'd better tell Superintendent Ross the whole
story, Mr. Chepstow," Campden suggested, with an
impish glance at his colleague. "He's got half an
hour to spare just now ; and it's really in the Horston
district, you know, not in ours. The Horston people
are working on it ; and any details you can give
Superintendent Ross at first-hand will always be
a help to them."

Ross's glance at his colleague betrayed no particular pleasure at the prospect ; but when he turned
to the farmer only friendly interest showed in his
face.

"Let's hear all about the trouble, Mr. Chepstow,"
he said cordially. "No miracles promised, of course ;
but we like to do our best for people, you know."

"The trouble's just this, Mr. Ross," Chepstow
began, crossing one leg over the other and leaning
forward to enforce his story on his auditor. "Last
summer I bought an Oxford Down ram, Frolic VI.
You may have heard about it ; his picture was in the
Kempsford Advertiser at the time, and a very good
likeness it was, too. He was bred by Mr. Alford of
Richmond Maisey, in Gloucestershire ; and he took
second prize at last year's Royal Agricultural
Society's Show, so you can understand that he's
a fine beast. I've seldom seen a ram I liked the looks
of so well ; and I had to give a stiffish price for him,
I can tell you. He didn't come cheap ; but Oxford
Downs do well in this part of the country, and
I wanted him, and I could pay the price for him,
and I got him."

Chepstow's face showed that his pride was in his purchase and not merely in the fact that he had been able to afford its price. Superintendent Ross, unlike Campden, was not bored by these details. Rams he cared nothing about ; but he had an acute interest in humanity ; and, if Chepstow was interested in rams, then Ross was prepared to listen sympathetically to him. He was learning something about Chepstow ; and he was also smoothing down a man who evidently felt a certain grievance against the police because they had not managed to produce results.

"Well, that was how it was, Mr. Ross," the farmer continued. "I bought the ram and brought him up here. Most of my land's round about Kempsford ; but I've got a nice bit of pasture just on this side of Seven Sisters. Likely you've seen it yourself ; for the railway runs through it and you must have passed it often enough. I've got a very good man there ; and I put him in charge of Frolic VI. Tarland's got his head screwed on right ; and I'd trust him just as soon as I'd trust myself—thoroughly reliable, I've always found him. Now, that was all right ; and the ram did very well down there."

Chepstow's face grew clouded as he continued his tale. It was clear that he was both puzzled and deeply wounded by the turn of events.

"I've no enemies that I know of, Mr. Ross. I treat people well, and they treat me well, and I never had reason to think that anyone wished me ill. That's just the plain fact ; and that's what puzzles me and worries me so much over this affair. This last week, I've turned it over and turned it over in my head and tried to think of anyone who could even think I'd done him a bad turn, and I can't bring to mind a single case. Not one. I'm not saying that by way of a boast, you understand, Mr. Ross ; it's just the honest truth. I don't know anyone that has a grudge against me. That's what makes it so perplexing."

He broke off and stared at the two officials in obviously honest perturbation and bewilderment. Campden, who had heard the whole story before, hardly concealed his boredom ; and the farmer turned directly to Ross as he continued his story.

" It was just a week ago to-day, on the 16th November, Mr. Ross. Tarland has the ram in a field close to his cottage ; and he says that he saw Frolic VI. about eleven o'clock in the morning— within a few minutes one way or the other—and Frolic was all right then, just grazing quietly some- where between the house and the railway. Tarland was cutting down a tree in his garden that morning ; it had got a bit shaken by a storm a day or two before, and he was afraid of it coming down alto- gether if the wind got up again. He was busy with that, and, while he was working, Frolic VI. moved a bit across the field and got out of his sight. Tarland went on with his job, and after a while he knocked off to rest himself, and to keep himself from catching a chill—he was pretty hot, you understand—he took a turn up the garden. The wind was blowing pretty cold, he told me. When he came in sight of the ram again, there was the poor beast lying on its side, kicking like anything, and anyone could see something had hurt it. So Tarland jumped over the fence and made for it as hard as he could go."

" Has he any idea of what time it was then ? " Ross demanded.

" It would be somewhere about twenty past eleven, he says," Chepstow answered. " Well, as I was saying, Mr. Ross, he ran to where poor Frolic was lying ; and then it was plain enough what had happened. The poor beast had been shot. There was a wound in his side and some blood on the fleece."

" Not a shotgun then ? A single bullet, eh ? "

" A single bullet, as you say. Well, you can guess how Tarland felt, being in charge of the ram. He was just completely taken aback, and I don't blame him for that—or for anything else, either. There's no question of blame in the matter, so far as he goes. He sent off post-haste for the vet. at once ; and in the meantime he did what he could for the poor beast. By and by Mr. Lorton—that's the best vet. in that neighbourhood, as I expect you know—he came along and examined Frolic VI. There's no question about it—the beast has been shot with a fairly heavy bullet, to judge from the size of the wound ; and it's touch and go whether anything can be done for the ram. He's alive still ; but the bullet's gone pretty deep—Lorton won't risk trying to extract it—and he frankly won't answer for anything. All we can do is just to let things take their course and hope that the poor beast will pull himself together again."

"The ram's insured, of course?" Ross asked. "You're not going to lose financially over it, I suppose?"

Chepstow confirmed this with a nod.

"Frolic was insured, just as you say; and, at the worst, I daresay the company'll pay up without a word. It's not that that's worrying me, Mr. Ross. Just look at it from my point of view for a moment. Here's somebody shot a ram of mine that was well known all over the countryside——"

"Just a moment," interrupted Ross. "Did Tarland see anyone in the neighbourhood when he went down to the ram first of all? Could anyone have shot the ram and got away without being spotted?"

Chepstow shook his head.

"That's the funny bit of it, Mr. Ross. From Tarland's garden you get a fair view over the neighbouring fields, and he says there was no one in sight anywhere. I've fences on my ground, you see, and no hedges; so there wasn't any cover to speak of anywhere. Tarland's quite convinced that there wasn't anybody lurking about anywhere. Now, coming back to what I said before, there's only three ways out of it: either it was malice or it was mischief or it was an accident. You'll agree with that?"

Ross nodded in agreement, without making any comment.

"Well, then," Chepstow went on, "suppose it was

just an accident. Somebody with a rifle must have been shooting away off in the distance and not caring a damn—excuse me !—where his bullets were going. If that's how it happened, then I want that man found and warned about his foolishness. It's bad enough having a valuable ram killed, but it might just as easy have been Tarland or any of his family— just as easy. That sort of thing needs putting down. And the insurance people will likely have something to say, too, if the man's laid by the heels."

The tone of his voice showed, however, that he regarded this hypothesis as being unlikely.

" We can't trace anyone owning a rifle in the neighbourhood," Campden contributed. " Shotguns if you like, but not a rifle ; and the wound wasn't made with a shotgun. We've accounted for all the military rifles round about there. It wasn't done with one of them."

" It doesn't look like an accident, then, does it ? " Chepstow pursued. " Not to my mind. But, if it wasn't an accident, then it was mischief or else malice. If it was mischief, then the man who makes mischief ought to pay for his fun ; that's my idea about it, and I want him caught before he does any more in that line. I've heard of these cattle-maiming cases before now ; and, if it's that, then it's a public danger. If it isn't mischief and if it isn't accident, why, then, it can't be anything else than personal spite. That's what makes me so uncomfortable, Mr. Ross. How would you like it if you'd gone on think-ing for years that everyone liked you and that you'd

21

always dealt straight with everyone—and suddenly you'd found that someone had a grudge against you, a bad grudge? I don't like the idea. I don't want to think about it. If I did, I'd soon get to asking myself when I met anyone : ' Is this him ? ' And that would be the end of any peace of mind to a man like me. That's what makes me so desperate keen to get this thing sifted to the bottom."

Ross nodded understandingly.

" I quite see it," he assured the farmer. " You can count on us doing our best. But," he added, with a whimsical expression on his face, " I've got to repeat what I said at the start. We don't promise miracles. And you haven't given us much to go on, remember."

" That's all admitted," said Chepstow cordially. " And, if you don't mind my saying it, you've seen my point of view, I'm sure. It's a worrying sort of thing to have happen, isn't it ? It's not a money matter at all, with me ; I'm covered, so far as that goes. But I'd been counting on that ram, you understand ? And, over and above all that, it's the mysteriousness of it all that bothers me. I'm a man that likes to have things plain ; and this business isn't a bit plain to me. It leaves a taste in my mouth that won't go away until the whole thing gets cleared up."

" Well, you can count on me to do my best in the matter," Ross assured him.

At this moment came an interruption. A constable hurried into the room and gave some message to

Campden in an undertone. Campden nodded, and
then turned to Ross.

" That's a message from the station," he explained. " A man's been shot on the 10.35 train from
Horston."

Chepstow's face expressed rather mingled emotions, which were explained by the comment which
broke from him involuntarily :

" There ! Now, wasn't I right in saying the sooner
you got to the bottom of this affair the better it'd
be ? Here's some more of this shooting going on,
right under your noses. First my ram, and now some
poor beggar or other."

Campden ignored the comment.

" It's been done on the Horston train, Ross.
Likely enough it may turn out to be linked up with
your district. You'd better come along with me now
to the station and have a look into things for yourself, just in case."

Superintendent Ross nodded a slow agreement
with this proposal.

" It may concern either your district or mine," he
admitted. " It won't do any harm if we both look
into it. If it's my case, I'll be all the better off if I've
had your ideas as well as my own at the start."

" The police surgeon's been rung up. He'll follow
on as soon as possible," Campden explained. " We'd
better go now."

CHAPTER III

THE BULLETS

" This isn't my show," Superintendent Ross pointed out to his colleague as they passed through the booking-hall. " I'll stand by, while you do the questioning. There's no use both of us butting in."

He left Campden's side for a moment and crossed over to the bookstall.

" Here, boy. Give me a local time-table—the penny one."

Stuffing the booklet into his pocket, he rejoined Campden, who was making his way, under the guidance of a porter, to the bay platform at which the carriages of the 10.35 train were still standing.

Under Campden's incisive questioning, the main facts in the case were elicited from George Mossley, the stationmaster, and the constable.

" That's that, then," said the Superintendent as he turned away, greatly to George's relief. " Now we'll have a look at the carriage. Lucky nothing's been touched."

Ross noted that the train was composed of a first-class carriage sandwiched between two pairs of thirds. The body lay in what had been the rearmost first-class compartment. Campden walked towards it, opened the door which the constable had shut, and looked keenly about the interior for a few moments. Then he pulled an inch-tape from his pocket and made some measurements before picking up a small object from the floor.

" Looks like half a spectacle-lens," he said, after examining it.

Ross took the glass fragment from his colleague, held it up to the light and looked through it, turning it this way and that as he did so.

" Now, that's rather interesting," he pointed out. " It looks as if somebody mixed up in this affair was near-sighted and suffered from astigmatism."

" Sherlock ! " Campden commented ironically. " And how d'you make that out ? "

" It's a concave lens : therefore it's for near sight. If you reflect something in it—use it as a concave mirror to reflect the girders up above there—you'll find that one side of it gives a sharp image ; but you won't get a sharp image from the other surface, no matter how much you shift it about. That's the cylindrical grinding they use for correcting astigmatism."

Campden tried the experiment, and found that Ross's observations were correct.

" It may have belonged to the dead man, of course," he suggested, " but, if it didn't, it ought to narrow down the field considerably. There can't be so many short-sighted, astigmatic people about."

" More than you'd think," Ross retorted.

He glanced again at the broken glass.

" It looks to me rather like the sort of lens you

find in tortoiseshell-rimmed reading-glasses. But you can't bank on that very much, Campden. Perhaps we'll find the case or the frame in the carriage."

He handed the broken disc to Campden for safe keeping.

"We might do worse than take it round to an optician's by and by," he suggested as he did so. "He'd be able to tell us at once what sort of sight the owner had, and that might be useful if it belonged to the murderer."

The next object to attract Campden's attention was the soft brown hat lying on the floor of the compartment. He picked it up gingerly, turned it over, and inspected the lining.

"'Thursby & Son, Brazenhall Street, Horston,'" he read out. "'Best Quality.' And the initials inked on the band are *O. F. P.* It shouldn't be hard to identify the owner, at this rate."

As Ross made no comment, Campden laid the hat down on the seat for safety and continued his quest. Pulling out a pocket flash-lamp, he threw its light under the rear seat of the compartment.

"Somebody's been burning paper," he reported. "The ash is all scattered about."

Groping laboriously, he succeeded in retrieving two unconsumed fragments, which he handed up to Ross.

"The rest's all burned away, so far as I can see," he said at last, straightening himself up. "Make anything of it?"

"Not much," Ross confessed. "The irregular

bit's out of to-day's *Horston Advertiser*. The other bit
looks like a strip of the edge of a letter, but there's no
writing on the paper. It might be the margin of a
note or else it might have been torn off a plain sheet
of notepaper. Torn off, in any case, I'd say ; and
charred after it was torn, because it's singed on both
edges."

"There's nothing to be made out of the ash,"
Campden said regretfully. "It's all in flinders—
impossible to patch together now. I'll have another
look."

He peered about under the seat for a while, but
when he raised his face again it was clear that he had
found nothing of interest.

"It's all fine stuff," he announced. "Newspaper
ash is all I can see ; thin, light stuff with the
printing showing on it here and there when it isn't
too curled up in the burning. Now we'll take the
other side of the compartment."

He put his flash-lamp back into his pocket, stepped
into the carriage, and began to examine the upholstery.

"Ah, here's something ! " he exclaimed after
a second or two.

Ross saw him feel for some object which had
pierced the cloth at the back of the seat.

"This is something definite, at any rate," Campden said with a tinge of triumph, as he turned and
held out a nickel-covered bullet between his fingers.

Ross inspected his colleague's find.

"A .38 by the look of it," he commented. "The

kind of thing that fits these automatic pistols. I wonder, now——" He stopped abruptly, then continued in a rather different tone : " Are there any more of them about ? "

Campden was ferreting among the cushions.

" Here's a second one," he announced. " I found it lying loose between the cushion and the side of the carriage. Same calibre as the first one, apparently."

He handed it to Ross for comparison.

" Yes, the same calibre," Ross confirmed, placing the two missiles side by side on his palm, so that the constable and the stationmaster could inspect them. " Pretty things, aren't they ? A bit dented at the point, but otherwise as good as new. Not a scratch on them. Have a good look at them in case you're asked to identify them," he suggested, with a faintly sardonic glance at his colleague, as the two spectators wrinkled their brows in an effort to memorise the appearance of the projectiles.

" Now, I think we'd better get him out from under the seat," Campden suggested. " I've gone over everything that might have got disturbed while we were moving him, so we can do as we like. Here ! Porter ! "

George Mossley woke suddenly from his torpor.

" Get a long luggage-truck," Campden ordered. Then, turning to the constable, he added, " You'd better go and clear all those gaping idiots away from the gate, there. Shove them right out of the station for a minute or two. We'll need to take him into one of the waiting-rooms, and I've no use for a lot of rubbernecks pushing around as if it was a circus procession. Some people could do with a bit more manners and decency. Give them a lesson."

The constable set off, nothing loath ; and succeeded in dispersing the crowd of would-be sightseers who thronged about the gate of the platform. The last of them were still arguing their right of access to the station when the rumble of wheels announced George's return with the truck ; and this stimulated the constable to more drastic measures. With the assistance of the grinning Ketton, he personally conducted the ultimate pair of Paul Prys to the booking-hall entrance, put them outside, and turned the key in the lock.

By the time they reached the train, George Mossley had again retired to the bench on the platform, where he sat with averted eyes, looking even paler than before. Superintendent Campden was covering the body on the truck with a tarpaulin.

" I'll have one more look round," he said to Ross as he completed his task. " There might be something left under the front seat."

Examination with the help of the flash-light, however, revealed nothing fresh.

" No bag, or umbrella, or anything of that sort," Campden reported as he switched off his lamp. " We seem to have got all that's to be found. Now we'd better take him to the third-class waiting-room."

When the dead man had been transported there and laid out, Campden posted the constable outside to keep off intruders and despatched Ketton to unlock the closed door.

"We can go through his pockets while we're waiting for the surgeon," Ross suggested. "It may save time."

"I'd just like to have a look at the wounds," Campden said, going over to the body. "The surgeon'll give us an expert opinion after he's done his P.M., but we may as well see what's what before he starts on his job."

He stooped over the body and scanned it closely, turning it as he did so.

"Five wounds, so far as I can see ; and all of 'em in the head," he reported at length. "It seems to have been a fair bombardment the poor beggar went through. Slight wound behind right ear—like a glancing shot. Serious wound under left eye— the surgeon'll be able to tell us more about it. Another wound on left forehead . . ."

He bent closer, and passed his finger lightly over the dead man's face.

"Look here, Ross, the bullet's lying just under the skin. I can feel it ; it's just the same calibre as the ones I found in the carriage."

"Is it ? " said Superintendent Ross.

If his tone sounded slightly absent-minded, Campden paid no attention to it, but continued his enumeration.

"And two wounds below the left ear : one of them looks a good deal worse than the other. There's some sign of singeing, I think, round about the wound on the forehead."

" Is there ? "

This time Superintendent Ross's voice betrayed quite clearly that something was puzzling him ; but Campden had discovered a fresh detail which arrested his attention to the exclusion of other matters.

" Poor devil ! " he exclaimed, startled out of his professional stolidity. " The shots—or some of them —seem to have been fired from behind ; and the poor beggar had pulled up his coat collar—trying to protect himself. See ! the shot's gone clean through the cloth, before it got into him. He was alive when that shot was fired, anyhow. Lord ! how helpless the average man is against a really determined murderer. Think of what the poor soul must have gone through in that carriage. And yet, if we get our hands on him, there'll be plenty of well-meaning blighters who'll sign petitions for a reprieve, you bet. Well, I'm all for the Frenchy who said : ' Let Misters the. Murderers commence.' If they don't like hanging, then, damn it, let them stop before they start murdering."

Superintendent Ross had a more vivid imagination than his colleague. He could conjure up the scene well enough : the helpless victim shrinking from his assassin and pathetically sheltering himself with the collar of his overcoat, as though the bullets had been hailstones.

" We'd better see if we can identify him," he said brusquely.

Campden agreed with a nod, and began an examination of the dead man's personal belongings,

laying each article down by itself as he proceeded
with his enumeration.

"Right-hand pocket of overcoat," he began, " a
pair of gloves, fur-lined. *Made in France* on one metal
clip, and a lot of hieroglyphics and *J. R.* on the other.
Nothing much there."

He laid down the gloves.

"Left-hand pocket, a box of Swan vestas, half-
empty. Ticket pocket of overcoat—ah, here's something useful !—a first return ticket, Horston to
Hammersleigh, outward half snipped by the ticket-
examiner. Now ! "

"It looks as if he'd been killed between Horston
and Hammersleigh, on the face of it," Ross admitted.
"But, of course, he may have overshot his station,
or changed his mind and gone on past Hammersleigh
of his own free will before he was murdered.
Don't let's get too many preconceived notions,
Campden."

His colleague grunted rather contemptuously ;
read out the ticket's number—6431—and the current
date, 23rd November, which was stamped on it ;
and then put the ticket along with the rest of the
collection.

"Right-hand breast-pocket of jacket," he continued, " a leather case with some papers in it. This
is what we want."

He opened the case, extracted some documents,
and from a second compartment took several
Treasury notes.

"Eight pounds ten," he commented. " Doesn't

look like robbery at that rate, unless he had a bigger lot of notes in a separate case. Oh, here are some visiting-cards in a compartment by themselves. *Oswald F. Preston, Hillcrest, Abbey Road, Horston.* That accounts for the initials on the hat ; evidently it's his."

He turned over the letters and glanced at the superscriptions on them.

" Some of them are addressed to O. F. Preston, Esq., and some to Preston's, Ltd., Great Deacon Street, Horston. H'm ! Preston's ? Isn't that the firm that manufactures weighing-machines for shops, Ross ? Scales and so forth ? You ought to know."

Superintendent Ross nodded.

" Yes, that's the firm. Their head office is in Deacon Street ; but their factory's out at Hammersleigh, which would account for the Hammersleigh ticket you found in his overcoat pocket. He must have been going out to the factory on business this morning."

" That limits things down a bit, then," Campden pointed out, as he pursued his search. " If he was going to get out at Hammersleigh, then he must have been shot before the train reached there, somewhere between Horston and Hammersleigh. He would know the line well enough not to get carried past his station, even in a fog like the one this morning, one would think."

A moment or two later he added :

" There's nothing more of any importance in his pockets : just keys, fountain-pen, cigarette-case, some loose money in the trouser-pockets, cigarette-holder, and handkerchief. Well, we've got something definite to start on, at any rate : we know who he is."

The constable put his head in at the door to announce the arrival of the police surgeon. Dr. Kegworth was a clean-shaven, hard-faced, competent-looking man, who wasted no time.

"All the wounds are in the head, the constable says," he said as he took off his hat and put down his bag. "We'll need to make sure of that. I don't want to be biased by suggestions, if you don't mind, Superintendent. I'll hand you my report as soon as possible. You don't want to stay now, do you ? All right."

And with very little ceremony he dismissed them from the room.

"The constable here can give me a hand if I need it, I suppose ? " he said, as he ushered them out.

Superintendent Ross glanced round the station and picked out a remote bench on one of the platforms.

"Suppose we postpone lunch for a while ? " he suggested to his companion. "I'm not exactly keen on food at this moment, somehow. Let's spend a minute or two trying to pull this thing into shape, first of all. Then I think we might do worse than drop into an optician's shop and see what he can tell us about that bit of spectacle lens. By that time, perhaps, we'll be more in a mood for lunch."

Campden made no objection ; and they walked over to the isolated seat, where they could talk

THE TWO TICKETS PUZZLE

without the risk of being overheard. As he sat down, Ross took from his pocket the time-table he had bought at the bookstall, opened it at the page showing the service between Horston and Kempsford Junction, and ran his finger across the columns until he reached the figures for the 10.35 a.m. train. Alongside them were the times for the express by which he himself had travelled that morning.

	Local	Express
Horston	10.35	10.47
Acton Holm	10.42	—
Poppleford	10.49	—
Nottage	10.53	—
Ingstone	10.58	—
Summerfield	11.05	—
Hilton-le-Gay	11.10	—
Seven Sisters	11.16	—
Hammersleigh arr.	11.22	11.10
„ „ dep.	11.25	11.14
Morpledene	11.29	—
Nether Kinton	11.33	—
Forest Forge	11.40	—
Menham	11.47	—
New Keyling	11.53	—
High Catton	11.59	—
Kempsford Junction	12.04	11.37

Campden leaned across and examined the figures. " Must have been pretty quick work, that murder, wherever it was done," he pointed out, after a few seconds spent in mental arithmetic. " The longest time between stops anywhere on the line is seven minutes."

" Less than that," Superintendent Ross corrected. " Your seven-minute difference includes the stop

at the station, and that would be round about a
minute on the average, I should guess. Besides, he'd
have to be well away from the station before he
started ; and he'd have to get everything cleared up
by the time he ran into the next station. Allow
another minute for these two items, and your
maximum time-allowance drops to five minutes."

" Five minutes to shoot a man. several times and
then stuff his body under the seat ? It's quick work.
But hold on a moment ! That fog held up the local,
you said, didn't you. Perhaps he had more time
than that, really."

" Possibly he had," Ross conceded, " but, whether
he had or not, he's a cool card and he backed himself
to manage it even in the five minutes that the time-
table allowed him."

" You seem to know a lot about him," Campden
commented, with a tinge of irony. " An old friend of
yours who took you into his confidence beforehand,
perhaps ? "

Superintendent Ross grinned broadly.

" Just for that, Campden, I'll leave you to worry
this out for yourself, instead of telling you now. I'll
give you my views, just the inferences without the
evidence. First, this affair was deliberately planned
beforehand by a rather clever—— No, I'll stop there.
I'm practically sure of that much, on the evidence
we've got up to the present ; and I'll be very much
surprised if Kegworth's P.M. doesn't confirm what
I say. Just wait till you see his report on the fatal
wounds."

" I'll wait," said Campden sardonically. " It'll be a treat to look forward to, won't it? A bright spot in my young life. Go on."

" Well, it's obvious enough that, if the thing were planned in advance, the fog was outside the calculation. No one could predict that beforehand. A fog in town doesn't imply a fog all along the line, so that, even if the preparations had been made that morning, the fog was an unforeseeable factor at the point on the line where the murder had been pre-arranged. But the preparations weren't made this morning. So the time-table was the schedule for the scheme."

" Ah, indeed? " Campden interjected in a sceptical tone.

" Indeed, indeed," Ross retorted chaffingly. " And, if you admit all that——"

" Not I," said Campden bluntly. " I never was keen on fairy stories, not even when I was a child."

" Who's telling you fairy stories? I'm giving you the plain facts of the case in a way suitable to my hearers, leaving all the hard parts out. And the fact that this was a prearranged affair limits it a good deal. For one thing, the murder must have been done before the train reached Hammersleigh, because Preston's ticket took him only that length, and there was no foreseeable chance that he'd go past his station. Ergo, Campden, we needn't pay much attention to the strip of line between Hammersleigh and here, so far as the murder itself goes. All we can look for there is traces of people leaving the train after the murder was done. And that reminds me, you'd better arrange for an S.O.S. on the wireless, asking all passengers to communicate with the police. That's our best chance of raking in evidence on that side."

" I'll see about that," Campden agreed. " Go on with the fairy story. I'm beginning to get a taste for these things. I'll have a look at my little girl's Hans Andersen to-night, like enough."

Superintendent Ross ignored this.

" If the murder took place before the train reached Hammersleigh, then it must have been done on one of three stretches of line : between Horston and Poppleford ; or between Ingstone and Summerfield ; or else between Hilton-le-Gay and Hammersleigh. On all the rest of the line the stops are too frequent to allow time for a man to be shot and stuffed under the seat and a piece of newspaper to be burned to ashes."

" That newspaper ash puzzles me a bit," Campden admitted grudgingly. " What would any man want to burn a bit of newspaper for ? If it had been letters or anything like that, one could understand. But newspaper——"

Ross laughed at the expression on his colleague's face.

" I don't know why it was burned," he volunteered, " but I can make a guess at it, perhaps. Suppose somebody got blood on their hands in manhandling the body when it was pushed under the seat. It needn't have been much blood, if care was taken ; but it would be safest to get rid of it. The natural thing to do would be to clean it off with a handkerchief, if you were a man—a woman's handkerchief wouldn't go far in that job. But whoever planned this affair had brains ; and blood on a handkerchief sometimes takes a bit of explaining away. Why not use a newspaper—and burn it afterwards to destroy both the blood traces and any finger-prints you may have left on the paper ? That's what I'd do myself, I think ; and I should think that's just what happened in that carriage."

"That sounds all right," Campden conceded readily enough. "In fact, it sounds pretty certain. I almost begin to think you've got your reputation honestly, Ross. Ah ! but what d'you make of the second bit of paper—the edge of the sheet of notepaper ? That needs explaining too. You don't tell me the murderer wiped his hands on a bit of notepaper when he'd got newspaper handy. That won't wash."

He glanced up, and detected, with some irritation, a quickly suppressed smile on Ross's face.

"The notepaper ? " Ross retorted. "You want everything explained at once, Campden. This case has hardly begun yet, you know. Did you notice anything interesting about the bit of notepaper, by any chance, apart from its being singed ? "

Campden pondered over his recollections for a few moments, as though he were trying to visualise the scrap of paper.

"It was about half an inch wide," he announced

39

at last, weighing each statement as he uttered it. " It was plain white notepaper. It had a sort of curl on it, as if it had been rolled up into a spill. And it was singed at both edges, though the straight line of the paper-edge wasn't burned into on the original edging side."

" Quite accurate," said Ross approvingly. " You have a sound pair of eyes in your head, Campden. I'll say that for you. It's what's behind the eyes that counts, though, in a case like this."

" Meaning brains, I suppose ? " Campden said indignantly. " I haven't the kind of brains that make up fairy tales, I admit. I suppose, by your way of it, the murderer, after he'd done his job, felt he wanted a smoke. So he screwed a bit of paper into a spill, walked over to the drawing-room fire, and lit his pipe with it. Funny world you must live in, with chimney-pieces and railway carriages all mixed up together."

" That nasty sneering habit ! " said Ross deprecatingly. " Don't let it grow on you, Campden. Here it's robbed you of another bit of priceless information ; for now I'll just wait till Kegworth's finished his job before I tell you what I think. I can't be quite sure myself till I see his results ; so we're not losing anything by waiting. But I bet I'm right."

He rose to his feet as he spoke.

" Now, what about an optician's shop ? You know the nearest one where we're likely to get the information we want."

CHAPTER IV

THE LENS

As they emerged from the station, the sight of a telephone-box suggested a fresh ramification of affairs to Superintendent Campden.

"Now that we're sure it's Preston," he pointed out, "we ought to notify his relations, whoever they are. Someone will have to identify him, just to be on the safe side."

Superintendent Ross had followed Campden's glance towards the telephone-box. Before answering, he paused for a moment to make a mental calculation.

"Rather a brutal way to break news of that sort," he suggested, with a gesture towards the telephone-box. "It's not a pleasant job ; but someone has to do it, and it may as well be me. I'll be back in Horston again quite soon enough to go over to his house and explain things before they see it in the evening papers. No one but ourselves knows who he is yet, and, if a reporter tackles you, you can always forget that point for an hour or two, can't you ? "

"I daresay I could," Campden agreed. Then, with a change in tone, he added, "Talk of the devil ! Here's one of them already. You can do your own lying, Ross. I'm off to ring up our people and get them to 'phone Scotland Yard about that S.O.S. on the wireless."

He walked off in the direction of the telephone-box, but before he had taken half a dozen steps he was intercepted by a middle-aged man who had just come up.

" Sorry, Mr. Wolvey, I can't spare a moment just now," Campden apologised. " You'd better speak to Superintendent Ross here ; he knows all about the affair. Ross, this is Mr. Wolvey of the *Kempsford Herald*. I won't keep you a minute ; and then we must hurry along," he added meaningly, as he turned away towards the public telephone.

Ross had often been indebted to newspapers for help in his cases ; and he believed in keeping on the right side of the Press. He dictated to the reporter a concise account of the whole affair so far as it had gone, with the exception of the name of the murdered man.

" You can amplify that if you get hold of the porter who found the body ; and the stationmaster can probably give you further information. Of course, you won't mention anything specific in the way of clues. We don't want the murderer to learn how much we know, naturally."

" Who's the victim ? " Wolvey demanded. " You forgot to tell me that."

" The body hasn't been identified yet by anyone who knew him," Ross said, covering his evasion with a firm tone. " But I tell you what, Mr. Wolvey. The *Herald's* a morning paper, isn't it ? And there's no evening paper in this place ? Well, if you'll look up Superintendent Campden about six o'clock, I think we'll be able to give you the name. That'll be in plenty of time for your purposes, so you're losing nothing. Awkward for all of us if you published the wrong name, you know ; and deuced awkward for us, at any rate. Call him a well-known business man and you'll be quite safe. It's a good general description."

Wolvey had the sense to see that nothing more was to be extracted from the Superintendent at the moment ; and Ross took care to make it clear that no one else would get the information before the hour he had named.

" So you needn't be afraid of being done out of a scoop," he pointed out.

" I'd meant to wire one of the Horston evening papers," Wolvey explained regretfully, " and it makes a poorer story without the name."

" Nobody here recognised the poor beggar," Ross responded disingenuously. " He doesn't belong to this neighbourhood."

Campden emerged from the telephone-box and rejoined them.

" Well, what about it ? " he demanded. " Time we were moving along, isn't it ? "

He turned to Wolvey with a broad smile.

" No use sleuthing around, Mr. Wolvey, to see what we're going to do next. We're on the road to Palmer's restaurant ; and then Superintendent Ross is going to take the first train home."

Ross explained the matter of the six o'clock appointment to his colleague, who reassured the journalist.

" Come and see me at six o'clock and I'll probably have some news for you. And now, Ross, I'm hungry."

Wolvey went into the station to hunt for further details.

" And now," said Ross, " what about this optician's ? I sort of gathered from your frank and honest statement that his shop's on the road to Palmer's Restaurant."

" It is. I'm always strictly truthful. We go down this street here."

Their call at the optician's did not occupy much time. There was quite enough glass left to identify the type of lens.

" Write down the technical formula for the thing, please," Campden asked the man behind the counter after the examination had been made.

When the slip of paper was passed across to him, he read on it :

$$- 5.50 \text{ sph. } + 0.50 \text{ cyl.}$$

" Of course, I can't say what the position of the axis may have been," the optician pointed out. " You need to see the thing in the frame to tell that."

" What sort of sight would a person have who needed a glass of this sort ? " Campden inquired.

" From the look of the lens, I'd be inclined to

44

think it came out of a pair of tortoiseshell-rimmed reading-glasses. I can't swear to that, of course ; it's just an opinion. But, in that case, the lens would suit somebody with fairly short sight and a quite perceptible amount of astigmatism."

" I'm not quite clear about astigmatism," Ross interjected. " Suppose these are reading-glasses. I take it that whoever wore them was short-sighted and would need other glasses for his ordinary use in the street. Now, would these other glasses have a cylindrical curve on them too, or would ordinary spherical lenses serve well enough ? "

The optician looked rather doubtful.

" I think it's likely that both sets would need to be made to suit the astigmatism ; but I shouldn't care to swear to it. You'd better try an oculist for an answer to that ; all I do is to test people's eyes and give them the lenses that seem to fit their sight. I'm not an expert, really."

Campden recovered the lens fragment, picked up the paper with the technical description on it, and bade the optician good afternoon.

" Now, we'll have some food," he suggested. " That'll leave us just time to get back to the station and hear if Kegworth's found anything startling, so far ; and then it'll be time for your train."

Their meal did not take long ; and they reached the station again in plenty of time for the Horston train. Dr. Kegworth was still engaged on his gruesome task ; but he had already a fair amount of information to give them.

45

"All the wounds are in the head," he explained curtly. "Five of them. If only four shots had been fired, the man might have lived, though one of the wounds is serious. The fifth shot was fired from behind and below. The bullet went in behind the left ear and lodged somewhere in the anterior part of the brain. It killed him. As to the other wounds, one of them is purely superficial. The shot entered the tissues, but didn't damage the bone. A scalp-wound, merely. I haven't found the bullet. Probably it glanced off the bone and emerged again."

"That would be one of the bullets we found in the carriage, likely," Campden confirmed. "Yes, go on, doctor."

"There's another wound, much the same, behind the right ear. I found no bullet there, either."

"We found two bullets in the compartment."

"Then there's a third wound on the left fore-head," the surgeon continued. "There was no injury to the bone. It's a purely superficial wound. Here's the bullet. I found it lying just under the skin."

He held up a nickelled bullet similar to those which had been found in the compartment.

"Same calibre as the others," Campden commented, taking it from the doctor and inspecting it closely.

"The fourth wound's much more serious," Kegworth continued. "It's under the left eye. I've extracted the bullet. It's not the same as the others —a leaden one, not nickel-covered, and bigger calibre. Here it is."

46

He produced the projectile and handed it to Campden. But Campden, instead of examining it, turned to stare at Ross with marvel in his eyes.

" You guessed something of this sort ? "

Ross nodded.

" It was fairly simple, if you just happened to look at the facts in a particular way," he said.

" This complicates things a bit," Campden mused, turning the leaden projectile absently between his fingers. " Two pistols of different calibre—does that mean two murderers or was it one man with two pistols ? "

" Neither," said Ross, with a suppressed smile.

" Neither ? " echoed Campden, in unashamed surprise. " It must be one or the other."

" The whole thing was done by one man with one pistol," Ross asserted confidently. " Look at the facts and you'll see the thing staring you in the face. There are five wounds in all. The fatal one was probably made by a leaden bullet, but, as we haven't got it in front of us yet, we'll leave it out and confine ourselves to the four projectiles that we've actually seen with our own eyes."

" Three nickelled bullets from an automatic pistol and one heavy-calibre leaden bullet fired from a revolver, I should say," Campden emphasised. " You said the automatic bullets were .38's yourself ; and this leaden one looks to me like a .45 or thereabouts."

" I'll come to the bullets immediately," Ross explained. " First of all, consider the wounds made

47

by the nickelled set. One hits him behind the left
ear, but doesn't damage the bone at the place.
Same in the case of the wound behind the right ear.
Then, in the third case, the bullet strikes him on the
left forehead, doesn't injure the bone, and actually
comes to rest under the skin. And in this last case the
shot was fired so close to the head that there were
actually slight signs of burning on the skin and hair.
You'd never make me believe that a normal automatic would produce results like that, Campden.
It's got a fairly high muzzle-velocity, and you
couldn't persuade a village idiot that a bullet from
it would stick in the skin six inches from where the
pistol was fired. The shot might have glanced off
the bone ; but it would have had far too much
speed on it, even then, to lodge under the skin
of the forehead. It's simply incredible, that's all
about it.

" Damn it ! I ought to have seen that ! " Campden admitted frankly. " And I suppose you've got
something further ? "

" Take the nickelled bullets themselves, that you
were so eager about a moment or two ago. Where are
the marks of the pistol's rifling on their casings ?
There's hardly a scratch on them, so obviously they
never were fired from the pistol they were meant to
fit. They must have come through a barrel of a much
bigger calibre ; and the leakage of gas between the
bullet and the barrel accounts for the low penetrating power. They had nothing like the full
energy of the cartridge behind them ; and one shot

—the one that made the forehead wound—was hardly better than a misfire."

" Now I see what that strip of paper was for," Campden interrupted. "You mean that the murderer used a heavy-calibre revolver and he rolled strips of paper round the .38 bullets to bring them up to the diameter of the revolver-barrel ? Then why did we find only one strip ? "

" Perhaps he picked up the rest ; or perhaps they stuck in the revolver rifling. I expect he picked them up, and missed the one we found, because it had blown under the seat somehow. He was in something of a hurry, remember, Campden, with a five-minute time-limit on his work."

" I think I see how it was done now," Campden went on. " The murderer had a .45 revolver. The first chamber was loaded with an ordinary .45 cartridge with a leaden bullet ; the next three had the paper-rolled .38 bullets in them, and the fifth chamber had a .45 normal cartridge. He attacked Preston suddenly and shot him in the face with leaden bullet No. 1. It wasn't fatal ; and Preston turned round and buried his face in the corner of the carriage. Then the murderer came up close to him. Preston instinctively turned up his overcoat collar, poor beggar, to shield himself ; and the murderer blazed thrice at him at close range without doing much damage, since the .38 bullets had no penetrating power. Then he finished the job with leaden bullet No. 2, fired upward from somewhere on the left side. Is that it ? "

" It's as near as we're likely to get, I expect,"
Ross confirmed. " And now you see why I said it
was a put-up job, all thought out beforehand ? A
man might have a revolver in his pocket by accident. But he wouldn't accidentally have a revolver
ready loaded in a peculiar way like this. Pre-
meditation's as plain as the nose on your face, thank
goodness. We've so much to go on. It isn't merely
a homicidal lunatic on the loose. And I expect to
get some more evidence yet—perhaps in a day or two.
If it turns up, then we can convince any jury that
this was a completely cold-blooded affair, thought
out long beforehand—and that helps a lot towards
a conviction."

Superintendent Campden's nod gave assent to this
view of the case.

" It's going to be a matter of pure circumstantial
evidence," he said reflectively, " and that's always
a tricky thing to put to a jury unlesss you've plenty
of it and all hanging together nicely. The bother is
that, except for that bit of spectacle lens—which
may belong to Preston after all—there doesn't seem
to be a single thing in the compartment that puts us
on the track of the criminal, not one."

" He's had plenty of time to think things out,"
Ross said confidently, " and he's made no mistakes,
apparently."

Campden thought he saw a possible flaw in his
colleague's assertion.

" H'm ! " he grunted, " I'll admit that he must
have made his arrangements before he got on to the

train—the bullets more or less prove it. But that carries you back only to about 10 a.m. this morning, and you talk as if you thought this had all been planned much longer ahead than that."

" I can't prove it," Ross confessed frankly, " so there's no use going into it, just now. But I expect to get the evidence before long, from what I've seen."

He turned to the police surgeon and took his leave. Campden followed him out on to the plat-form.

" My train's in a minute or two," Ross said, glancing up at the clock-dial. " Let's run over the next moves. If the murder was done on the stretch between Horston and Hammersleigh, then it's a case for us in Horston. We'll need to hunt up all the information we can at intermediate stations along the line, to see if we can pin down the murderer amongst people who left the train at any of these places. I'll put a detective-inspector on to that job —Mornington's a good man. He'll work up from Horston to Hammersleigh, including Hammers-leigh station. Would you put someone of your lot to do the same for the stretch between here and Hammersleigh ? It'll save time to work from both ends. We'll need to get the ticket-collectors and porters while their memories are fresh, or else they'll begin recollecting dozens of things that never happened at all."

" They'll do that, anyhow," Campden interjected morosely.

Ross glanced again at the clock.

51

"Would you mind ringing up Mornington now and telling him to meet me on the platform at the terminus when my train gets in? Then I can start him on his job at once, before I go out to Preston's house. It'll save time."

"All right," Campden assured him, as Ross turned to hurry towards the waiting train, "I'll fix that up for you; and I'll send a man down the line from this end."

CHAPTER V

IN SEARCH OF A MOTIVE

Superintendent Ross secured a carriage to himself ; and, as the train steamed out of the junction, he lit his pipe and settled down to an undisturbed consideration of the Preston case. Very little reflection satisfied him that he had extracted from the known facts everything that he judged valuable. So far as he had gone, he felt on firm ground.

Dismissing that side of the subject, he began to turn over in his mind the points which were still lacking in the story of the crime, and the type of evidence which would be needed to fill the gaps.

Obviously, the murderer and his victim had travelled together, for some part of the journey at least. Inquiry would have to be made in the hope that someone who knew Preston might recall seeing him in company with the criminal. Superintendent Ross had little real hope in this direction. He knew too well the unobservant nature of the ordinary town-dweller when in a crowd at a railway-station. Still, there was always a chance, he reflected. Mornington could be trusted to rake through the whole station staff at the terminus and unearth any information that could be got.

It was on the cards, though, that the murderer

had not joined the train at Horston, but had got into Preston's compartment at one of the stations farther along the line. Putting himself mentally into the murderer's shoes, Ross felt inclined to dismiss this hypothesis. A man might pass unnoticed at a big terminus ; but on the platform of some sleepy little wayside station he would be conspicuous and easily remembered. The murderer had evidently laid his plans skilfully ; and Ross felt fairly sure that a point like this would not have escaped him. The chances were that he joined the train at Horston. But, in any case, Mornington's investigations along the line would throw some light on the subject, if they had any luck.

Where had the murderer arranged to leave the train after committing his crime ? Clearly enough, Ross concluded, he would get out at the next station. Nobody in his senses would travel a yard farther than he was forced to do in company with the body of a victim, and with the chance of a fresh passenger getting into the carriage at any stop. But that seemed to imply that the murderer would hold a ticket to the station just beyond the site of the assassination ; for, if he gave up a ticket for any other destination, it might attract the special attention of the collector, even if no excess fare had to be paid.

Remained the motive behind the crime. Ross knew quite well that, if circumstantial evidence is strong enough, the Crown need not suggest a motive in its case for the prosecution ; but he knew also that juries were apt to shy when no sound motive was put before them to account for the crime. A motive would have to be discovered, if the prosecution was to make a certainty of getting a conviction.

Superintendent Ross's experience had convinced him that at the root of almost every murder lay one of four primary causes : mania, revenge, money, or a woman ; and now he examined each of them in turn to see which could be eliminated. Homicidal mania he dismissed almost immediately : this murder had nothing in it to suggest a disordered mind acting on the spur of the moment. Revenge, also, the Superintendent felt inclined to exclude from his problem, or at least to leave in the background until he had explored the other possibilities. If it were a case of revenge, then—as things went in this country —a murderess seemed more probable than a murderer. But only an exceptionally cool and determined woman could have planned and executed a crime like that on the 10.35 train. On the face of things, Ross was inclined to doubt the plausibility of any such hypothesis.

This left only money or a woman as a probable cause of the murder. One was as likely as the other, so far as the available evidence went ; and Superintendent Ross was on the look-out for fresh indications pointing to either. It was, in fact, with this at the back of his mind that he had volunteered to carry the news to Preston's family. In the initial confusion produced by the announcement, something might leak out which would help him to choose the right trail. If money were at the root of the affair, direct questioning would bring out something of value ; whereas, if passion underlay the mystery, a hint might be got from even the demeanour of those who had been most closely associated with the murdered man.

At the Horston terminus, Ross found the Detective-Inspector awaiting him on the platform. Mornington was one of the Superintendent's favourite sleuth-hounds ; and Ross had once given three reasons for his preference. " Mornington looks more like the man-in-the-street than anyone else I know ; so he attracts no attention when he's at work. Then, he can pick up more bits of useful information in a given time than most people. And, finally, he never gets mixed up between the actual evidence he collects and the inferences he draws from it ; so I can rely on getting the plain facts apart altogether from any superstructure of theory, if I want them. Show Sergeant Sparkford—that cocksure devil—a basin of soapy water and a wet cake of soap. He'll tell you at once that somebody had been washing his hands, and he'll probably back it up by saying the towel was damp, too. How does he know anyone washed his hands in the basin ? That's not a fact ; it's an inference. But Mornington would have more sense. He'd say : ' There was soapy water in the basin ; the cake of soap was moist ; and the towel was damp. I should imagine somebody had been washing his or her hands ; but it's quite possible that somebody had been shaving without a shaving-pot : either notion would fit the case.' By the Mornington method you never get confused between what's definitely provable and what's only surmise."

A few minutes sufficed to lay before Mornington the rough outline of the investigation which was needed to clear up, as far as possible, the railway side of the case. When he had finished this, Superintendent Ross added what seemed to the Inspector an unrelated piece of work.

" By the way, since you're going down there, you might kill two birds with one stone. Just beyond Seven Sisters Station a prize ram was shot a week ago; it belongs to Mr. Chepstow and it's in charge of a man called Tarland—you'll easily find out about it. Make any inquiries that occur to you—the more zeal you show, the better ; Chepstow's under the impression that we're not doing enough. Now, here's the important point. If that ram dies, we're to be notified at once ; and the vet.'s not to start any investigation on his own. I want the bullet out of the beast ; and we must have it taken out in such a way as to leave no doubt about its identity. You understand ? Then that's all just now."

Hailing a taxi, the Superintendent drove off to Preston's address. Now that he was actually on the verge of it, he began to wish he had left to someone else the task of breaking the news.

Abbey Road was a broad avenue in the best quarter of Horston, and Hillcrest proved to be a good-sized house standing in a roomy garden. Telling his taxi to wait, Superintendent Ross walked up the drive and rang the front-door bell, feeling even more uncomfortable at the emotions which he expected to rouse by his tidings.

A neat maid opened the door, and Ross looked into a wide hall with Persian rugs scattered about the parquet. On one side was a broad, thick-carpeted stairway ; and, as Ross moved forward, a pretty, dark-haired girl of about twenty ran lightly down the steps, glanced in passing at the figure in the doorway, and vanished into one of the rooms leading from the hall. As she opened the door, Ross heard the notes of a piano, obviously reproduced from a loud-speaker.

" I'm Superintendent Ross," he explained, bringing his attention back to the maid, who was looking at him rather doubtfully. " Is Mrs. Preston in ? I've an important message for her."

He had taken the chance that Preston was married, to save explanations to the maid, and he was relieved to find his guess was right.

" Mrs. Preston's at home," the maid admitted, with a glance of curiosity at the unexpected visitor. " I'll give her your card."

She held out her hand. But this did not suit Ross's plans. He had no intention of being shepherded into a room and left there to wait while the mistress of the house used the maid as a go-between. If he was to learn anything, he would need to be there when the blow fell. He produced his card ; but as the maid examined it he put an end to her obvious hesitation.

" This is urgent," he said authoritatively. " Take

me to your mistress at once. I must see her immediately."

His manner convinced the maid, and she led him
towards the door through which the dark-haired
girl had disappeared. As she opened it to usher him
into the room, the loud-speaker within lifted its
voice.

" *This is London calling. Here is an S.O.S. message
which has just come in. Will any passengers on the* 10.35
*a.m. train from Horston to Kempsford Junction this
morning, please communicate immediately with the Chief
Constable, Horston, (Telephone number, Horston* 3981),
or with any police station ? "

The maid hesitated for a moment on the threshold.
Then, when the machine paused and allowed her
voice to be heard, she announced the
Superintendent.

Ross found himself in a drawing-room softly lit
by shaded lamps. At his entrance, the girl whom he
had seen on the stairs rose from a chesterfield and
crossed over to switch off the wireless. Beside the
bright-burning fire, a second girl was sitting in a big,
comfortable easy-chair with a fashion paper on her
knee ; and as the Superintendent appeared at the
door she looked up swiftly with a blend of surprise
and misgiving in her expression. Then, as he came
forward, she put down the paper and rose to her
feet. Her attitude made it clear that she expected him
to address her and not her companion. Apparently
she was Preston's wife. Who the other girl might be,

Ross could not guess ; for she was obviously not a daughter of Mrs. Preston, and there was no resemblance to suggest that the two might be sisters.

Though he did not betray it, the Superintendent was momentarily taken by surprise. Preston was a man in the fifties ; and Ross, naturally enough, had formed a mental picture of a Mrs. Preston about the same age. This fair-haired young beauty would not fit into the frame. Disconcerted, he took in with an unobtrusive glance the girl's lithe figure, her beautifully kept hands, her clean-cut features, with their faint suggestion of plaintiveness.

" She'd be a pretty toy for any man," he reflected crudely. " And she looks just the sort that might like to be played with."

Superintendent Ross believed in telling the whole truth as soon as possible in cases of this kind ; and now he gave his message with as little beating about the bush as he could.

" Mrs. Preston ? I'm sorry I've brought you bad news. You'll need to prepare yourself for a severe shock—very severe. Mr. Preston was found dead in the train at Kempsford Junction this afternoon."

The Superintendent had but little belief in facial expression as a guide to mental processes ; but he watched keenly to see the effect of his thunderbolt. Mrs. Preston's reaction to the news gave him something to think about ; but it certainly failed to yield any definite information. The startled gesture, the twitch of the lips, the whole attitude of the girl spoke clearly of a shocking surprise. But in her eyes there seemed to be something more. Their look gave Ross the impression that apprehension was mingled with the other emotion. She seemed to have grasped his news and instantly to have fallen afraid.

" Dead ? " she exclaimed incredulously. " How did it happen ? Quick, tell me ! "

Again Superintendent Ross found himself confronted by the unexpected. The tone was one of acute anxiety rather than of the grief which might have been anticipated. Some people have the faculty of facing bad news courageously and keeping their feelings under iron control even when confronted with the worst ; but Ross doubted if Mrs. Preston was one of these. Her voice suggested that her interest was concentrated almost entirely on the manner of her husband's death, to the exclusion of any great sorrow at the event itself.

" She was completely staggered by the news. Therefore, she had no foreknowledge of the murder." This flashed through Ross's mind on the instant. " And yet, by the look of her, she must have had an inkling that something of the sort was on the cards, or, at least within the possibilities. And, what's more, she's afraid. Afraid of what ? That someone she's interested in may have had a hand in the business ? "

Superintendent Ross's attention had been so concentrated on Mrs. Preston that the personality of the other girl had escaped his attention. She recalled herself to him by coming over to Mrs. Preston and putting an arm round her as though to soothe her. As she did so, the two exchanged glances ; and Ross

61

had the feeling that the younger girl guessed the real reason underlying Mrs. Preston's attitude. And in that unguarded silent communication he caught something in the older girl's face and in her wide-opened eyes. Fear was plainly there, now : fear verging on panic.

Whether it was the sympathetic touch of the younger girl or merely that she had reached the end of her resources, Mrs. Preston's self-control suddenly failed. She made two unsteady steps to the chair and then buried her face in the soft cushions while her whole body shook with the violence of her sobbing. Her companion knelt beside her for a few moments ; and then, failing to calm her, turned to Ross.

" How did it happen ? " she asked, in a trembling voice.

" I don't know," the Superintendent admitted. " I'm sorry to have to tell you that Mr. Preston was found shot—no, not suicide. His body was dis-covered when the train reached Kempsford Junction. It was identified by some letters he had in his pocket. That's really all we know at present."

The girl nodded, without commenting directly. After a few seconds she made a suggestion.

" I think you'd better go and wait in the study for a minute or two, while I look after Mrs. Preston. Then I'll come and talk to you, if there's anything you want to know. You can't worry her just now ; and I can tell you anything just as well as she could. Please ring the bell, and the maid will show you where to go."

Superintendent Ross raised no objection to this course. Mrs. Preston was clearly on the verge of hysteria ; and no good could come of any attempt to question her at that moment. Besides, he thought, he could spend his time better in dealing with other witnesses just then. An indirect approach would probably yield quicker results than any attempt to go too fast along the direct path. He allowed himself to be conducted to the study.

During the quarter of an hour he was kept waiting, he had considerable difficulty in refraining from theory-building. It all looked so simple, if one examined the facts from one point of view. But Ross had an ingrained mistrust of solutions arrived at before all the facts were available ; and now he held his imagination in check lest it should run away with him.

At last the younger girl came into the study, and, seeing the Superintendent still on his feet, she invited him by a gesture to find a chair.

" I don't want to be away from her too long," she pointed out. " It's been a terrible shock to us both, as you can guess ; and she's not really fit to be left alone just now. So would you mind being as quick as you can ? "

Superintendent Ross acquiesced at once.

" I quite understand," he said sympathetically, " and I'll not detain you long just now. I want to ask only a few questions. It's rather awkward, though, for, you see, I don't even know who you are."

The girl forced a faint smile.

" I'd forgotten that," she said. " My name's Madge Winslow, and I'm a sort of ward of Mr. Preston—no relation at all, but I've no one in the world now, so he asked me to stay with him. That's all you need about me, isn't it ? "

" I suppose he's your trustee ? " the Superintendent asked, ignoring her obvious attempt to cut his personal questions short.

" He and Mr. Iverson the lawyer. Is it really necessary to ask these questions ? I don't want to be rude, but I'd like to get back to Mrs. Preston as soon as possible."

Superintendent Ross took her rebuke in good part.

" It makes it easier when I know exactly who you are," he protested good-humouredly. " You must remember, Miss Winslow, that you're all strangers to me. Now, have you any idea—any idea at all ?— who could have had a grudge against Mr. Preston ? "

Madge Winslow looked down at the carpet as though reflecting on the question. At last she lifted her eyes to meet those of the Superintendent.

" I really can't say," she answered in a colourless tone.

Ross was not taken in by the form of words she had used.

" Do you mean you can't or you won't, Miss Winslow ? It's not quite the same thing, you know," he said bluntly.

" I can't say," she repeated, with more than a touch of stubbornness.

The Superintendent forbore to press the point.

He expected to have less prejudiced evidence on the matter very shortly ; and there was no need to drive the girl into open antagonism by baiting her when she had obviously decided to give no help.

" We'll say no more about it," he conceded, as gracefully as he could. " Now, I want, if possible, to find out exactly what Mr. Preston did to-day. You probably know something of his routine. What did he usually do ? "

Madge Winslow again looked at the carpet, as though to occupy her eyes while her mind was concentrated on the question he had asked. When she looked up this time, however, it was with a different expression ; and Ross gathered that she was giving him the truth to the best of her knowledge.

" This is Friday, isn't it ? " she began. " Then he usually left the house after breakfast and walked to the tram going into town."

Superintendent Ross was slightly surprised.

" Didn't he drive in to business ? "

Madge shook her head.

" He had a motor accident a year or so ago, and nearly killed someone. After that, he sold the car, and he would never use a motor if he could help it. He always took the tram into town."

" Ah, that explains it ! You see, I told you that I did not know anything about any of you ; and it seemed strange that a man like Mr. Preston should go in by tram. Please go on."

Madge Winslow nodded and continued.

" He used to go first to his office. Then, when the

bank opened, he went there and drew a cheque for the amount of his employees' week's wages at the factory. That left him just enough time to catch the train to Hammersleigh. The factory's at Hammersleigh, you know."

"You mean he used to take the money down to the factory himself? Surely a clerk could have done that."

"He was faddy about a good many things," Madge retorted in an impatient tone. "That was one of his fads—taking the money down himself and handing it over to the manager. That's why I asked if to-day was Friday—I wasn't sure. Friday was his day for going down to Hammersleigh, every week."

"Then he would have this money with him to-day?" Ross demanded, recalling that no such amount of cash had been found at Kempsford Junction.

"Oh, yes. The men's wages would have to be paid, so of course he'd have the money for that."

She paused for a moment, and then added :

"You think it might have been a case of robbery?"

"I can't say," Ross answered, repaying her in her own coin. "Do you suppose anyone knew that he carried such a sum? Did he never delegate the money-carrying to someone else?"

"Never," Madge declared in a tone of conviction. "He had his own way of doing things, and nothing would make him alter that. I'm quite certain he would have the money with him."

The Superintendent did not feel inclined to lay too much weight on this opinion. He had seen a faint sign of relief in the girl's face when the money point was brought up ; and he inferred that she wished to lay stress on it in the hope that she might be spared further probing into the possible motives in the case. He decided to make a pretence of sharing her views.

" If I understand things, Miss Winslow, the case is this : there was no concealment of the money being secured at the bank ; anyone might have got that information by watching him when he cashed his cheque ; he travelled always with the money on Fridays ; and he went down to Hammersleigh invariably by the same train each week—the 10.35. Is that right ? "

" That's quite right. I see what you mean, Mr. Ross. Anyone might have laid plans to secure the money, since they would know every move beforehand ? "

" If he never diverged from that routine, as you tell me."

" Except when he was on holiday. Then the factory manager carried the money."

Ross had made up his mind that nothing of value was likely to be extracted from Madge Winslow. Quite obviously she had decided to be guarded in her answers until she had time to consider the situation ; and he had the impression, rightly or wrongly, that she had not been over-fond of her trustee. From the stress laid upon Preston's fads and adherence to

67

routine, the Superintendent suspected that he had been a person with but little give-and-take in his methods ; and possibly he had antagonised Madge Winslow by making her conform to his ideas whether she liked them or not.

" Can you give me the name of his lawyer ? " he asked. " There will be a number of things—legal affairs—which he could take off your hands. I don't want to trouble Mrs. Preston more than is necessary."

" It's Mr. Iverson of Arthur Street."

Ross had no desire to detain Madge Winslow any longer. He had another source of information in reserve ; and now he led up to this in such a way as to avoid suspicion of his real motive.

" There's just one question I wanted to ask Mrs. Preston," he explained. " We must have every detail checked as far as possible, you understand ? Now, can you tell me when Mr. Preston left the house this morning—I mean within a few minutes of the exact time, if possible."

Madge Winslow shook her head, and Ross was delighted to find that his excuse for questioning the servants was ready-made.

" Mrs. Preston would know nothing about that," the girl answered frankly. " She always breakfasts in her own room, and never sees—never saw him," she corrected herself hurriedly, " in the morning at all."

" Then perhaps you could tell me ? " Ross asked.

" No, I can't, as it happens. I was at a dance last

night, and didn't get up for breakfast at the usual time this morning."

" That's a pity," the Superintendent said in a regretful tone. " You see, I must get the information somehow. Perhaps one of your maids could tell me ? "

" Quite possibly," Madge Winslow answered coldly ; but she did not offer to summon the maid.

" Then, with your permission, I'll ring the bell," Ross said, suiting the action to the word, before the girl had time to raise any objection. " And now, Miss Winslow, I won't keep you any longer ; Mrs. Preston should have someone with her, as you said."

The girl bit her lip. Quite obviously she had intended to stay in the room while Ross examined the maid ; but he had turned her own weapon against her so skilfully that she could not protest. After having laid so much stress on Mrs. Preston's need for her, she could hardly linger, now that the Superintendent had released her. She took her dismissal rather ungraciously ; but, when the maid appeared, she left the room, throwing a suspicious glance behind her as she went.

Superintendent Ross believed in suiting himself to his company when he went in search of information ; and, if Miss Winslow could have watched him, she would have seen a sudden transformation in his manner when he came to deal with the maid, who now stood waiting in the doorway.

" Come in, come in," he said genially, " and shut

the door, please. Don't be afraid, now. It's nothing
to do with you. Mr. Preston's met with an accident
—a bad accident ; and we're looking into the
matter."

He had made up his mind to keep the news of the
murder from the maid for the present. Later on, he
might be able to use it with effect.

" I suppose Mr. Preston left the house as usual this
morning ? That would be about—what o'clock
would you say ? "

" It would be about five or ten past nine. What
sort of an accident has he had ? "

" I'll tell you all about it in a minute," the Superintendent assured her. " Just let's get things clear,
first of all. By the way, what's your name ? "

" Poole's my name."

" Thanks. H'm ! Five or ten past nine."

He made a note ostentatiously.

" By the way, what sort of a man was Mr. Preston ?
I mean, does he get on well with people and all that
sort of thing ? "

" He's a bit fussy for that," the maid declared,
with some bitterness. " It's not the sort of place I've
been used to, not by a long way. I've given notice at
the last—simply couldn't stand any more of it. How
would you like, now, if you had a man always prying
about to find something done wrong by his way of it ;
rubbing his finger on the picture-frames to see if
there was any dust, complaining about a finger-
mark on the silver, poking his way into the scullery
to see if the taps needed new washers, and all that

sort of thing? That's the kind of man he is, and I don't care who knows I said it."

"It's not my way of doing things, certainly," the Superintendent admitted sympathetically. "A bit of a trial, eh? But you're lucky, you know. You can get away if you want to. It must be worse when you can't give notice."

The maid rose to the bait immediately. She was obviously a thoroughly spiteful person, only too glad to get rid of her venom.

"Ah, there you're right," she confirmed. "If I was married to a man like that, I'd think I'd made a poor bargain, for all his money. Not but what there's ways of squaring the account," she added, with a sly glance.

"This is the kind of talk I like to hear," the Superintendent encouraged her. "It needn't go any further, of course ; just between you and me, eh? I can make a guess at what you mean. Mrs. Preston's a bit younger than the man she married."

Evidently the maid's spiteful tongue carried her away.

"That's another reason why I'm leaving here. It does no girl's character good to be mixed up in a divorce case, no matter if it's no affair of hers. That's the way I look at it, and I don't see as how you can blame me for it. No one wants a maid that's been up in the divorce court giving evidence. 'Might be my turn next,' they say, and whose fault's that? Not that I mind a bit if she amuses herself with that doctor, it's no affair of mine and I wouldn't throw

a stone at her, not me. Preston's just been asking for
it, with his red-tape sort of way of doing things. Nice
and convenient, isn't it ? when you can tell to a tick
when your husband's coming home; no chance
of being caught out, is there ? Fine goings-on there's
been in this house, I can tell you. It's high time
I left it, I think."

The Superintendent's expression suggested that he
was revelling in the baser aspect of these disclosures.
He was not inclined to credit Poole with exactitude ;
she was too obviously the sort of person who can
make a mountain out of a molehill at a moment's
notice. But he believed that probably there was a
substratum of fact below her flood of gossip.

" This doctor—what's his name ?—pays visits on
the Q.T., does he ? "

" It's Dr. Selby-Onslow ; you know, the one with
the house in Prince's Square. Well, if I had to choose
between them myself, I'd rather have the doctor, by
a long way, in spite of that hard face of his. More
about my own age, for one thing, and good-looking,
too, in a kind of way. It must be a handy thing being
a doctor. ' May '—that's Mrs. Preston, you know—
' May telephones she's got a sore throat. I'll just drop
round and have a look at it.' That's how it's done,
mostly. Real convenient, isn't it ? Sometimes it takes
an hour and a half to get that throat properly seen
to."

She tittered sardonically.

" Quite so ; we understand, don't we ? " the
Superintendent assured her. " But what about this

Miss Winslow ? Doesn't she spot the nigger in the fence ? "

" Oh, her ? She's a bit of a fly-by-night herself, if you ask me ; one of these cool ones, you know. She's out most of the time—dance-mad, if you ask me, always supposing that it's dancing she goes for. She wouldn't see anything ; and, if she did, it would take a lot to put her off her balance, I can tell you. Besides, she's as thick as thieves with May ; they both hate the old man, d'you see ? I don't blame them— he fusses so. He's always criticising Madge's clothes and finding fault with her for going out to dances so much—enough to set any girl against him, take my word for it. And, of course, he has the whiphand of her over her money till she's twenty-five. She'll come into a pile then—my word !—but just now he cuts the money down as low as he can. He just hates seeing people enjoying themselves."

Superintendent Ross reflected for a moment. Facts—if they were facts—were pouring in on him now quickly enough ; but he wanted something more definite than this mass of scandal.

" About Dr. Selby-Onslow," he demanded, as the maid stopped to take breath after her tirade. " When did you see him here last ? Within the last day or two ? "

" He hasn't been here for a couple of days," Poole admitted. " He rang up this morning, though, before May got out of her bed."

" What time was that—when he rang up, I mean ? "

" After the old man had gone off to business, as you can guess," Poole answered, with a meaning smirk. " It was about a quarter past nine or so. I took the message, that's how I know what it was."

" And what was it ? "

" Oh, nothing much. Just that he'd been called away unexpectedly to Morpledene and wouldn't be able to get back in time to see her this afternoon. She was more than a bit sulky when I took that message up to her room—a bit of a disappointment for my lady, that was."

Superintendent Ross paid no apparent attention to the incident.

" Now, there's another thing I want to know," he pursued. " When Mr. Preston left the house this morning, was he carrying anything—an umbrella, or a bag, or an attaché-case, anything of that sort ? "

" He had an attaché-case with him—a thing about that size." She illustrated with her hands. " He always takes it with him on Fridays. He hadn't an umbrella with him that I remember."

Ross had secured all the information that he expected to get from this source, and he had no further time to waste.

" I want to use your telephone for a minute," he said. " You might let me see where it is, will you ? "

Rather reluctantly, Poole allowed herself to be ushered out of the room.

" To-morrow's my evening out," she volunteered as she led the way across the hall. " If there's anything else that you'd like to know, perhaps we'd have more time then. I generally go to the pictures."

Superintendent Ross ignored the tacit invitation. Poole, apart from her use as a mine of information, was not a very attractive personality.

" I'll let you know in good time if there's anything further," he said, leaving the matter apparently open.

" The telephone's in the cloak-room—in here," Poole directed.

Rather to her obvious annoyance, the Superintendent closed the door after him, leaving her outside. He had quick ears ; and a smile twitched his lips as he realised that the maid was waiting outside in the hope that she might catch what he said over the 'phone.

" A bit dry for her, poor thing," he reflected whimsically, as he took up the directory. " She's welcome to all she hears."

He looked up Iverson's address in Arthur Street, and from the next entry he obtained the lawyer's home telephone number.

" This is Superintendent Ross, of the central police station, speaking," he explained when he had got his connection. " Is Mr. Iverson in ? "

There was a moment's hesitation at the other end of the wire ; then came the formal reply :

" Mr. Iverson is speaking. What do you want ? "

" I should like to see you for a few minutes, as soon as convenient, Mr. Iverson."

The lawyer appeared to be considering this request. After a few seconds he demanded again :

" What do you want ? "

" I can't explain fully over the 'phone. An accident's happened to one of your clients, and I must see you about it as soon as possible. It's a serious matter."

Superintendent Ross had reverted to his more formal style of conversation.

Again there was a pause, then the answer came in a tone of some annoyance.

" I'm just going to sit down to dinner. Is it important enough to interrupt that ? "

" I'm afraid it is," Ross assured him, smiling sardonically to himself over the 'phone.

The Superintendent had no idea when he would get his next meal himself, and it gave him a faint satisfaction to disturb someone else.

" Very well, then," Iverson answered ungraciously. " Come as soon as you like."

With that, he put down the receiver.

" Fond of his food, apparently, this Iverson," was Ross's not unnatural reflection. " Well, he'll just have to interrupt his dinner for once."

CHAPTER VI

THE LAWYER'S EVIDENCE

At the gate of Hillcrest, Superintendent Ross directed his taxi to drive to 83 Warlingham Road ; and in about a quarter of an hour he found himself outside a small villa set back from the street. Evidently he was expected, for the maid admitted him at once, without asking either his name or business.

An old-fashioned hat-and-coat stand in the hall attracted the Superintendent's glance, and he noticed that it held only men's sticks and umbrellas.

" Bachelor, apparently," Ross inferred almost mechanically, as the maid led him to a room and switched on the light.

" Mr. Iverson's at dinner just now," she explained. " He left a message that, if you thought the matter urgent, he would come out and see you ; but he's got three guests to-night, come to play bridge ; and if it's convenient, he'd rather not be interrupted for twenty minutes or so."

Ross glanced at his watch. After all, he reflected, what did twenty minutes matter ? So far as he could see, there was nothing further that he could do that night. Mornington's facts would not be available till the following day. If he insisted in dragging the

77

lawyer away in the middle of dinner, he would gain
nothing vital ; and he would certainly be faced with
a man in a bad temper, who would be only too
anxious to cut the interview short in order to get
back to the dinner-table. If anything of value was to
be extracted from Iverson, it was worth while to fall
in with his obvious wishes at this point.

" Don't interrupt him on my account," he told the
maid. " I'm quite prepared to wait till he's finished
dinner."

The maid had evidently received instructions
which provided for this.

" Mr. Iverson told me to ask you to smoke, if you
wished," she explained, bringing a couple of silver
boxes from a table near at hand. " These are cigars,
and here are cigarettes, if you'd prefer them."

She offered him his choice, but Ross declined both.
He put his hand in his pocket for his pipe ; then,
thinking better of it, he pulled out a cigarette-case
instead.

" Thanks, I'd rather have my own," he said.

" Mr. Iverson said perhaps you'd care to see
Punch or some of the other papers. They're over on
the table at the window, if you'd like to look at
them."

" Thanks. I'll get them for myself."

The maid withdrew ; and Ross, left to his own de-
vices, began to pass the time by examining his surroundings. His eye fell on the silver boxes, and he
inspected their contents.

" H'm ! Abdullah, Cairo, No. 2, Special. These

must run him into about £1 a hundred. Imported Havanas, the cigars. There must be a lot more money in the law than I ever got out of it, if he can afford to splash that kind of stuff on a casual visitor."

He lit his own Gold Flake cigarette with a satisfaction that was mainly moral. It was against his principles to accept any gifts while he was on official work ; but Iverson's tobacco tempted him sorely. He turned away from the boxes and cast a glance round the room, which was lined with bookshelves.

Superintendent Ross was one of those peculiar people who are fond of books ; and the sight of this ample library made him even more envious than the cigars had done. Also, he guessed immediately that this was the library of a reader, and not merely a collection of complete editions of the classics, bought as furniture and never opened after their purchase.

Having time on his hands, the Superintendent moved over to the nearest set of shelves, vaguely wondering what sort of books he would find there. Books, he believed, gave a fair indication of their owner's tastes and character ; and it amused him to guess, from an inspection of a library, what sort of man collected it.

The first tier suggested nothing except Iverson's profession, for it was stacked with purely legal works, among which Ross noticed a number of volumes on Medical Jurisprudence.

"Funny line, that, for a solicitor in private practice," he mused. "He can't find much use for books of that sort in his work, one would think."

Farther along the shelves, he chanced upon something unexpected : a *Newgate Calendar*, the first complete set he had ever seen. Close to this, his eye caught a row of yellow paper-bound books : Bataille's *Causes criminelles et mondaines* ; and beyond them stood Gross's *Archiv für Kriminalogie*, cheek by jowl with volumes of the *Notable Trials* and some of the *Scottish Trials*. Then came technical manuals by Gross-Höpler, Reiss, and Locard.

" That accounts for the Medical Ju. books," Ross reflected, with the satisfaction of a man who has solved a simple problem swiftly. " He's evidently made a sort of hobby of that side of the law. I wish he'd give me the run of his library. That set of Bataille's out of print and can't be got nowadays."

He put out his hand and pulled down one of the volumes.

" It'll pay to handle Iverson nicely," he concluded, as he turned over the pages enviously. " If this is his hobby, he ought to have a lot of useful information stored away in his head ; a lot of sound precedents, perhaps, if one could manage to set him talking. I'm thankful I didn't rasp him by dragging him away from his dinner."

He retired to an easy-chair by the fireside, and was soon so engrossed in one of Bataille's cases that he was startled by the sound of the door opening as Iverson entered the room.

From the peculiarities of the lawyer's library, Ross had unconsciously pictured Iverson as a keen-faced man with perhaps a suggestion of that spruceness which characterises the fashionable surgeon ; and it was almost a disappointment to find that his involuntary host was a very ordinary-looking person who would have passed quite unnoticed in a crowd.

Iverson's annoyance seemed to have passed away under the influence of his dinner ; and, as he came forward to greet the Superintendent, he half-apologised for keeping Ross waiting so long.

" When you rang me up, I thought at first it was this business of my car," he explained, " and naturally I wasn't over-pleased at being bothered about it just at dinner-time."

" Your car ? " Ross said interrogatively.

" Yes. It was stolen to-day while I had left it standing outside a house—a most annoying business. Of course, I rang up the police and gave them the particulars ; and naturally, when you 'phoned, I took it that someone was coming to make further inquiries."

He dismissed the matter of the car with a gesture and turned to the immediate business.

" What's this about an accident to one of my clients ? "

" Accident was only a word to use over the 'phone," the Superintendent explained. " It's a murder case, Mr. Iverson. Mr. Oswald Preston was found shot on the 10.35 train to Kempsford Junction this morning."

" Found shot ? " Iverson echoed, raising his voice half an octave in his excitement. " Well, I'm——"

He bit off the expression in the middle, with the evident feeling that it was hardly the proper phrase to use.

" Let's hear about this," he demanded.

Superintendent Ross gave the lawyer a summary of the facts, including the bald statement that he had already visited Hillcrest. Iverson had the knack of listening without interrupting ; and he gave Ross his full attention while the narrative unfolded itself. When the Superintendent had finished, Iverson with a movement of his hand invited him to sit down, while he himself walked to and fro for a moment or two, apparently reconsidering the various points which Ross had detailed.

" A bad business," he summed up at last, sitting down in an easy-chair opposite the Superintendent.

" The 10.35, of course. I shouldn't be surprised if I was the last man—bar the murderer, of course— to speak to him alive. That's a strange coincidence, isn't it ? I haven't been near that station for weeks, lately ; and to-day of all days I went there—to see Preston, too. It's a weird world."

He looked up, and noticed that Ross was examining him sharply. At the sight of the Superintendent's expression, the lawyer allowed a faint twinkle of amusement appear in his eyes.

" No, you haven't got the murderer, Superintendent. I didn't travel by the train at all."

Ross, rather annoyed at having let his suspicions appear so plainly in his face, laughed a little to cover his vexation. Iverson smiled in his turn.

" No offence taken, Superintendent. It's your business to suspect, I know."

He settled himself in his chair, and then, after a moment's consideration, spoke again.

" I think it would save time if I told you what took me to the station ? Very well, then. Poor Preston and I are trustees—funny how one's tongue betrays one ! *were* joint trustees in the matter of the estate of Miss Madge Winslow. You met her just now at Hillcrest, didn't you ? Well, as it happens, some stock that we held for her has been redeemed ; and we've had to think of re-investing the cash that came in from it. Preston's a busy man ; so am I ; and we hadn't had an opportunity of discussing the matter thoroughly lately—couldn't hit off a time when we were both at leisure. And we did not see quite eye to eye over the business. He wanted to put the money in Water Board stock, and I had a fancy for the 4 per cent. Funding Loan. That's by the way."

The Superintendent interrupted him for a moment.

" You don't mind my taking notes of this ? "

" The Judges' Rules, eh ? Certainly take notes, and I'll sign them afterwards if you wish it. A lawyer doesn't need to be in criminal practice to know that part of the procedure."

Ross availed himself of the permission, pulled out his notebook, and, resting it on the chair-arm, looked up to show he was ready.

" As it happened," the solicitor continued, " I had to go out this forenoon to look over a house belonging to a client—out Hammersleigh way. My client's abroad, the place is shut up at present, and some alterations are wanted ; so I'd arranged to see the contractor on the spot this morning and talk things over with him."

The Superintendent made a jotting, and Iverson paused until he had finished it.

" I was going down in my car, naturally, since the place is rather out of the way ; and it occurred to me that I might kill two birds with one stone if I could get Preston, poor chap, to come along with me in the car and talk over the investment affair on the road. Do you know anything about Preston ? "

" Not much," the Superintendent admitted.

" Well, one mustn't speak ill of the dead, of course ; and I'm not depreciating him. But he was a creature of routine—a perfect slave to prearrangements. For instance, for years past he's travelled every Friday by the 10.35, although the express starts later and gets to Hammersleigh sooner. His reason was that the express was sometimes late, and that didn't suit him. He insisted on carrying down personally the money for the men's wages at the Hammersleigh factory. I don't know how often I've pointed out to him the risk he ran in dragging that attaché-case full of notes and silver about with him every week and travelling invariably by the same train on the same day. Any unscrupulous devil could have held him up on one of these prearranged journeys and got away with the loot easily enough. That's by the way, though."

He paused to give Ross time to make a jotting.

" As to-day's Friday," he continued, " of course I knew that poor Preston would be taking the 10.35 as usual ; so I went to catch him at the station. I meant to take him down to his factory at Hammersleigh, discussing the investment affair *en route ;* and then, after dropping him, I intended to cut across to keep my appointment with Tenbury, the contractor, at Oxenden Grange—my client's place. It wouldn't really have taken me much out of my way ; Oxenden Grange is about a couple of miles on this side of Hammersleigh, you know.

" Preston banked with the United Mercantile and Trinity Bank—the branch in Garfield Street ; so I knew he'd go into the main entrance to the station in Grosvenor Street. I didn't see any sign of him as I went in ; so I walked over to the bookstall, thinking he might go there. Then I remembered that he had some fad about not reading in the train—afraid of hurting his eyes."

" Did he wear glasses ? " the Superintendent interjected.

" Glasses ? No, he'd perfectly good sight. This no-reading-in-the-train idea was just one of his health crotchets. That's by the way. The 10.35 was at the platform waiting—it starts from No. 1—so, as I didn't see him anywhere about, I took a platform ticket, went through the barrier, and walked up the train. He was one of those people who are always about a quarter of an hour early for a train, even if it's a local. ' Making sure,' and all that sort of thing, you know. I knew where to look for him, for he always travelled in the last first-class compartment in the train—another of those cranky ideas of his. He was sitting in his usual place, back to the engine, with an attaché-case on the seat beside him."

" About what size was the attaché-case ? " inquired the Superintendent.

" Oh, quite a small one : a foot by eight inches, or thereabouts. One of those smooth leather things. I expect he carried the money in it. I spoke to him through the carriage-window and made my suggestion about the car ; but he wouldn't hear of it at any price. What a pity ! He'd have been alive now, if he hadn't insisted on sticking to that train. It seems he'd had an accident with his own car ; and he'd lost his nerve so far as motors were concerned ; so there was no persuading him.

" There was nothing to detain me there, so I didn't wait long ; just made an appointment with him for to-morrow to square up that investment business and get this money off our hands. Then I said good-bye to him and went away to pick up my car. I'd parked it just outside the station ; and I didn't care about being away from it too long. There's no one in charge of that parking-place ; and I felt a bit uneasy about it, owing to the amount of car-snatching that's been going on lately. And now I've lost it after all ! "

" About what time did you leave Mr. Preston ? " Ross inquired.

" Only a minute or two before the train was due to start—about 10.30 or later, I should think."

" There was no one with him in his compartment when you saw him, I suppose ? "

Iverson shook his head.

" No, he had the place to himself."

Superintendent Ross seemed to consider for a moment before asking his next question.

" Did you see anyone you knew on the platform or on the train, by any chance ? "

The lawyer hesitated, as though doubtful about replying. Then something crossed his mind, apparently.

" I don't—oh, well, I heard your S.O.S. on the wireless to-night, so he'll be speaking for himself, no doubt. Just as I was turning away, I caught sight of Dr. Selby-Onslow coming along from the front of the train towards me. He'd come in at the Campbell Street entrance—the one under the railway bridge, you know, at the other end of the platform from the main entrance. Now I come to think of it, I noticed him as he came up the stairs from that lower booking-hall, just beside where the engine was standing."

" You didn't see him get into the train, did you ? "

Iverson shook his head.

" No, he was a few doors away from me when I turned to walk back to the entrance. I happened to look round a second or two later, but by that time he'd found a carriage and got in."

" Had he got into the same carriage as Mr. Preston ? " Ross demanded bluntly.

" Can't say ! " Iverson retorted, with equal bluntness. " That's just what made me hesitate about answering your question at the start. I won't be made to suggest something that I don't mean to suggest, Superintendent ; take that for granted ! I tell you what I saw ; but I'm not going to have it twisted further than the words go. Besides, you've sent out your S.O.S. It's up to the doctor to come forward and tell you what he saw himself."

Superintendent Ross accepted the rebuke without comment. He had no desire to rasp a man who would obviously be called as a witness for the prosecution, and who was quite alert enough to prevent words being put into his mouth.

" Was *he* carrying anything—an attaché-case or anything of the sort ? " he inquired, as though to slip away from the contentious matter.

" He had an attaché-case in his hand," Iverson admitted. " A thing about twenty inches by ten, or so—rather larger than Preston's, I should say. But I won't swear to figures on the strength of a casual glance, remember."

Superintendent Ross seemed to have gone off on a fresh line of thought.

" I don't know much about Dr. Selby-Onslow," he explained. " I understand that he keeps a car and a chauffeur too, perhaps. Rather curious that he should take the local train, surely, seeing that Morpledene's only about twenty miles away. His car would have got him there more comfortably and just about as quick, one would think."

Iverson looked up quizzically.

" You officials always try to pretend that your short suit is brains. I can't imagine that you've over-looked possibilities like a breakdown or an overhaul, or even a car-theft. Any one of these would account for Dr. Selby-Onslow preferring to take the train, wouldn't it ? "

Superintendent Ross turned the point by asking another question.

" Was the 10.35 crowded this morning ? "

" Crowded ? " the lawyer said doubtfully. " That's one of those words that might mean anything, really. If you want facts, I should say that I saw one or two empty compartments in the third class, and the first next to Preston's was empty when I turned away."

" Was it ? " the Superintendent said, with a touch of eagerness, as though he had got a fresh idea from the fact.

He made a note in his book before continuing.

" You're supposing that the murderer may have been next door at the start and got along the foot-board while the train was in motion ? " Iverson asked.

" Or *vice versa*," Ross amplified. " One's as likely as the other, isn't it ? "

" I suppose so, provided the murderer kept his eye open for people entering the next-door compartment during the journey."

" He was quite sharp enough to do that,"

Superintendent Ross declared. " Now, Mr. Iverson, this isn't a civil law business. It's a serious affair ; and it's everyone's duty to help. You were associated with Mr. Preston——"

" I was his solicitor."

" Oh ! I didn't know that. It was the trustee business I meant. But, if you were his solicitor, so much the better. Now you must have known something of his affairs. Can you think of any motive for this affair—anything, no matter how remote, that might put us on the track ? Murder isn't done without some reasonable cause—not this kind of murder, at any rate."

Iverson's eyes wandered to the bookshelves.

" There was a case rather like this in France in 1886 : the Barrême affair. Barrême was shot in the head in the railway carriage and then pitched out on the permanent way. It was never cleared up ; but the general idea was that he had been carrying a fair sum of Secret Service money, and that someone knew it and murdered him for the sake of the cash. Of course, the Government kept quiet about the money, and on the face of it there was no motive. Then, again, there was that case up in the North a while back—you remember it ? "

Superintendent Ross nodded.

" That was money again—and little enough at that when you put it against a man's life," Iverson pointed out.

" So you think Mr. Preston was murdered for the money ? "

" How should I know ? " asked the lawyer, rather irritably. " What is obvious is that it was taking a fair risk to carry a decent sum of money every week by a regular route where a criminal could be sure of finding Preston if he wanted the cash. I spoke to him about it ; but he was one of those people who'll never listen to anything that goes against their routine, unfortunately."

Superintendent Ross put out a feeler in his next question, though he did not expect to get much, in view of what Iverson had already said.

" Money's often at the root of these things ; but I've seen other cases where a woman was at the bottom of the business. What about that aspect of the affair ? "

" Oh, women ? Women are the very devil," Iverson replied, with all the contempt of a case-hardened bachelor.

He paused for a moment or two, as though thinking over something ; then at last he evidently made up his mind to speak out.

" It doesn't take much to see what's in your mind, Superintendent. Well, I think you're barking up the wrong tree ; that's my honest opinion. You're hinting that Mrs. Preston had a hand in this affair, if I'm not misreading you. Take my advice and look elsewhere. I grant you that she married him for his money—that stares you in the face. And he's anything but an ideal husband : he's made her miserable with his routine and his fussiness and all the rest of it. And she'll come out very well under his

91

will ; I know that, because I witnessed it myself. But she's had a dog's life of it, poor girl, and it would be the last straw now if people begin to chatter and suggest that she had any hand in this business. I'm sure she hadn't ; she hasn't enough backbone for anything of the sort. I know her fairly well ; and, like everyone else, I was sorry for her. She couldn't stand up to Preston, even over trifles ; she just caved in for the sake of peace, every time—not that it helped her much."

Superintendent Ross's eyes ranged over the book-shelves for a moment.

" I see you've got the Crumbles case and the chicken-farm affair amongst these trials, up there," he remarked, with apparent irrelevance. " In both these affairs a man murdered a girl because he couldn't screw himself up to tell her he was tired of her. Found it too difficult to say ' No ! ' and cut the knot by killing her instead. Human nature's a rum affair, Mr. Iverson."

The lawyer's gesture was that of a pinked fencer ; there was no denying the aptness of Ross's parallelism.

" I'll need someone to identify Preston's body, just for form's sake," the Superintendent pointed out. " I suppose you won't mind doing that ? It may save Mrs. Preston and Miss Winslow from having to give evidence at the inquest, perhaps."

" I don't mind," Iverson said, by way of consent.

Ross rose to his feet, but paused before taking his leave.

" About this motor-car of yours—you've lost it ? "

" I left it standing at the gate of this house I had to go over with the contractor—Oxenden Grange. We drove up to the place together, and, as we had to look about the grounds as well as the house, we left our cars at the gate. When we got out again, his car was there, but mine was gone. I've given your officials all the facts already and a description of the car."

" I mustn't keep you any longer from your guests," Ross said, half-apologetically, as he moved towards the door. " Thanks for the help you've given me."

He cast a final glance of envy at the bookshelves.

" I wish I'd that library of yours," he confessed.

Iverson caught his meaning.

" Oh, the criminology stuff ? " he said. " I never lend books to anyone—that's one of my principles. I've lost too many volumes through generosity in that line. But, if there's anything here that you'd like to consult, I've no objection to your coming up and having a look at it. That's absolutely as far as I ever go with anyone, nowadays."

The Superintendent expressed his gratitude for this unexpected favour ; and then, being anxious to leave a good impression, took himself off with the least possible delay, so as to allow the deferred bridge-party to begin.

Before going to bed, Ross took a sheet of paper, and, as was his habit, set down in diagram form the characters in the tragedy, so far as they had come within his purview :

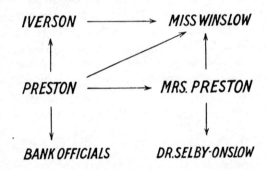

He examined the result discontentedly. It seemed a very meagre gleaning after these hours of hard work.

CHAPTER VII

THE BANK

On the morning after the murder, Superintendent Ross found that his S.O.S. on the wireless had yielded a fair crop of responses, some by letter, others over the telephone. These he turned over to Mornington for checking and comparison with the facts which the Detective-Inspector was gathering from the personnel of the stations along the line. He himself proposed to follow up some of the lines of inquiry suggested by the facts he had acquired from Iverson and at Hillcrest.

His first objective was the branch of the United Mercantile and Trinity Bank in Garfield Street, which the lawyer had indicated as the place where Preston drew the money for the factory wages. Here, as soon as the staff were on the premises, Ross interviewed the manager, and asked for an opportunity of questioning the person who had actually paid over the cash to Preston.

After a few minutes, an alert-looking man with eyeglasses came into the manager's room.

" Mr. Sancroft ? " the Superintendent inquired. " I think you attended to Mr. Oswald Preston when he came in to cash a cheque yesterday morning ? About what time was that, can you remember ? "

" Between ten and a quarter past—about ten past
ten, as near as I can make it. You see, he always came
on Fridays almost as soon as the doors were opened."

" What was the amount of the cheque he cashed?"

" He cashed two cheques yesterday," Sancroft replied, to Ross's surprise. " One of them he presented to me direct ; the other one was brought me
by the manager, Mr. Linsey."

" Let's take them in turn," Ross suggested. " What
was the amount of the cheque he cashed with you
across the counter ? "

" A hundred and thirty-three pounds, nine and
sixpence. Here's the cheque he presented ; I thought
you'd like to see it, so I got it for you."

" Was that about the figure he used to draw weekly
—his wages bill ? "

" It was."

" Can you remember how you paid him ? "

" I can. I gave him this."

Sancroft produced a jotting on a scrap of paper,
and Ross read :

	£	s.	d.
One Pound Notes	83	0	0
Ten-Shilling Notes	38	0	0
Silver	11	8	0
Copper	1	1	6
	£133	9	6

" You haven't the numbers of the notes, I suppose?"

" No, I have not. I have the numbers of the notes
I gave for the other cheque."

" We'll leave it aside for a moment," the Superintendent suggested. " I want to keep this transaction by itself. Can you remember anything further about this £133 9s. 6d. ? "

" I can. I handed him the copper in a paper bag —like this one here."

He produced a small square paper bag and handed it to the Superintendent.

" The silver I gave him in a white canvas bag with the name of the bank on it and ' *Please Return this Bag* ' as well. Here is a bag like the one I gave him."

" Do you always get these bags back ? " the Superintendent asked sceptically.

" Not invariably."

" Then they may get into the hands of people who are not clients of yours ? H'm ! Then bags like these won't be much use as clues, I'm afraid. Now what about the notes ? "

" I counted them and handed them across to Mr. Preston. He re-counted them twice—he was always very particular about his money. Then he slipped each set between two cardboard strips and snapped a couple of rubber bands over them to hold them tight. Then he put the whole cash into his attaché-case."

" You saw the attaché-case close at hand ? "

" I did. It was about twelve inches long by eight inches broad, I should say. I remember that, because once I happened to wonder whether it would hold a piece of foolscap paper without crumpling, and I couldn't make up my mind about it."

" Did you see any initials on the outside ? "

" I did not. But he had one of his visiting-cards gummed to the lid inside, I remember."

" And after cashing that cheque he left the bank ? "

" He did."

" Had you any conversation with him during the transaction ? "

" We spoke about the fog that morning and the weather. That was all."

" H'm ! " said Ross. " Now about this second cheque. What do you remember about it ? "

" That was brought me by Mr. Linsey before Mr. Preston came to the counter at all. Mr. Preston saw Mr. Linsey in his private room. Mr. Linsey came out with the cheque in his hand and told me to give him notes for it, and make a jotting of the numbers of the notes I gave him. He particularly asked me not to give him notes in a series—he wanted the numbers to be at random."

" What was the value of the cheque, do you remember ? "

" I have it here for you to examine. It was for £5 10s. I handed over four one-pound notes and three ten-shilling notes. Here is the memorandum I made of the numbers :

Treasury Note (£1)	S1 /85	809241
,, ,, ,,	S2 /77	314665
Bank of England Note (£1)	D50	157128
,, ,, ,, ,, ,,	D45	174236
Bank of England Note (10s.)	X14	920646
,, ,, ,, ,, ,,	T12	147563
,, ,, ,, ,, ,,	X10	177972

Mr. Linsey took the notes away with him to his private room."

Superintendent Ross refrained from asking any further questions on this point, since obviously he could get fuller information at first hand from the manager himself. He copied the two memoranda which the teller had presented.

" I suppose you didn't notice whether there was anyone else at the counter when Mr. Preston presented his cheque ? "

" There were two or three other people waiting their turn. I didn't notice them particularly, but I daresay I might recall them if you give me time. They were all known to me, and none of them had any interest in Mr. Preston, if that's what you mean."

" That's what I meant."

" Well, I hope you'll get the murderer, Superintendent. But, if you ask me, I think Mr. Preston was just asking for trouble by his methods. Anyone could have got to know about his carrying that money up to the factory each week—just like clockwork. I'd never think of doing a thing like that myself."

Superintendent Ross made no comment on this criticism.

" Thanks, Mr. Sancroft. I wish everybody could be as clear about things as you've been. It's a pleasure to get someone who can say what they mean and stop when they've said it. And now I'd like to see the manager again, if you'll let him know."

When Linsey re-entered the room, Ross took up

the matter of the second cheque ; and again he was delighted to find he had come across a man who could tell a plain story.

" There's no difficulty in giving you details about that," the manager answered the Superintendent's question. " Mr. Preston insisted on my making a special note of the affair, because he wanted to leave no loophole for any misunderstanding later on, if it came to a police-court case. Here are the facts.

" He came in here yesterday morning as soon as the bank opened, and explained that he had been troubled by thefts in the office at the Hammersleigh factory. It was a small matter—a few shillings now and again, with occasional rises to a pound or thirty shillings once or twice. They hadn't been able to trace the thief, though they had some suspicions ; so he made up his mind to try marked money and then get the possible people to turn out their pockets. He was rather fussy in some ways, poor fellow ; and he insisted on doing this sort of thing himself instead of leaving it to his subordinates.

" Well, the upshot was that he gave me a cheque for £5 10s., and got us to take the numbers of the notes. The teller has a list, but Mr. Preston insisted on my taking the numbers as well. Not only that, but he asked me to put private marks on the notes, so that I could identify them even if the numbers were torn off—quite excessive precaution, obviously. To please him, I put a pinhole through the eye of the horse on note No. 809241, a blot of ink on the left-hand leaf on the back of note D50 157128, and so on. Here's the list of the marks, if you want them."

" I may as well make a note of them, since you have the list there," Ross said, picking up the paper. " What became of these notes, by the way ? Did he put them in his note-case ? "

" No. I remember that he opened his attaché-case and dropped them in. I suppose he wished to keep them separate from any notes he had already in his pocket."

Ross nodded.

" That would be all right," he admitted. " The teller told me that Mr. Preston put the notes he got from him between bits of cardboard. That would keep the marked ones independent, since they were loose in the case, whilst the others were in two bundles."

The bank manager made a gesture of agreement.

" I read about the whole affair in this morning's paper," he said, dismissing the subject of the marked notes. " A shocking business, isn't it ? I suppose you haven't got to the bottom of it yet ? "

" Not quite," Ross admitted, in a defensive tone. " We're not clairvoyants, you know ; we have to collect a few facts at the start, to have something to go on. There's a lot in this case that I don't understand. For instance, why did he draw his cheque here every week and carry the cash all the way to Hammersleigh ? You have a Hammersleigh branch, haven't you ? He might just as easily have cashed his cheque there, and saved lugging all that money about with him in the train."

" He had a disagreement with the people at Hammersleigh a long time ago," Linsey explained, " and after that he boycotted the Hammersleigh branch completely—wouldn't deal with them even for the sake of convenience."

The manager's tone showed that his sympathies in the matter lay entirely with his colleagues ; and Superintendent Ross noted mentally that, so far as he had gone in the case, Preston's death had yielded only the most perfunctory expressions of regret from those whose evidence had been taken.

" He can't have been a very likeable creature, evidently," was his inference. " And quite clearly his wife must have had a thin time of it—the Winslow girl, too, probably. But if unlikeableness justified murder, I suppose a fair proportion of the human race would be out of existence to-morrow."

CHAPTER VIII

THE PASSENGERS

Detective-Inspector Mornington fingered the mass of papers which he had laid on the desk before Superintendent Ross.

" That was a bit of a job," he said ruefully, by way of prelude to his report.

Ross, who knew that his subordinate revelled in intricate details, was not deluded by Mornington's tone.

" I knew as much when I put you on to it," he pointed out blandly. " Now tell me something fresh. Go ahead."

Mornington's method of presenting a report was characteristic. In a series of curt sentences, each ascertained fact stood isolated, so that it could be discussed independently if it gave rise to a question.

" I went first to the booking-office at the terminus here," he began. "I asked them to find out what tickets for stations up to Kempsford Junction had been sold on Friday morning before the 10.35 a.m. train started. They were able to tell me that they had sold forty-seven third-class tickets and five first-class tickets. That total includes the sales at the main booking-office on the platform level and also the sales at the low-level booking-office under the bridge at the Campbell Street end of the platforms. That makes fifty-two people who could have travelled by that train."

" Fifty-two people at least," Ross interrupted. " Some others might be using the return halves of tickets bought the day before at Kempsford Junction and the other stations on the line."

" I'm coming to that," Mornington explained. " Next, I got hold of the ticket-collector who was on duty at the far end of the platform, where the stairs come up from the lower booking-office. Rather a stupid chap called Smith. He could remember nothing about anyone who had passed the barrier. He was quite certain that he'd punched no return halves of tickets. My impression was that he was probably accurate.

" Then I got hold of the collector who was on duty at the other end of the platform. He's quite a live wire. But he might be inclined to embroider a bit, I think. He'd punched no return halves either. That disposes of return halves."

Mornington allowed himself a faint expression of triumph as he refuted the Superintendent's suggestion. Then his face relapsed into its customary woodenness, and he continued :

" The second ticket-collector is James Hutton. I questioned him about the ticket-holders who had passed his barrier. In addition to ordinary tickets, two platform tickets had been presented. I asked him if he could describe the holders. One was a man

in a brown suit. Hutton remembered him because
he saw him bump into a man just at the gate. The
man in the brown suit was looking back as he came
to the barrier, and he ran full tilt into a passenger
entering through the gate. I had some difficulty in
identifying the man in the brown suit. I find he's a
lawyer of the name of Iverson. The collector
remembers him passing the barrier outwards.
Iverson confirmed this without knowing I'd seen
the collector.

" The other holder of a platform ticket was a girl,
Hutton says. He can't describe her accurately.
Dark haired, smartly dressed—that's about as far as
he goes. He didn't see her after the train left. I
haven't got her identified."

Superintendent Ross's face betrayed a slight disappointment at this admission, but he made no
comment. Mornington, he knew, had done his
best.

" I went back to the other ticket-collector, Smith,"
the Inspector continued. " When I put it to him
direct, he remembered that two people had presented platform tickets at his end. He could give no
description of them, whether they were men or
women. That makes fifty-six people on the platform,
fifty-two of them with tickets entitling them to travel
by the train.

" I got hold of the stationmaster. He gave me a
description of the train as it was made up every
week-day. I made a note of the position of the
compartment in which Preston's body was found.

A man might have got into it from the next first-class compartment, while the train was in motion, without much risk. With more risk, a man might have got into Preston's compartment from the forward third-class compartment of the next carriage."

" The windows were heavily frosted that morning," Superintendent Ross contributed. " There would not have been much chance of a man on the footboard being seen by anyone in adjacent compartments. He might have been seen from the projecting window of the guard's van ; but, after all, a guard can only be on one side of the train at a time."

Mornington waited until his superior had finished, and then continued his report :

" That finished the job here in Horston for the time being. I'd got a list of the tickets sold. The next thing to do was to check the collection of them at the different stations along the line. I did that by telephone, first of all. All the forty-seven third-class tickets were given up. Four out of the five first-class tickets were collected. The fifth first-class ticket must be the one you found in Preston's pocket. That accounts for all the tickets.

" All the first-class tickets had been given up at the proper stations. One third-class passenger had got out at Hammersleigh and had given up a ticket entitling him (or her) to travel to the next station : Morpledene. That may have no importance in the case. Morpledene and Hammersleigh are only two miles apart. The passenger may have been bound for a spot halfway between them. He (or she) may have meant to get out at Morpledene when the ticket was taken, but changed his (or her) mind at the last moment and got out at Hammersleigh instead.

" Over the telephone, I checked the point about return halves of tickets previously sold. Nothing of the sort had been collected. All tickets surrendered bore that date of Friday. Any return tickets were outward halves. That checks up with the statements by the ticket-punchers at this end. No excess fares had been paid by any passengers on that train.

" I made inquiries about tickets sold at intermediate stations along the line. No first-class tickets had been sold for the 10.35. Here's a list of the third-class lot. I've checked the collection of them also. They've all been collected at the proper stations. They throw no light on the matter, as you'll see immediately."

" Wait a moment," Ross interrupted. " Let's see if I've got this right. Leave the intermediate station tickets out of account just now. The Horston booking-offices issued fifty-two tickets in all for the 10.35. One of these was Preston's. That leaves fifty-one. Fifty of these were given up at the proper stations, and no excess fares were paid. One ticket for Morpledene was given up at Hammersleigh instead. That's right ? "

" That's right," echoed Mornington. " Now about the pistol. While I was on the telephone, I got all the surfacemen warned to search for it. It hasn't turned up anywhere on the permanent way or within throwing distance of the line, so far as we've gone. So, if it was thrown out of the carriage window after the murder, it must have been missed by the search or else the murderer hunted it out himself and collected it."

Superintendent Ross seemed rather downcast at the news.

" I'd feel more comfortable if we could lay our hands on it," he admitted.

" It may turn up yet," Mornington argued, though in a doubtful tone. " They're still searching. I'd better get on with this report. I went down to all the stations between here and Hammersleigh and questioned the staffs. Dyce from Kempsford covered the ground between his end and Hammersleigh. We got nothing suspicious. Barring Hammersleigh, they're all tiny wayside stations, where the porters know everybody in the neighbourhood by sight. No strangers—except Dr. Selby-Onslow—joined or left the train at any of these places. Dyce and I got lists of everybody. There's nothing in it. Hammersleigh's the only weak spot, being a bigger place ; but I don't think we've missed anything there. I checked up the tickets received at Hammersleigh with my list, and there's no sign of anyone landing there who's not accounted for one way or another, so far as the wayside stations go."

Superintendent Ross was taking a certain intellectual pleasure in the Inspector's report, quite apart from its criminological importance. He liked to see a piece of work done methodically and described accurately ; and, of all his subordinates, Mornington was the man who could be most relied on for both of these features.

The Inspector turned over the papers on the table, and extracted one or two of them before he continued his statement.

" I concentrated on the people who joined the 10.35 at Horston. Fifty-two passengers—fifty-one plus Preston—had to be accounted for. That's a bit of a job. But I had a fair amount of information. First of all, the S.O.S. on the wireless brought in seventeen messages. I saw these people. Some of them knew other people whom they'd seen at the train, or else they were travelling with a friend or two. That brought the total up to twenty-nine. The extra dozen were able to give me more names. That brought it up to thirty-seven. Then the station staff remembered some regular passengers not on the list ; and, when I got hold of them, I got one or two more names. Then I took the other end—the stations where the tickets showed that people had got out. That brought the final total up to forty-nine. That leaves three unaccounted for still. Here's the list of the forty-nine names and addresses."

" I don't wonder you took some time to get all that stuff together," Ross commented, as he glanced over the list.

" Most of it was time wasted," Mornington admitted glumly. " Hardly any of these people had so much as heard of Preston before the murder. Obviously they're just ciphers in the case."

He cleared his throat, as though coming to something more important.

" Once I'd got on the track of the passengers, I concentrated on their places in the train. Extraordinary how little people remember about where they really sat in a train. At the front or at the back is about as much of it as most of them can tell you. Luckily it was only a case of two carriages : the one a first class, with Preston's compartment at the back end of it ; and the other the third class just behind it in the train. Each carriage had six compartments. Here's the list of the occupants, so far as I can fill it in."

Mornington laid down a paper in front of the Superintendent.

FRONT OF TRAIN

FIRST CLASS	1. Empty compartment.
	2. Miss Ackworth.
	3. Empty compartment.
	4. Mr. and Mrs. Sowerby.
	5. Dr. Selby-Onslow.
	6. Mr. Preston.
THIRD CLASS	A. ?
	B. Mr. Hadlow, Mr. Sibsey, and Mr. Gilsland.
	C. Mr. Yardley and Mr. Cromford.
	D. Mrs. Dymock and child.
	E. Empty compartment.
	F. Mr. Fenton.

REAR OF TRAIN

" I've found out something about each of them,"

110

Mornington explained. "Take them as they come on the list. Miss Ackworth's a sort of late Victorian old maid. She's still all in a twitter because she travelled in a train with a murderer, though she knew nothing at the time, naturally. She heard of Preston first through the newspapers. Mr. and Mrs. Sowerby are an old couple, very well off. He's half crippled with rheumatism, and physically incapable of getting into or out of a railway carriage without help. Then there's Dr. Selby-Onslow. I'll deal with him later.

" So far as I can make out, no one saw anyone in Preston's compartment except Preston himself. That means nothing much. People don't notice things much unless they've a reason for observing. Besides, the windows were frosted and difficult to see through. We can't be sure whether he was alone in the compartment at the start or not.

" That finishes the first-class coach. Take the third-class one now. I can get no information about compartment A, the one next Preston's. Nobody seems to have noticed anything about it. There may have been someone in it or there may not. In the compartment B there were three men. They were all going through to Kempsford Junction. They were old acquaintances, and they spent the time playing cut-throat bridge. One of them knew Preston by sight, and remembered seeing him on the platform. They heard fog-signals going off frequently, but nothing suggested a pistol-shot to them. In compartment C, the two men were strangers to each other, but their stories tally completely. One of them got out at Forest Forge ; the other at High Catton. That's checked. Compartment D gave me some trouble. This Mrs. Dymock couldn't remember exactly where she was in the train, except that she was at the back. But she did remember showing a picture of Densmore Abbey to her kid. I've seen the train, and the only picture of Densmore Abbey is in compartment D. That fixes that. Mr. Fenton's a commercial traveller, well known on the line. He knew Preston by reputation only."

" What about the three so-called empty compartments ? " demanded the Superintendent. " What grounds have you for being so positive about them, while you can't be sure about compartment A ? "

" The doors of compartments 1 and 3 were open as the train moved off. I found the porter who slammed them. He was quite sure both compartments were empty. This man Fenton told me he came up late for the train, just as it was going to start. He opened the door of compartment E, and was going to get in, when he noticed it was a non-smoker. I've checked that. So he went next door, into compartment F. He looked out of the window at once, as he was expecting a friend who might be travelling by the 10.35 ; so no one could have got into compartment E without being seen by Fenton."

Mornington's face, as he closed this part of his report, showed that he knew he had done his work well and was quite confident that it would stand scrutiny.

" And now what about this Dr. Selby-Onslow ? "
inquired the Superintendent. " He was next door to
Preston, you say."

" I'll give you facts, first of all, if you don't mind,"
the Inspector suggested. " I'd rather keep the
inferences separate. It was Iverson, the lawyer, who
put me on to Selby-Onslow being at the station.
He'd caught a glimpse of him as he was looking
back towards Preston's carriage—just when he ran
into someone at the barrier, you remember. No one
else recognised the doctor at the station. He's
a fashionable physician but he holds no hospital appointment, and doesn't come into contact with the
working man much, except by accident. Naturally
no one would pick him out, unless a patient of his
happened to be travelling, or a friend of his happened
to be on the train.

" I haven't gone to see him. I left that to you. It
seemed best. I got my information about him from his
servants, mostly. He's got a fine wireless set. He
invariably switches on for the news at 6.15 p.m. He
was at home at 6.15 on Friday. His maid heard the
wireless going. He reads the newspaper at breakfast every day. Both our morning papers had a big
splash heading on Saturday morning dealing with
the murder. But he did not reply to the S.O.S.
message. And he did not trouble to let us know that
he was a passenger on the 10.35."

" Anything else ? " Superintendent Ross inquired,
as Mornington paused for a moment.

" When he came to the station, he was carrying

an attaché-case rather larger than the one Preston
had the notes in. He travelled to Morpledene, and
got out there. The station staff didn't know him personally, but they noticed him particularly. After
he gave up his ticket, he hung about for a while. They
say he looked worried about something. Then, after
a while, he crossed the line and waited for the next
up train. When it came along, he travelled in it back
to Horston."

" Rather curious," was all that Ross thought
necessary in the way of comment.

" I've made some inquiries about his personal
affairs," the Inspector went on. " He's got a fine
expensive practice, makes a big income, and spends
every penny of it. He's a bachelor. He knew Preston.
He knew Mrs. Preston even better. Rumour is that
she's his mistress. Facts are that he and Preston were
on bad terms, though not openly enemies."

" And your inferences ? " Ross inquired, as the
Inspector seemed to have completed his summary of
the facts.

" Well, then, No. 1 : He hoped he hadn't been
spotted on the train and identified ; so, although he
knew we wanted every passenger, he decided to keep
quiet. That's not inconsistent with innocence, of
course. But it's a rum procedure. And he can't complain if it leads him into trouble. No. 2 : His attaché-
case was a bit bigger than Preston's. Preston's case is
missing. It might have gone inside of Selby-Onslow's
and no one would have been the wiser. Even if it
wouldn't go in whole, a surgical knife would make

short work of it and the bits would fit into the doctor's case all right. In other words, he could have carried off the case and left no trace. And, if he did that, the affair would look like a murder for loot. No. 3 : He's got a motive for clearing Preston out of the way. I'd prefer a safer method myself ; but nothing surprises me when a man gets mixed up badly with a woman. They seem to lose their heads, poor blighters," the Inspector concluded in an almost sympathetic tone.

Superintendent Ross made no remark for a few moments. He seemed to be reconsidering the evidence which Mornington had laid before him.

" I don't say anyone could have done more," he said at last, " but we're left still with a loophole in the business. Three passengers unaccounted for— one of whom may have been the murderer—and the matter of that third-class compartment next to Preston's. It's unfortunate. Still, we're lucky even in getting as much as this. If it had been an express instead of a local, the passengers would have been scattered to the four winds by this time, and half of them quite untraceable."

He paused again, while Mornington waited stolidly. Then in a doubtful tone he made a suggestion.

" I suppose there was no hanky-panky between the local and the express. I was on the express myself, and I remember that it was held up alongside the local just as we were passing."

He shook his head, rejecting his own idea almost as soon as he had voiced it.

" That won't wash. If anyone had done the murder and slipped over into the express, there'd be a ticket missing amongst the local set. And the other way's impossible. No one would have had time to cross from the express to the local, kill Preston, shove him under the seat, and get back into the express again before the two trains separated. There simply wasn't time for that, from what I remember of the length of the stop the express made when it was held up by the signal."

Mornington made a gesture of agreement.

" It was done by someone on the local. That's my view."

" Then we're down to three possibilities. It must have been done by the doctor in the next carriage, or else by someone who was in Preston's carriage, or else by someone in compartment A. It's damned annoying we can't be certain about compartment A, Mornington. One can't ask for impossibilities ; but it is an infernal nuisance that the one vital spot is the one we can't get sure information about. If it hadn't been for the frost that morning, someone would have looked into the compartment window and we'd have had the evidence."

" It may have been someone in Preston's own compartment that did the trick," Mornington contributed. " I did my best to find out if anyone joined the train at the very last moment ; but no one had bothered to note that, of course. According to the guard, two or three people were hanging about on the platform till the last moment, and jumped in just as he blew his whistle ; but he couldn't tell me exactly which carriages they got into. That's the botheration of dealing with the public ; they never seem to use their eyes, except at the pictures."

Superintendent Ross shrugged his shoulders. The deficiencies of witnesses were all in the day's work. He turned to a fresh subject.

"What about that prize ram of Chepstow's—the one that got shot ? Campden, up at Kempsford, shunted the whole affair on to our shoulders ; and Chepstow has been ringing up here every day, wanting the blood of the man who shot it. Did you find anything special when you went down there ? "

Mornington shook his head definitely.

"Nothing whatever," he admitted gloomily. "It seems to have been either an accident or a bit of wanton mischief. The ram was a sound article, so it wasn't insurance that Chepstow was after. The man Tarland has an excellent character. Quite above suspicion, I should say. Chepstow's in a great state, with all the signs of working up further if nothing's produced to satisfy him."

"What about the ram ? Isn't it dead yet ? "

"Not yet," Mornington explained. "But if it recovers, it'll give the vet. the surprise of his life, I'd imagine. I made it quite clear that, if it died, we'd send a representative to the autopsy. Nothing will be done except under our eye, so far as hunting for

117

the bullet's concerned. They understand that quite well."

He looked inquisitively at the Superintendent.

"You've got some notion about this ram. I can see that, or you wouldn't have given me that job on top of all this other stuff. Anyone could handle the ram case, for all that's come out of it so far. There's something behind it, isn't there?"

Superintendent Ross's good-humoured face showed a faint smile.

"Between ourselves," he confided, "I'm practically certain that Chepstow's ram was killed with the same revolver as Preston. That's why I want the bullet—for comparison. But I'm not sure about it; and to cut up a prize ram, even a deteriorated one, might come a bit expensive. So we'll have to wait till the brute dies, as it seems likely to do. If it doesn't, the bullet's always there, ready to be fished out and used as evidence when we've laid hands on our friend with the revolver."

"But the ram was shot a week before the murder of Preston," Mornington objected.

"Of course it was," Superintendent Ross conceded gracefully. "That's what gives me some notion of the murderer's character. He was a person, Mornington, who was prepared to take devilish big risks—the biggest, in fact. But he didn't take any more risks than he absolutely had to. Hence the ram-shooting. A sort of preliminary canter. At least, that's how I read it."

"Oh, indeed?" said Mornington in a blank tone,

as though the Superintendent's words had given him a good deal to think over.

" There's another point you'd better look into," Ross directed. " You spoke about a girl on the platform. ' Dark haired, smartly dressed,' was the description you got. Suppose you go and have a look round Preston's house—Hillcrest's its name, in Abbey Road. There's a dark-haired, smartly-dressed girl lives there—a Miss Winslow. See if she was at the station that morning. And you can have a talk with the maid Poole, too, about the ' fine goings-on,' as she calls them chastely, at Hillcrest in the past. She'll open her mouth wide enough if you give her half a chance, and probably throw in a trip to the pictures as well. That's a treat for you."

" I'll see about it," said Mornington in a sour tone, which augured ill for Poole's chance of visiting a picture-house in his company.

" Let's see, now, what else there's to do," the Superintendent went on. " I'll take over Dr. Selby-Onslow myself ; you needn't bother further about him. I suppose you're still trying to trace these unidentified passengers on the 10.35 ? We ought to get every name, if it's possible at all. And, finally, I think you'd better make a big hunt for any news of these marked notes getting into circulation—the ones Preston had in his attaché-case along with the wages money. If it really was a murder-robbery business, they're almost sure to drift out amongst the general public some time or other."

" Very good," Mornington agreed, checking over

119

the items. " See Miss Winslow : interview the maid ;
finish up the list of passengers ; and keep the hunt for
the notes going : that's all ? "

Something in the Inspector's tone showed that he
thought he had quite enough on his hands ; and
Ross saw that the implied criticism was sound.

" You can drop Miss Winslow and the maid," he
revised. " I'll look into that part of the affair myself."

CHAPTER IX

THE DOCTOR'S EVIDENCE

In the collection of evidence, Superintendent Ross bound himself by the Judges' Rules, but by no others. In some cases it paid best to give a witness due warning, so that he might have time to put his ideas in order before examination. In other circumstances, a sudden pounce on an unprepared man was more likely to elicit the truth. Ross considered that Dr. Selby-Onslow stood in the second category ; so he descended on him without warning at a time when he knew the medico would be at home and disengaged. His card gained him immediate admission to the house ; and he was shown into the doctor's study without delay.

If Dr. Selby-Onslow was surprised by the Superintendent's unheralded appearance, he showed no outward sign of it. In his student days he had read Osler's *Æquanimitas* ; and from that essay he had drawn the lesson that one of the best weapons in the medical armoury was a mask-like facial expression, behind which a man could conceal his real nervousness or uncertainty. A doctor may permit himself to look grave at times. That impresses his patient's relations at the moment, and enhances the credit of the ultimate cure, if one be achieved. But no medical man can risk appearing unmanned or embarrassed if he wishes to retain public confidence ; still less can he afford to be obviously puzzled.

Having absorbed this idea from Osler, Dr. Selby-Onslow had applied himself whole-heartedly to carrying it into practice. In his professional hours he deliberately cultivated a sphinx-like appearance, behind the screen of which he could conceal his real emotions. The battered copy of *Æquanimitas* still stood on his bookshelves ; for even now he had recourse to it from time to time.

As the Superintendent was shown into the room, Dr. Selby-Onslow put down a book and rose to his feet. Before greeting his visitor, he deliberately removed a pair of horn-rimmed reading-spectacles, deposited them on the mantelpiece beside him, and replaced them by gold-rimmed glasses. Through these, he inspected Ross with a certain professional gaze which was among his assets.

" Well ? " he inquired at last, in a perfectly noncommittal tone which was something of a masterpiece.

The Superintendent guessed that Dr. Selby-Onslow preferred, in this case at least, to let the other man do most of the talking.

" Dr. Selby-Onslow ? We haven't met before, doctor . . ."

" No."

The tone faintly suggested that the doctor would have felt it no loss if the Superintendent had never come across his path. Quite obviously the underlying suggestion was that Ross should get straight to business and not waste time over preliminaries. The Superintendent took the hint.

" I'm in charge of the investigations which are being made in the Preston case—the murder on the 10.35 train."

" Ah ? Sit down."

Dr. Selby-Onslow made a gesture towards an easy-chair on the other side of the hearth, re-seated himself in his own chair, and waited for Ross to continue. If the Superintendent had expected to surprise anything in Dr. Selby-Onslow's expression, he was completely balked by the sphinx-like mask which had served the doctor so well in his career. For a moment or two Ross considered whether he should hold up his trump card and keep the doctor in ignorance of the fact that he was known to have been on the 10.35 ; but finally he decided on more direct methods.

" You were a passenger on the 10.35 train that morning, I believe, doctor ? "

" Who told you that ? " Dr. Selby-Onslow demanded, though with no particular emphasis.

Ross was becoming faintly annoyed by the doctor's methods. " Damn the man, one would think *I* was the witness and he was cross-examining me ! " he reflected. " We'll never get on at this rate."

Aloud, he answered curtly :

" We received information to that effect. It's correct, I believe ? "

" It's quite correct," Dr. Selby-Onslow confirmed, in a tone which simulated indifference fairly well. " And what then ? "

Evidently the doctor intended to keep the initiative in the conversation so long as it suited him. Ross, after an instant's reflection, changed his ground.

" You were a friend of Mr. Preston's, I understand."

" Indeed ? Who told you that ? "

The doctor's tone was almost one of faint curiosity ; but Ross thought that it was overdone.

" We received information to that effect," he stated. " Of course, in a case of this kind we start from scratch. We have to find out what sort of man Mr. Preston was, and all that kind of thing. It might lead us somewhere. Can't you tell me something about him—anything you think might be of use to us ? "

Ross was in hopes that by this road he would be able to make his way round some of the doctor's defences. His host stretched his legs, leaned back in his chair, put his finger-tips together, and seemed to sink into a fit of abstraction. It was an attitude which Dr. Selby-Onslow habitually adopted when considering the case of a new patient—impressive without being exactly rude. It merely irritated the Superintendent. At last, after a brief period of brooding, the doctor pronounced his opinion :

" Preston was a crank—a disagreeable crank. He wasn't a patient of mine, though his wife was. He was a homœopathist. A vegetarian, too, of the propagandist type."

Suddenly the doctor became almost communicative.

" That man's mind was simply a confusion of complexes. He had a money-complex—a penny out in his accounts would have sent him half crazy till he'd found the error. He had complexes about his food—he lived almost entirely on fruit and raw vegetables, and quarrelled acrimoniously with anyone who didn't share his ideas. He had another complex about routine—he seemed to live by time-table and expect everyone else to do the same. And he had about a dozen other complexes as well—he was hagridden by them. I wouldn't have shared rooms with that man if you'd paid me five thousand a year. It wouldn't have been worth it."

The Superintendent noted that the doctor had not taken the trouble to feign any regret at Preston's tragic end. After all, he reflected, the affairs of Dr. Selby-Onslow and Mrs. Preston were evidently sufficiently obvious ; and in such circumstances any expression of pity for Preston's death would have rung false from the lips of the doctor. That meant neither one thing nor another, except that it showed Dr. Selby-Onslow to be something better than the worst brand of hypocrite.

As to the repressed animus behind the doctor's description of Preston, that was easy enough to understand. Every one of the facts mentioned was something which would affect Mrs. Preston closely,

and the whole thing was evidently merely a summary of the grievances of Preston's wife which had
been poured into the sympathetic ears of Dr. Selby-
Onslow.

"A difficult man to live with, evidently," the
Superintendent admitted. " Mrs. Preston can't have
had an easy time."

The doctor refused to rise to this too obvious bait.
He kept silence, and waited for Ross's next remark.

" Miss Winslow . . ."

" She loathed him," said Dr. Selby-Onslow
abruptly, and then looked as though he regretted this
display of candour.

Superintendent Ross stared at the doctor for a
moment or two. But the professional mask was on,
and he gauged that he would gain nothing by pushing inquiries further along this line. He was learning
little that he had not already guessed. Without
troubling to arrange for a gradual transition, he returned all at once to the original subject.

" You were on the 10.35 train that morning,
doctor. I need the evidence of every passenger we
can identify, naturally ; and I'd like to hear what
you have to say."

Dr. Selby-Onslow, whose attention had seemed
concentrated on his joined fingers, turned his
head slightly and gave the Superintendent a cold
glance.

" Well, ask your questions," he suggested, in a
tone which faintly betrayed the hostility he was
striving to conceal.

Superintendent Ross accepted with satisfaction the opening given him. The doctor would have been wiser if he had volunteered a statement and refused to amplify it. By suggesting questions, he threw the game into Ross's hands. The Superintendent made no attempt to conceal the notebook which he drew from his pocket.

" Thanks," he said. " I'd prefer to have the whole facts at once, then, in case I'm questioned myself on some point or other. It's easier to take things in chronological order ; it keeps one straight."

He reflected for a moment, then put his first question :

" What took you to the station that morning ? "

Instead of replying, Dr. Selby-Onslow reverted to his practice of asking a fresh question.

" Is that information necessary ? "

" I shall probably be asked something on the point," the Superintendent replied evasively. " Counsel for the prosecution often ask all sorts of odd questions."

" Very well," said Dr. Selby-Onslow ungraciously. " That morning I got a wire signed ' Whitacre,' of Morpledene, summoning me to a consultation—an urgent consultation—about one of his patients. Whitacre I know casually; I've acted in consultations with him before. The wire upset some of my arrangements for the day ; so naturally I went to the 'phone at once and rang Whitacre up, to see if the affair really was urgent. I could get no reply ; the Exchange said his line was out of order. So there was nothing for it but to go. It might have been a touch-and-go case for all I knew."

"But Morpledene's less than twenty miles from town," Ross pointed out with an assumption of innocent incredulity. "Why didn't you take your own car down, instead of going by train?"

"Because the wire asked me to come by the 10.35. Whitacre was to pick me up at Morpledene in his own car."

"I see," Ross admitted. "So you went straight down to the station in your own car, I suppose?"

"I don't see the point of these questions," Dr. Selby-Onslow said testily. "What does it matter how I went to the station?"

"It's just the stupid sort of thing I might be asked," Ross explained apologetically. "I don't want to have to come back and trouble you again, doctor."

"Well, then, if you think it's important, I wanted a pair of gloves; so I told my chauffeur to drop me at Crossens' shop in King Street and take the car home without waiting for me. I bought a pair of gloves at Crossens'; and after that I went round to the station."

"Which entrance did you go in by?" asked the Superintendent. "Crossens' shop's about a hundred and fifty yards from the front entrance."

"And about a hundred and forty-nine from the low-level entrance in Campbell Street. It's six and half a dozen. I went in by the low-level entrance in Campbell Street,[1] took my ticket at the booking-office

[1] See diagram at the front of the book.

there, and went up the stairs to the platform. But what's that got to do with you ? "

" I was just going to ask you if you noticed anyone you knew going by the train," Ross explained. " We're trying to identify every passenger, if possible."

" I saw no one on the way upstairs—no one that I knew."

" What part of the train did you get into, doctor?"

Dr. Selby-Onslow shrugged his shoulders.

" Somewhere at the back end of the firsts. I never notice exactly what compartment I get into."

" Anyone in the carriage with you ? "

" Nobody. When we came to Morpledene, I got out."

" You heard nothing suspicious on the journey, did you ? Nothing like a pistol-shot ? "

" I heard a lot of fog-signals going off—at least, I took them for fog-signals and not pistol-shots."

Superintendent Ross nodded as though satisfied.

" And when you got out at Morpledene ? " he pursued.

" When I got out there, I found nobody to meet me. Whitacre hadn't turned up. Naturally, I was angry. I'm not used to having people let me down in that way. I waited about for a long while, expecting his car to come. It was a cold morning—bitterly cold. I went into a telephone box and tried to get on to Whitacre—he lives three miles out of the village —but his 'phone was still out of order. I couldn't leave the station for fear he turned up. I didn't know the name or address of his patient. At last it was pretty clear he wasn't coming ; and by that time my temper had gone. There was nothing more for me to do at Morpledene, so I crossed over to the other platform and took the first train back to town."

" Yes ? " said the Superintendent, in a tone of friendly interest.

" When I got back here, I rang up Whitacre again. His line had been repaired by that time. He knew nothing of the telegram I'd got ; he'd never sent any. He's a fidgety man, and he seemed more interested in his 'phone than in my time having been wasted. He told me some long story of how his line had broken down on the Thursday afternoon, late ; and all the bother he'd had to get the telephone people to fix it up. When they did come, they found some-one had snipped off about ten feet of the wire and carried it away. It looks as if there was a gang of practical jokers infesting that countryside."

" Haven't you made any inquiries ? " demanded Ross. " What about the telegram ? It might throw some light on the business."

Dr. Selby-Onslow rose from his chair, searched in a drawer, and produced a telegram form.

" There it is," he said. " I don't see what inquiries you can make. A piece of paper can't talk."

Superintendent Ross picked up the form.

" I'll make some inquiries about this," he said, folding it up and slipping it into his pocket. " People have no right to use the post office for practical jokes."

He watched Dr. Selby-Onslow narrowly as he spoke, to see how his proposal was received.

" I'm not sure I want that done," said the doctor, in a hesitating tone. " I've kept the thing to myself ; I don't want it to get about. It makes me look rather undignified, having been hoaxed like that. I think you'd better let the matter rest where it is."

He put out his hand for the telegram, but Ross affected not to see the gesture.

" I'll take good care it doesn't become public property," he said reassuringly. " You needn't be afraid of that."

On entering the doctor's study, the Superintendent had noticed a typewriter standing ready for use on a side-table ; and now his glance swung in its direction. He seemed to find himself in trouble with his fountain-pen. The trouble was genuine enough, since he had taken care to rub his forefinger over his hair as though by accident, and had then surreptitiously transferred some of the film of natural oil to his pen-nib.

" I see you've got a typewriter there," he said. " My pen seems to have gone wrong. Do you mind if I use your machine to copy this wire, and then I needn't take it with me ? "

Without waiting for a refusal, he stepped over to the typewriter and, taking up a sheet of paper, did as he had suggested. Dr. Selby-Onslow's face was not sufficiently mask-like to conceal what he thought of the Superintendent's manners.

Having completed the copy, Ross turned back to

the fireplace and handed the official form to the doctor, who received it with a bad grace. Then, instead of re-seating himself in his chair, Ross turned his back to the fire and rested his elbow on the mantelpiece for a moment. An apparently un-conscious movement of his arm dislodged the doctor's reading-glasses and sent them tinkling on the tiling of the hearth.

The Superintendent seemed completely taken aback by the mishap. He swooped down on the spectacles, discovered that the lenses had been shattered in the fall, and broke into a flood of apologies and self-reproaches for his clumsiness.

"Don't worry about it, please," Dr. Selby-Onslow said icily, though a quiver in his voice showed that the dicta of *Æquanimitas* were being subjected to an exacting test. "It's nothing. These things are always giving trouble. I lost my last pair a week ago."

But the Superintendent refused to let the matter drop.

"Extremely clumsy of me," he asserted, with considerable injustice to the deftness with which he had contrived the mischance. "You must let me replace these, doctor ; I'd no right to be so careless. I've got all the pieces ; and luckily the frame—no, I'm afraid it's got a crack in it, too. Most unfortu-nate ! "

Dr. Selby-Onslow objected strongly.

" I really shouldn't feel comfortable if I didn't replace them," Ross insisted, running his eye

along the mantelpiece in search of something. " Ah !
Here it is ! "

He picked up the spectacle-case and read the gold-
lettered address on the flap :

" Irlam & Holmes, King Street. I'll call there on
my way down town and tell them to send you a fresh
pair as soon as possible."

And, as though closing the matter, he slipped
the spectacle fragments into the case, which he
thrust into his pocket, without paying the slightest
attention to Dr. Selby-Onslow's protests. Then,
with a complete change of tone, he demanded
abruptly :

" And now, doctor, tell me this. Why did you not
come forward with the other passengers and say you
were on the 10.35 that day ? "

Dr. Selby-Onslow's practice of the principles of
Æquanimitas came to his rescue under this direct
attack. His face took on a sphinx-like impassivity, and
his voice was well under control as he replied :

" What advantage would it have been to anyone
if I had come forward ? You've questioned me for a
considerable time, and you've secured absolutely
nothing that helps you in the case, obviously.
We've both wasted our time, to put it bluntly. I
knew I had nothing worth telling, so I didn't volun-
teer evidence which had no value."

" No value in your eyes, perhaps ; but it had some
value to us," Ross pointed out. " We have to identify
every passenger if possible. Preston's murderer must
have been on the train, and, if we have a complete

list, his name will be on it. By not coming forward, you left a blank on my list."

Dr. Selby-Onslow glanced shrewdly at the Superintendent.

" But before you came into this room you knew I was one of the passengers. Therefore my not coming forward didn't hinder you in any way. And since you came here you've learned nothing of the slightest importance."

He suddenly changed his tone.

" If I'd had anything to tell, I'd have rung you up at once. I'd nothing to tell. And if I went to you, then I'd have had to explain all about this hoax which someone has played on me. I'd rather have kept that to myself, obviously. People talk—even the police—and it's the sort of story that would make me look ridiculous. I can't afford to look ridiculous, in my position."

Ross had to admit that the doctor had the logic of facts on his side, from a purely personal point of view. But he inferred that Dr. Selby-Onslow must be a peculiarly self-centred man if he weighed factors of this sort when murder was in question. There was something rather repulsive in the doctor's thought for his own reputation at that particular moment.

It was clear that any further inquiries would be useless. He had got all the information that Dr. Selby-Onslow intended to yield ; and there was no point in prolonging the interview.

After leaving the doctor's house, Ross's first visit was to Irlam & Holmes's shop in King Street.

" I've broken a pair of reading-spectacles," he explained to the assistant behind the counter. " Here are the bits. I suppose you can make me a new pair ? "

He displayed the broken lenses, and the shopman pieced them together roughly on the glass-topped counter. Fortunately, they were not badly smashed.

" Could you write me a copy of the prescription for these things ? " Ross inquired. " It's handy to have it, in case of another accident."

The assistant picked up the fragments and took them away to the testing-room. In a few minutes he came back with a piece of paper. Ross took it, and a glance showed him that the first figures were the same as those he had got from the optician in Kempsford :

R.E. — 5.50 sph. + 0.50 cyl.
L.E. — 5.50 sph.

" Thanks," Ross said, slipping the paper into his pocket-book. " You might send the new glasses to Dr. Selby-Onslow as soon as possible. You know his address ? I'll pay for them now."

CHAPTER X

THE MARKED NOTES

On most official occasions Inspector Mornington's face suggested that he, like Dr. Selby-Onslow, had once been influenced by *Æquanimitas*; but at times, when he had scored an obvious success, his expression relaxed considerably. As he entered Ross's room, the Superintendent saw at a glance that Mornington had good news for him.

The Detective-Inspector made his report in his customary staccato fashion, isolating facts from inferences :

" It's the Preston case. The Bank of England one-pound note numbered D50 157128 has turned up. It was reported to us by a pawnbroker, Leo Allen. He got it from a man who was redeeming some pledges. Allen handed it over to me. I took it to the United Mercantile and Trinity Bank in Garfield Street. The manager identified it at once by a blot of ink he'd made on the back. The teller confirmed this from his list of the numbers of the notes in Preston's packet. There's no question about it being one of the notes Preston had in his attaché-case that morning.

" Allen knew by sight the man who handed it in. We got the fellow identified, after some trouble.

136

He'd been pawning things under a false name. Nothing much in that ; lots of people do it. His real name's Maddox—John Henry Maddox. I went over the records in Allen's books. So far as I can trace, Maddox began pawning stuff on 10th September, and he went on pawning one thing after another right up to 28th November, five days after the murder. He was hard up, obviously. Amongst other things, he'd pawned his wife's engagement ring, a suit of clothes, boots, some silver spoons—things he could take to Allen's without anyone knowing—light stuff.

" Five days after the murder, the pawning stopped. Then, a couple of days ago, he came round and redeemed a lot of things at once—his wife's ring, his clothes and boots, the spoons. Amongst the money he handed over in payment was that marked Bank of England note.

" When I got him identified, I went round the shops where he'd been dealing and got them to let me look at any notes they'd taken over the counter lately. I found a Treasury note amongst them—a pound note numbered S1/85 809241. The horse's eye had a pin-hole in it. The bank officials identified it as one of those in Preston's packet.

" That seemed pretty fair. I made inquiries about Maddox. He was a clerk in Preston's Hammersleigh factory. It appears Preston suspected him of thieving, and dismissed him without a character in August. That's confirmed by the factory manager so far as the dismissal without a character's concerned. They also say that Maddox was quite aware of Preston's routine in bringing down the wages-money each week. Maddox and his wife used to live with an aunt of hers at Morpledene. After he was dismissed, they came up to Horston. No one at Hammersleigh Station recognised him if he travelled by the 10.35 that day. He wasn't a regular traveller at any time. He walked over from his aunt's house to the factory, when he was at work there.

" I've identified every passenger on the 10.35 now bar one. None of them travelled in the third-class compartment next Preston's. If Maddox was on the train, then he may have been in that compartment."

" Even if he was, that doesn't prove that he was the murderer," Ross cautioned his subordinate.

" No," Mornington admitted, " it doesn't. But at any rate I've got fifty-one out of the fifty-two passengers identified. That's better than I expected at the start. And since the notes were on the train, and one of them at least was in Maddox's possession, there's a very fair likelihood that he was number fifty-two."

" Well, go ahead," the Superintendent suggested. " What else do you know about him ? "

" To-day I went round to his house," Mornington continued. " I asked him to account for the note D50 157128 which he had had in his possession. He turned white about the gills as soon as I mentioned it. Apparently he thought he'd got away with it, and it was a bit of a shock to find the game was up.

I suggested he might like to make a statement to you. At that he pulled himself together a bit. I suppose he'd expected to be arrested at once. So as soon as he'd got his boots on—under my eye, of course—I brought him along here. He's outside now, if you'll see him."

" Bring him in," the Superintendent directed.

Mornington went out, and in a few moments ushered the suspect into Ross's room. The Superintendent was case-hardened to situations of the sort, and his swift examination of the newcomer's aspect was untinged with any obvious prejudice. Maddox was a little man of about thirty-five, plainly of the clerk class. He was neatly but rather shabbily dressed ; and his stiff collar was slightly frayed and obviously home-laundered. It needed no second glance to diagnose him as a man down on his luck. He was, naturally enough, very nervous, and seemed hardly to know what to do with his hands.

" Sit down, Mr. Maddox," the Superintendent directed, with a gesture towards a chair facing the light. " Inspector Mornington tells me you wish to make a statement. I'm going to have your statement taken down in writing ; and after it's finished I'll give it to you to read over and check. You understand ? Good. Now, what we want to know is how you came into possession of a Bank of England one-pound note numbered D50 157128, which you handed over to Leo Allen, the pawnbroker."

Maddox, like a trapped animal, glanced mistrustfully from the face of one official to the other ; and his Adam's apple worked convulsively once or twice before he could find his voice.

" I don't quite know where to begin," he said faintly, at last.

" Then we'll go back to the beginning," Ross suggested in an encouraging tone. " Not a bad place to start from, usually, Mr. Maddox. Let's see. You were employed in the office at Preston's factory down at Hammersleigh, weren't you ? And at that time you were living—you and your wife—with a relation of yours at Morpledene ? Then there was some trouble at the factory, wasn't there ? Suppose you tell us about that."

The kindliness of Ross's tone seemed to take Maddox by surprise ; evidently he had not expected to be handled in quite this fashion ; and, though it by no means put him at his ease, it took the sharp edge off his alarm.

" It was this way," he began, clearing his throat and speaking with some difficulty. "I mean, I was a clerk in the office there ; and there was some thieving going on ; money was missing now and again— not big sums, but just a few shillings now and a few shillings again. I had nothing to do with it, I'll swear that any time you like ; I was as innocent as you are ; that's the honest truth, and nothing but the truth, really. But Mr. Preston got it into his head that I was to blame, though he hadn't an atom of proof to show for it ; and he was that sort of man that, if he once got an idea into his mind, nothing would ever get it out again—nothing. He was a hard

man, Mr. Preston—just as hard as a bit of stone—
if you came up against any of his notions. So one
day he called me into his office and he said : ' Maddox, I shan't require your services after to-day. The
cashier will pay you instead of notice. And,' says
he, ' you needn't send anyone to me about your
character.' "

In the recital of his grievance, Maddox had lost
some of his nervousness ; and his repetition of Preston's speech was evidently a not wholly unsuccessful
attempt at mimicry.

" Well, that was a nice tale to take home to the
wife," he went on. " Wasn't it, now ? Discharged
without a character ! I knew pretty well what would
happen, I can tell you. Preston was a vindictive
swine—oh, yes, he was, even if he's dead now—and
I knew pretty well he'd got it in for me. He wouldn't
give me a bad character—oh, no ! He was a bit too
clever for that, and wouldn't risk me having him
up for slander. He'd just look down his nose and
say nothing, if anyone asked if I was trustworthy ;
just do the thing in the meanest little way it could
be done. But if you look down your nose just the
right way, you can say a lot without opening your
mouth, can't you ? Of course you can."

He paused for a moment and moistened his lips.
Now that he had got fairly into his tale, he showed
no sign of cutting it short.

" Well, there it was, and a nice affair for a man
with a wife to keep and only a few pounds
saved. What chance had I of getting another job in

Hammersleigh after that? Just about as big as you could put in your eye and not feel it tickle you. I knew Preston well enough for that. He'd got a down on me because I told him what I thought of his methods when he flung me out; and he'd take mighty good care that Hammersleigh was closed so far as getting work went.

"I went home to the wife and we talked it over. Horston seemed the best chance, so we shifted in here so's I could look for a fresh job. When we got here, it was worse than we'd expected. What chance have I of getting a job, when the town's full of clerks walking the streets looking for work, and all with good references behind them? Again and again I was nearly taken on, and then : ' Where were you last ? '—and they'd make a note of it, and that was the end of it so far as I ever heard. They went to Preston, I expect, and Preston looked down his nose, the way he used to do, and said nothing at all. So they turned me down. And what could I do? Nothing, just nothing."

He broke off bitterly and stared at the floor, as though to allow his anger to pass before he spoke again. It seemed as if his original nervousness had been swamped by his rekindled rage against his late employer.

"That's what Preston did for me," he went on in a quivering voice. "And what's more, he tried to stop my getting the dole, even, though he didn't manage it. Wouldn't that sort of treatment turn an honest man into a Bolshevist most days? It would me, I can tell you, if it hadn't been for the wife, and no great wonder, either. We got hard up ; our savings went, bit by bit ; and we had to take and pawn things from time to time, just to keep things going. Then the wife says to me at last : ' There's nothing for us here in Horston, and we're spending money and getting nothing for it. What about getting Aunt Emma to take us in for a bit ? She won't want to make a profit off us, with things like this.' So we talked it over, and she got me round to her ideas, and we settled that I'd go down to Morpledene and talk it over with her aunt and see if we could go back there for a bit."

Maddox's anger seemed to have died down again, and now a tinge of nervousness reappeared in his voice as he approached the crucial part of his statement. He glanced doubtfully from Mornington to the Superintendent, as if momentarily undecided whether to go on or not. Mornington, who was taking down his words, merely glanced up, as though he was impatient at the interruption ; but Superintendent Ross showed a more human expression, which seemed to encourage the clerk.

" That was what took me down to Hammersleigh the day that Preston was done for," he continued. " I'd come to the end of things here in Horston— so far as I could see, anyway ; and, for all I was getting out of it, we might just as well be at Morpledene, and it would cost less to live there. So I made up my mind to take the 10.35 that morning ; see Aunt Emma at Morpledene ; and then have a look round Hammersleigh on my way back and see if I couldn't pick up a job, no matter what it was. I was fair desperate by that time ; I'd have taken nearly anything that offered.

" I went down to the station and took my ticket. Then, as I was going along the train, I saw Preston coming along the platform towards me, carrying his little attaché-case ; and I remembered this was his day for bringing down the factory wages. I was up against it hard then, just about cracked up with the worry of getting no job ; and when I saw him I'd half a notion to stop him and sort of throw myself on his mercy—anything to get a fresh start, you understand ? That'll give you an idea of how bad things had got with us. But, when he came abreast of me, he just looked down his nose, the way he used to do, and I could see him grinning in a sort of self-satisfied way—you know what I mean—like as if he was saying : ' Well, I've fixed *you*, my lad.' And when I saw that on his face, I knew it was no good ; and I walked past him and got into the next compartment I came to ; and he got into the first-class carriage next door to me ; and that was the last I saw of him —or ever shall, now."

" Just a moment," Ross interrupted. " I want to be clear about this. You were in the third-class compartment immediately behind Preston's first— next door to him ? "

" Yes, next door," Maddox admitted. " There was nobody else in my compartment all the way. I don't remember anything much on the journey till we got past Seven Sisters station : and then I happened to let down the window and look out. Just as well I didn't look out very far ; for the next thing I knew was a big thing flying past my face along the train, and that gave me a bit of a jump, I can tell you. I'd just time to see what it was when it pitched amongst some bushes by the side of the track ; but I didn't need two looks at it to know it well ; for it was Preston's attaché-case—the one he used to bring the cash down to the Hammersleigh factory, the one I'd seen in his hand when I met him on the platform."

Maddox paused after making this last statement, evidently in the expectation that the two officials would voice their surprise ; but neither the Superintendent nor the Inspector betrayed any special interest. Mornington took advantage of the interlude to scrutinise his pen-nib and remove a minute hair from it. The lack of astonishment in his hearers seemed to excite Maddox's misgivings again, and it was in a more nervous tone that he pursued his narrative.

" I was more than a bit surprised to see that attaché-case flying out of the train that way," he went on. "My idea was that Preston had let it drop out of the window somehow ; and I just wondered how he'd managed to be such a clumsy ass as to do it. Then . . ."

He broke off sharply, as though he had sudden doubts as to the wisdom of going further with his story.

145

Superintendent Ross seemed to wake up all at once.

" You'd better go on, Mr. Maddox," he suggested in a neutral tone. " We have definite evidence that you got hold of that attaché-case, so it's no use trying to pretend you didn't. You may as well make a clean breast of things while you're at it."

Maddox apparently digested this advice for a moment or two before making up his mind to accept it.

" Well, that's just how it happened," he said, with a tinge of defiance in his tone. " You may not swallow it, but it was so. I saw that attaché-case flying through the air and landing in a clump of bushes ; and I did some quick thinking on the spur of the moment. First thing I did was to pull in my head from the window, in case Preston was looking out and noticed me. I'd marked the spot where the attaché-case fell pretty fairly. Then I . . . Well, you know how Preston had treated me. I didn't owe him much except a grudge ; and here was a grand chance to get square with him. If I could get out of the train at Hammersleigh and beat him back to where the case was lying, then I could collar it before he got on the scene, and hold it up until he had to offer a reward for it. That idea just flashed through my mind as the train was running into Hammersleigh ; and, as soon as we stopped at the platform, I hopped out of the carriage and scurried off to the gate, so as to be out of the road before Preston got out. Naturally, I didn't want him to see me and be reminded of me at Hammersleigh Station, for then, when the attaché-case turned up missing, he might think of me."

"You'd taken a return ticket to Morpledene, hadn't you ? " Superintendent Ross interjected.

The question seemed to increase Maddox's nervousness. It was clear that he had not imagined the police knew quite as much as this.

"Yes, I'd taken a Morpledene ticket. I told you I was going down to see my wife's aunt, didn't I ? And she lives at Morpledene. I told you that, too. I'm not keeping anything back ; I'm giving you the whole story, just as it happened. I know it sounds funny ; but that's just how it happened, as far as I can remember."

"Go on," Superintendent Ross ordered. "What happened next ? "

"As soon as I got out of the station, I hurried round the first corner, for fear Preston was coming out behind me and might see me making a bee-line back along the line. After I was out of sight of the station, I doubled back and took the road to Seven Sisters. It's about two and a half miles from Hammersleigh to Seven Sisters, and I reckoned the case was dropped out of the carriage window about half a mile, or maybe three-quarters, after we'd left Seven Sisters Station. That meant I'd not more than a half-hour's walk in front of me ; and, to make sure of keeping ahead of Preston, I hurried for all I was worth. It was a misty morning, and I was pretty sure he couldn't spot me in front of him on the road, even at the bits where you can see a good bit ahead of you."

"How thick was the mist?" Superintendent Ross asked suddenly.

"Oh, pretty thick here and there, and sometimes there was a clear patch."

"How far ahead could you see? I mean, when it was thick?"

Maddox reflected for a moment or two.

"Where it was thickest, you could hardly see a couple of yards in front of you," he answered at last. "More like a ground-fog than a mist, in parts, it was; but patchy."

"Yes, go on," Ross directed, as though satisfied about the mist.

"Well, in twenty minutes I guessed I was somewhere near the place where I'd seen the thing fall, so then I got off the road into the fields and walked over to the railway line. I started to walk along it towards Seven Sisters when I heard someone coming in my direction, so I slipped off the permanent way and slid down the embankment a bit. Just about there the mist was very thick, and I didn't need to go far to be out of sight of the line."

"How far?" demanded the Superintendent. "Try to be accurate in that sort of thing."

Maddox's nervousness increased at the sharp tone of Ross's voice.

"Oh, it would be about ten feet or so—three or four yards, I should think. The mist was quite thick enough to hide me at that distance unless anyone was specially on the look-out."

Ross seemed satisfied with this, and gave a nod to stimulate Maddox to further revelations.

"A man came up the line, as I was saying," the clerk continued. "He didn't see me, because I was down the bank ; and all I could see of him was just a sort of outline in the mist against the sky. I suppose he was a platelayer or something of that sort, going along the line to make sure things were all right. Or he may have been laying fog-signals for all I know. I crouched down until he was past ; and then I got up and went along again towards Seven Sisters.

"I'd hit the place all right, more by accident than anything ; for I hadn't gone ten yards farther before I came to the clump of bushes I recognised at once as the spot where Preston's case had dropped. So I began rummaging around after it, and it wasn't another couple of minutes before I stumbled right on to it amongst a lot of evergreens close beside the line."

"Wait a moment," Ross interrupted. "How far was this clump of evergreens from the rails, as near as you can guess ? "

Maddox rubbed his cheek, as though rather perplexed by this inquiry.

"I'd say it was about six feet or eight feet from the nearest rail," he hazarded at length. "Eight feet, perhaps, or . . . well, about eight feet or nine at the most, I should think. But you can find the place for yourself if you want to measure it ; it's about fifty or

sixty yards on the Seven Sisters' side of a road-
bridge over the line, and there's only one road-
bridge between Seven Sisters and Hammersleigh, so
far as I remember. There's a bit of embankment just
before you come to the bushes, just as I told you."

" Very well. Go on with the story."

" When I got my hands on the attaché-case, I went
off the line into the fields at once, for fear the plate-
layer—or the surface-man, whichever it was—might
come back and catch me with it. When I was well
into the mist and out of sight of the line, I opened up
the case ; and there were the notes, right enough.
Besides, Preston's visiting-card was stuck to the
leather of the inside of the lid. I scraped that off
with my finger-nail. There weren't any initials on the
outside of the case to give me away if I was seen
carrying it."

" What about the notes ? "

" Some of the notes were done up in packets with
rubber bands round them, and some of them—just
a few—were lying loose in the case ; and there were
a couple of bags of money as well. Out in the field,
I opened them, and found one had coppers in it and
the other was full of silver.

" I thought for a bit what to do next. I didn't much
care to carry the case back through Hammersleigh
in daylight, for someone might notice it and mention they'd seen me with an attaché-case. I knew
there'd be sure to be a hullabaloo raised about it,
and I wanted no risks. The best thing to do would
be to hide it securely somewhere and come back for

it later on, in the dark, when no one would be likely to notice it in my hand. And then, just as I was standing there in the fields, the sight of all that money was too much for me. The wife and I were at our wits' ends to pay some accounts we were owing in Horston ; and here was I with all this cash in front of me, and nobody to know I had it. Why not cop the lot ? I thought to myself. Preston owed me more than a bit for the way he'd treated me. Well, I stood there like a dummy for minute after minute, trying to make up my mind what I'd do about it ; and at last it was more than I could do to go back to the wife with empty hands when there was all this stuff here, just for the picking up, as you might say."

He broke off, and his glance roved from one hearer to the other as though he were trying to gauge the effect he was making. Met by complete impassivity on Mornington's part and a grave look from the Superintendent, he hurried on with the rest of his narrative.

" I just couldn't leave that money. And then, besides, no matter how well I hid it, somebody else might stumble on the attaché-case, and where would I have been then ? Not a penny the better for all my trouble. So that turned the scale in my mind ; and I made sure that, come what might, I'd have something out of the business. I took some of the silver out of the bag and left the coppers alone ; and then it struck me that it might look queer to be paying everything in silver, and nothing but silver.

Preston would never know the numbers of the notes, I felt pretty sure ; and it would be safe enough to take a few of them. So at last I helped myself to some of the loose notes, as well as two or three pounds' worth of the loose silver ; and then I hunted about till I found a good place to hide the attaché-case in—somewhere safe. It took a while, that ; but at last I got it stowed away in the thick of a clump of bushes a hundred yards or two away from the line."

Again Superintendent Ross interrupted.

" And what about the pistol ? Wasn't it in the attaché-case ? "

Maddox seemed to shrink into himself at the Superintendent's question.

" The pistol ? " he said in a quavering voice. " I never saw any pistol. You don't think *I* murdered Preston, do you ? I never laid a finger on him, that's the whole truth."

Superintendent Ross avoided a direct answer.

" You say you found no pistol in the attaché-case ? Very well. Go on and tell us what you did next."

" I never killed him," Maddox persisted. " I didn't. I didn't."

Ross shrugged his shoulders.

" I'm not asking you whether you did or not. I want to know what you did after you hid the attaché-case. If you don't choose to tell me, it's your own look-out."

There was no mistaking the underlying menace in

the last few words ; and Maddox shrank again at the Superintendent's tone.

" Very well, then," he said, licking his lips to moisten them, " I'll tell you, for fear you think there was anything worse behind it ; and there was nothing wrong in it, anyway. I've told you the bad bit already. As soon as I'd hidden the attaché-case I got back to the road again without being seen, so far as I know ; and I started to walk in to Hammersleigh. I was on the look-out for Preston, because I expected him to be along on my heels, hunting for his case ; and I dodged off the road when I saw anyone come along to meet me. I only had to get out of the way twice before I got to the outskirts of Hammersleigh ; and after that it didn't matter if he saw me. I was a bit surprised when I saw no signs of him ; I couldn't make head or tail of it, for a man doesn't leave hundreds of pounds of money lying by the side of a railway line for anyone to pick up. I thought perhaps he'd got permission and walked back along the line itself to the place where the case fell out of the window."

Mornington interjected a question for the first time.

" See any motors on the road ? "

" One passed me just as I was getting into Hammersleigh," Maddox replied, after thinking for a moment or two. " A big closed car painted dark blue, it was ; and it had two fellows on board that looked like—well, like anybody else, so far as I saw when they passed me. They were driving fast, that's

all I really noticed ; and they hooted me out of the
way as if the road belonged to them."

" You didn't notice the car's number ? "

" No, I never bother about the numbers of cars ;
and, besides, it just came out of the mist and disappeared again before I had a good look at it. I'd
other things to think about just then."

As Mornington made no comment, the clerk continued his story.

" I went on into Hammersleigh and took the
Morpledene road. By and by I got to my wife's aunt's
house. It turned out she'd taken in a lodger after we
left, and she couldn't take us in until she'd given him
notice. She gave me some food."

" What time was it then ? "

" Round about two o'clock, I should think, but I
couldn't be sure. She'd had her own dinner before I
got there, I remember that. I stayed a while there,
talking to her ; and then I walked back to Hammersleigh, meaning to see if there wasn't a job to be
found there. But by the time I'd got there I wasn't
in the mood for looking for jobs. I was worried over
the—over the money business. All the way along the
road I'd been thinking it over ; and now I'd think it
would be best to put the money back and hang on
for a reward ; and then again I'd make up my mind
I'd go the whole hog and stick to the lot. I wish I'd
never touched the stuff now."

" You came back to Horston by train ? "

" In the end I did. I caught the 3.23 at Hammersleigh."

" Didn't you learn then that Mr. Preston had been murdered ? "

Maddox shook his head.

" How could I ? I talked to nobody. I was that worried over the business, turning it over and over in my mind and trying to settle what I'd really do, that I never noticed anything till I got home again. I was just in a sort of brown study—kind of dazed with what I'd done, if you understand."

" I don't understand this," the Superintendent pointed out. " You took the money from the attaché-case ; and yet for some days after that you were still pawning things. How do you account for that ? "

Maddox had his answer ready.

" What do *you* think ? " he replied, with a certain appearance of cunning in his tone. " I wasn't going to be such a fool as to tell anyone I'd been taking Preston's money—not me. I didn't breathe a word about it to the wife, even. That was just where the shoe pinched, you see ? She knew we were on the rocks ; and if I'd come home flush with money, she'd have wanted to know where I got it. So I had to wait till I could think of some way of accounting for that cash before I could produce it ; and that took me a while : and, in the meantime, I just went on pawning things to keep us going till we could get away to Morpledene."

" H'm ! " said Ross, not too encouragingly. " And what lie did your brilliant mind hit on, at last ? "

" I pretended I'd spotted a winner and had a shilling or two on an outsider," Maddox explained.

155

" That made it all right, for she knew I used to bet now and again. And that opened the way for me to go the whole hog ; for, if that yarn held for a shilling or two, it'd hold just as well for bigger money. So I told her I'd got some real straight tips for the next week's racing ; and then I went out to Hammersleigh again and picked up the money out of the attaché-case. I left the attaché-case where I hid it—no one had touched it, so the place seemed safe enough."

" And after that, I suppose, you began to take your pledges out of pawn again ? "

" Yes."

" And the bulk of the money's at your house now ? "

" Yes, I've spent very little of it—just a pound or two."

" You can tell Inspector Mornington where it is by and by. And now I'm going to arrest you for being in possession of a Bank of England one pound note, numbered D50 157128, knowing that it was the property of the late Mr. Oswald Frederic Preston. Do you wish to say anything in answer to the charge ? You are not obliged to say anything unless you wish to do so, but whatever you say will be taken down in writing and may be given in evidence."

For a moment, Maddox was unable to speak. He gulped once or twice, and then found his voice.

" And that's all you're charging me with ? " he asked anxiously.

" That's the charge I'm holding you on," Ross answered.

" I never murdered him—I'll swear that."

" I never said you did," the Superintendent pointed out. " Now Inspector Mornington will read over that statement to you and you can check it."

At a gesture from Ross, the Inspector led his prisoner out of the room, and Ross settled himself at his desk. In a few minutes Mornington returned.

" You ran the Judges' Rules pretty fine, didn't you ? " he suggested, with a sardonic smile, as he came into the room.

" Did I ? How ? " Ross demanded, with an assumption of innocent surprise.

" Well, hadn't you made up your mind to charge him, as soon as he confessed he'd taken the money from the attaché-case ? "

" You don't generally jump to conclusions like this," the Superintendent pointed out. " He confessed to taking the money out ; but, until we got his whole story, we didn't know whether he'd thought better of it in the end and put it back again. Then someone else might have lighted on the attaché-case and put the note in circulation. See ? "

" You're too deep for me," Mornington confessed. " I never had any doubts about what he did."

" Doubts come in handy at times," Ross said blandly. " Now, what do you think of that evidence of his ? I have my doubts ; but probably you've got none."

" A damned fishy story, if you ask me. It might be true ; but it sounds like the other thing. I didn't like his manner much."

157

" I doubt if my own manner would be quite satisfactory if I felt someone was just on the edge of arresting me for a murder," the Superintendent mused aloud. " It's always a rather trying experience, from what I've seen. I shouldn't lay too much stress on that, if I were you. Put yourself in Maddox's place, and you'll feel rather funny about the throat, too. if you've any imagination."

He reflected for a moment, and then turned to a fresh subject.

" If this story of Maddox's is true, then that attaché-case was flung out of the carriage-window by the murderer."

" Unless Preston himself dropped it out when he saw the attack coming," Mornington suggested as an alternative. " He seems to have been the sort of man who'd take care of his money in any circumstances."

" It wasn't dropped out of the window," Ross asserted. " If Maddox's yarn's true, it must have been flung out with enough vim to carry it nine feet away from the side of the train. The case itself weighed, say, three pounds ; the silver must have run to about another three pounds ; and a quid's worth of coppers comes to somewhere round about four pounds weight, I should guess. That's ten pounds in all, plus the weight of the notes. A ten-pound attaché-case isn't a bit of paper that can drift on the wind. It must have been flung out by someone who wanted to land it well of the permanent way. That's clear."

Mornington's gesture admitted the force of this.

" I doubt if Preston was given time to throw things out of the window," Ross went on. " If Maddox's story is true, then the murder took place between Seven Sisters and Hammersleigh ; and the train only spends about five minutes on that stretch. The murderer must have got to work almost as soon as the 10.35 left Seven Sisters station, and there wasn't time for a struggle in which the case could get pitched out of the window. I can understand the murderer pitching it out after he'd shot Preston ; for the attaché-case would be an awkward thing to carry with him when he left the train—too easily remembered by anyone who happened to notice it."

" So, if it was robbery at the bottom of it all, you think the murderer pitched the case out and went back to pick it up later ; and, if it wasn't robbery, the case was pitched out of the window to suggest robbery as a motive ? " Mornington questioned.

" Something of that sort," the Superintendent admitted in a cautious tone. " Now, there's another point. You've got fifty-two tickets sold ; and you've got fifty-two passengers. But I'm not sure that each person who bought a ticket used *that* ticket. It's just on the cards that two of them may have exchanged tickets."

" You mean a man might have bought a third-class ticket and swopped it for the first-class ticket of another passenger ? "

" Something of the sort," Ross repeated in an even more cautious tone. " Now, let's see what's still to be

done in the next stage of this business. I'll see Miss
Winslow myself. You needn't bother about her.
You'd better check up Maddox's story as soon as
you can : see if his aunt confirms the times he gave
us ; find out if a plate-layer or surface-man was on
the line at the time he said he saw one ; have a hunt
for the attaché-case at the place where he said he
hid it finally. Then there's another affair in the same
neighbourhood. You might kill two birds with one
stone while you're about it. Look into the case of
that motor that this lawyer Iverson lost at Oxenden
Grange. I've a use for Iverson ; and I want to
keep on good terms with him. And, when you're
at it, you'd better make inquiries at Dr. Whitacre's
—about three miles from Morpledene—about the
cutting of his telephone wire lately. It seems worth
looking into. Let's see. Morpledene, Whitacre's,
Oxenden Grange, the line between Hammersleigh
and Seven Sisters : they're all within a ten-mile
drive if you take a taxi at Hammersleigh. You can
make inquiries about the plate-layer at Hammersleigh and get him fished out in time to see you on
your way back ; then go on to Morpledene ; after
that to the doctor's ; then back to Oxenden Grange.
It's about a mile off the railway line, somewhere
between Hammersleigh and Seven Sisters ; so, after
you've had a look round there to see what the place
is like, you can cut across to the line and check
Maddox's statements about the bushes and so forth.
Then you can see the railway people again at Hammersleigh on your way back. It won't really take

long, and it's not worth while sending a second man down to deal with the motor theft separately."

" I'll have to search Maddox's house for the pistol and the notes," the Inspector suggested. " I'd better do that first ? "

" It would be just as well," Ross agreed. " Though I don't think you'll find much except the notes."

CHAPTER XI

MADGE WINSLOW'S EVIDENCE

" That mouth's just a trifle hard," was Superintendent Ross's inward comment as he examined Madge Winslow's face. The clean-cut features, the finely arched eyebrows, the natural wave in the girl's dark hair, all met with his artistic approval ; but the curve of the lips hinted at a stronger character than would have been inferred from the rest of the physiognomy.

" I'm sorry to trouble you again, Miss Winslow," Ross said in a semi-apologetic tone, " but the fact is, we haven't got to the bottom of this case yet, and we're still in need of more information."

Madge Winslow sat down, crossed one knee over the other, shook her skirt into position, and with a gesture invited the Superintendent to take a seat ; but she made no attempt to help him by volunteering anything. He noticed that, whether by accident or design, she had chosen a chair with its back to the light, whilst his own faced the nearest window.

" There are just two or three points I'd like to be clear about," Ross pursued, drawing his notebook from his pocket as he spoke. " When I saw you last, you explained that Mr. Preston breakfasted alone on the morning of his death."

Madge Winslow contented herself with a confirmatory nod.

" And Mrs. Preston had breakfast in her own room, which was her usual custom ? "

Another nod formally corroborated this.

" And you yourself were late in coming down, because you had been at a dance the night before ? When did you actually come downstairs, Miss Winslow ? "

If Madge Winslow was surprised by this question she succeeded in concealing it.

" Shortly after Mr. Preston left the house," she answered, without comment.

Ross switched off to a fresh subject.

" You told me that Mr. Preston and Mr. Iverson were your trustees. What is the exact state of affairs in that matter ? "

Madge Winslow's eyebrows arched slightly at the question.

" Are my private affairs really essential ? " she demanded.

" Everything connected with Mr. Preston is of value to us," the Superintendent pointed out in a neutral tone.

Madge Winslow seemed to consider this statement in all its possible bearings before she spoke again.

" Then the position is this," she said. " My father left a certain capital, and appointed as trustees Mr. Preston and the firm of solicitors of which Mr. Iverson is now head. The senior partner died last year, and now Mr. Iverson manages things. The arrangement under the will is that I have the life-rent of the estate ; and the capital will be distributed after my death among any children I happen to have, if I get married. I can't touch the capital itself. I'm not a trustee myself till I'm twenty-five. When I'm twenty-five I can draw the full interest on the capital ; but until my twenty-fifth birthday my trustees pay me what the will calls ' an allow-ance sufficient in the opinion of the trustees ' for my expenses."

Ross, in his turn, considered for a few moments before putting further questions.

" Perhaps you did not quite see eye to eye with Mr. Preston about the amount you were allowed ? Mr. Iverson may be more generous in his ideas, perhaps ? "

Madge Winslow's expression showed plainly that she regarded these questions as impertinent.

" I fail to see what my private affairs have to do with Mr. Preston's death," she said stiffly.

" Very well, then," Ross hastened to assure her, " we'll leave the matter. You say you came down-stairs that morning shortly after Mr. Preston left the house. Was that before or after a telephone message came for Mrs. Preston ? "

The Superintendent, keenly on the watch, detected a sudden dilation of Madge Winslow's pupils as he brought out this question. She kept her features composed ; but clearly the inquiry had touched a tender spot.

" I didn't answer the telephone," she pointed out.

" Did you know about that call ? " the Superintendent pressed.

Madge Winslow took longer than necessary before she replied.

" Yes."

" How did you hear about it ? "

Again there was a pause, as though the girl took time to consider.

" Mrs. Preston sent a message asking me to go to her room."

" And she told you about the message the maid had given her ? "

A nod confirmed this.

" Who telephoned to Mrs. Preston ? "

Madge Winslow examined her neatly-shod foot for a moment or two before answering.

" It was Dr. Selby-Onslow," she said, at last.

" Mrs. Preston told you what his message was ? What had he said ? "

" Hadn't you better get that from Dr. Selby-Onslow himself ? " Madge Winslow suggested coldly. " I understood that evidence should be first-hand if possible. You're asking me about a thing I could only know at third-hand."

" I'll put it differently, if you wish," Ross said patiently. " What did Mrs. Preston tell you about the message ? "

Madge Winslow evidently felt that she had made a slip in handling the situation. Her coolness did not desert her, however, and her voice was quite level as she answered.

" Mrs. Preston told me that Dr. Selby-Onslow had been called away unexpectedly, and might not be able to come here that afternoon as she had arranged."

" How did that information concern you ? "

" Because I intended to make arrangements that afternoon that Dr. Selby-Onslow and I could go to the Plaza that night."

Something in the manner of this statement excited Ross's suspicions.

" You and Dr. Selby-Onslow alone together ? "

" And Mrs. Preston," Madge Winslow amplified, reluctantly.

" This proposed arrangement was an after-thought, then. Why ? "

" Because we had just learned that Mr. Preston was going out to a Masonic dinner that evening," Madge Winslow admitted frankly.

Ross had no doubt whatever that this, at least, was the truth. Quite obviously Mrs. Preston had snatched at the chance of spending an evening with the doctor. Madge Winslow's part in the affair was merely subsidiary.

" You learned this from Mrs. Preston. What happened after that ? "

' I had some breakfast and then went out to do some shopping."

" When did you leave the house ? "

Madge Winslow's patience was evidently fraying under the strain of this continued examination.

" At about a quarter to ten. May I ask if you have

a roving commission to inquire into *all* my private affairs ? ''

But the Superintendent had guessed what lay behind this ; it confirmed his original vague surmise.

'' Don't fence with me, Miss Winslow,'' he said bluntly. '' You went to the station, to the 10.35. Didn't you ? Yes or no ? ''

This was evidently a home-thrust, as he could see from the girl's face ; but she did not lose her composure.

'' You seem to be fairly well informed,'' she admitted, with a faint sneer. '' I did go down to the 10.35. What of it ? ''

'' To meet Dr. Selby-Onslow ? ''

'' Yes.''

'' Because you could go there and give him a message which Mrs. Preston couldn't take herself, since her husband was in that train and she might have been seen ? ''

'' If that interpretation pleases you, I have no objection.''

'' You got on to the platform with a platform ticket ? ''

'' Naturally.''

'' After the train left, what did you do ? ''

'' I did some shopping in town.''

'' What shops did you visit ? ''

Madge Winslow favoured the Superintendent with something which could only be described as a stare.

'' How do you expect me to remember, after all

167

that time ? " she demanded coolly. " I was doing ordinary shopping—odds and ends. I don't profess to recall where I went or what I bought. Where were you yourself at half-past two on 23rd September ? You don't know, you see. Then how do you expect me to have a better memory than you have ? My impression is that I lunched in town, probably at Henley and Sutton's ; but I couldn't be absolutely certain even of that."

Superintendent Ross saw that here he had come up against a blank wall. If she chose to say that she could not remember, she had the whiphand of him, since now he had no further information which he could spring upon her. Besides . . . And, as a fresh thought occurred to him, he put another question.

" Dr. Selby-Onslow came here on the evening of Mr. Preston's death ? "

" Yes."

Ross decided that further questioning would not elicit much more. Evidently the doctor and the two women had discussed the whole case and made up their minds how much they could safely tell ; and they had done their planning at the earliest possible moment after the commission of the crime. Whether their stories were truth or lies, it was at least likely that they had been well thought out and would tally with each other. The Superintendent considered for a moment whether he should demand to see Mrs. Preston, but abandoned the idea for the present. Whoever had done the actual murder, he was fairly sure that she had no direct hand in it ;

and Dr. Selby-Onslow would have coached her carefully as to what evidence she could safely give.

" Then, I take it, that's all the help you can give us in the matter, Miss Winslow ? " he inquired in an almost perfunctory tone.

" I've nothing more to say," Madge Winslow assured him formally, as she rose and stepped across to the bell.

But by this dismissal she made an error in tactics. The Superintendent wanted to see the maid again, and Madge Winslow had saved him from disclosing that fact. As he followed Poole down the hall, he made no attempt to start a conversation. He knew his witness ; and he was sure that, left to herself, she would seize the opportunity.

" Just a minute," she said, stopping him at the door. " I've got something to tell you, something that'll perhaps put you on to the track. I didn't tell you it the last time I saw you, 'cause then I didn't know about the murder, you see ? And I didn't tell that wall-faced man you sent round here, 'cause I didn't care for the look of him. But I'll tell you about it. It's this."

She glanced back at the closed door of the room in which Ross had interviewed Madge Winslow, and dropped her voice a little.

" Just before the murder, Mr. Preston sent me on a message to the office of that lawyer of his, a Mr. Iverson. When I got there, I was kept waiting for a good while ; and, when I was taken into the lawyer's own room, there was Mr. Preston waiting for me.

169

Then the two of them started questioning me, fair trying to turn me inside out, all about the doctor's goings-on here, and had I ever gone into the room suddenly or had I ever happened to glance in at the window, and all that sort of thing, you understand. Well, they kept me there for a long while, and the lawyer taking notes of all that I said ; and after that they went over the whole story again, with the notes, and tried to trip me up, but they didn't manage it, for I'd stuck to the truth all the way through. And at the end of it the lawyer says to Mr. Preston : ' This young woman will make a valuable witness.' So then they packed me off, and they told me to say nothing about it."

" And when did this happen ? " Ross demanded. " The day before the murder or earlier ? "

" About a week—no, ten days or a fortnight before the murder. Call it a fortnight and that would be about it."

" What day of the week was it ? "

" I can't remember now."

" And what happened after that ? "

" Well, it's a free country, isn't it ? Nobody's got a right to tell me what I'm to say and what I'm not to say, have they ? If they'd given me something to keep my mouth shut, it might have been all right ; but Mr. Preston was too mean for one to expect that from him. So they'd no claim on me, not the very least bit."

" I see," Ross agreed. " I'd feel much the same myself, I'm sure. So ? "

" So I thought about it, and it was pretty plain what the two of them were after ; and I've no wish to be dragged into the witness-box in a dirty case of that sort, with my name in the papers to spoil my chance of getting a good place when I left here. I'm not so green as that, I can tell you. And, after I'd thought it over for a while, I just went and dropped a hint to Madge, seeing she's so thick with Mrs. Preston and would be sure to pass it on. And Madge—she's more of a lady than Mr. Preston ever was of a gentleman—she gave me a pound at once and told me not to say anything to Mr. Preston about having told her about it. So I guess she passed it on to May and the doctor double-quick, and I said nothing about it. But now I thought you'd like to hear the story, 'cause it looks a bit of funny work to me, what with one thing and another ; and perhaps you'll find it useful, so I thought."

" Quite right," Ross agreed heartily. " That's a thing we ought to know about, sure enough. Now try and remember what day it was that you had this business at Mr. Iverson's office. That's an important point."

For a few moments the maid stood cudgelling her memory ; then her face lighted up.

" I remember, now," she exclaimed. " It was the day I saw *Roses and Raptures* at the pictures. That would be a Tuesday, and it was about ten days or so before the murder."

" That would be Tuesday, 13th November then ? "

171

"That would be it," the maid asserted eagerly. "I'd swear to that, now I think of it."

Ross nodded approvingly.

"You'll remember that," he cautioned.

"Of course," Poole declared firmly. Then, with a change of tone, she added : "Are you going to *Passion's Slaves* ? It's on at the Scala this week, and a young lady friend of mine says it's the best thing she's seen for ever so long. I'd like to go myself."

It required all the Superintendent's tact to extricate himself without being too blunt in his refusal of the implied invitation.

CHAPTER XII

THE TELEGRAM

" There's no harm in having a second opinion on it," Superintendent Ross reflected, as he compared the two slips of paper.

One of them was the original form of the decoy telegram which he had procured from Morpledene Post Office. The other was the copy of its wording which he himself had typed on Dr. Selby-Onslow's machine.

" I may as well see if Iverson has really read all these criminology books of his, or if he just bought them to put on his shelves. Pity that fellow Groombridge never took up typewriting, or he might have helped me to make certain this time, just as he did in the Hyndford case."

Actually, the Superintendent had more in view than the decoy telegram. Since he had learned from Poole about the projected divorce case, it had been evident that Iverson knew more than he had divulged in his interview with Ross on the evening of the murder. He had said nothing about Preston's decision to bring an action against his wife and the doctor ; and yet, on the face of it, that was a non-negligible factor in the situation. And, at the recollection of Iverson's special pleading in favour of

Mrs. Preston, the Superintendent's lips twisted in a rather wry smile.

" He had a fair nerve to sit there with that thunder-bolt in his pocket and talk away about how sure he was that Preston's wife had nothing to do with the case ! "

Superintendent Ross rang up Iverson's office and made an appointment for the same evening at War-lingham Road. This time he took care to avoid the dinner hour and to make sure that the lawyer would be alone.

" Good evening," Iverson greeted him, when Ross was shown into the study he had seen before. " You've taken me at my word, apparently. Well, the books are there for you to consult if you want to."

His tone was rather more genial than it had been on the Superintendent's earlier visit.

Superintendent Ross looked rather blankly at the shelves.

" I'm afraid it would take me some time to find my way about a library of this size," he said diffi-dently. " I'd better tell you what information I'm after, and perhaps you could put me on the right track."

Iverson made a gesture offering the silver boxes of cigars and cigarettes. When they were refused by his guest, he took a cigar himself, cut it, and went back to his chair.

" My trouble is this," the Inspector pursued, when his host was ready to give him his attention.

" I want to know if two documents come from the same hand."

The lawyer's eye turned lovingly towards the bookshelves.

" H'm ! Gross isn't much good to you. You read German ? No ? Well, it doesn't matter. What about French ? "

" I think I can plough my way through that," Ross admitted modestly.

" Let's see, then," said Iverson, rising to his feet. " You might find something useful in Locard's books —I've got three of them there. My edition of Reiss hasn't got the length of the forgery volume yet, unfortunately. But I expect Locard might help you ; though I must say I'm not altogether sure about some of his methods unless they were applied by himself. If it's a matter of inks, or anything of that sort, his tests seem sound enough to a non-expert like myself. But that's by the way."

" It's a case of typewriting," the Superintendent volunteered.

" Oh, typewriting ? " said Iverson, in the tone of one who is relieved to find a problem easier than he expected. " There's only one book here that's of any use in that line. Here you are : Osborn's *Questioned Documents*. You'll get everything you could possibly use in it—and probably a good deal more," he added, as he passed the massive volume over to the Superintendent. " You'll find it all in the chapter called ' Questioned Typewriting.' "

Clearly the lawyer bought his books to read, and

175

not merely to fill shelf-room. Ross accepted *Questioned Documents* ; but, instead of opening it, he laid it on the table beside him, and drew from his note-case the two documents which he had brought with him. They had no obvious connection with the Preston case.

Iverson half-unconsciously held out his hand.

" If they're not confidential, I'd like to have a look at them, just to see if I can make anything of them," he explained, to account for his tentative gesture.

Ross showed no reluctance in the matter, but passed over the papers.

" *Please come for urgent consultation Friday morning. Shall meet 10.35 train with my car at Morpledene station. Whitacre,*" Iverson read out from Ross's copy.

Then, as he turned to the original telegram-form and saw Dr. Selby-Onslow's name and address at the head, his eyebrows rose sharply. Evidently it cost him an effort to refrain from a question. The Superintendent took compassion on his obvious curiosity.

" I may as well put my cards on the table," he said, " since I'd like your opinion on one or two points. You see, the original telegram-form is filled in by typewriting, not by hand. It wasn't handed in over the counter, I find, but came by post in an envelope, with stamps to pay for the transmission. Now it turns out that it's a hoax ; and naturally the post office people want to know who's been using their machinery to play practical jokes. I've come across a typewriter which may have been used to produce that fake wire ; and it's a question of seeing whether one can prove that these two documents were written with the same machine."

Iverson re-read the telegram thoughtfully.

" So Selby-Onslow was off on a wild-goose chase that morning when I saw him at the station ? " he commented. " That accounts for his being in the train. I couldn't understand why he didn't take his car, instead of going by rail."

Superintendent Ross fidgeted slightly, as though he had no wish to linger over this part of the problem. Iverson noticed his impatience and dropped the subject. He picked up Osborn's book, and turned over the pages until he came to the paragraph he wanted.

" Let's see. Here he collects all the points one ought to look for."

As he read, his face clouded slightly.

" The worst of it is, half these things don't apply to a telegram-form. ' Depth of indention of paragraphs,' ' arrangement of conclusion,' ' arrangement of heading,' and so forth : it's no good bothering about them. The spacing after punctuation's quite normal ; and there are no erasures that I can see. All that seems to be relevant is what he says about the use of the shift-key, heavy impressions of some letters and light ones of others, and the alignment, vertical or horizontal, of the type. Let's have a look at the two things side by side."

He placed the two papers in juxtaposition and

studied them intently for a time, while Ross patiently waited to see what inferences the lawyer would draw.

" The shift-key for capitals seems to be slightly out of adjustment," he said at last. " In both documents, the capitals P, F, S, M, and W are just a shade above the normal alignment. If you got these things enlarged photographically you might be able to show that the upward displacement was the same for the two documents—it's identical so far as naked eye-work's concerned."

" I daresay we could manage that, all right," Ross said, thinking of the microphotographic outfit owned by his former collaborator, Groombridge.

Iverson appeared to pay little attention, as he was engrossed in a fresh matter.

" There's a spot of dirt lodged in the loop of the lower-case letter a," he continued. " It makes the loop print almost as a solid block in all the a's of the telegram ; and there's precisely the same flaw in the corresponding a's of your copy. That's a bit beyond normal probability, surely, unless they're both from the same machine."

Ross was not particularly impressed by this display of observational power, for he had noticed the same thing himself, almost at the first glance.

" All the t's in the telegram have a very slight defect in their tails," Iverson continued. " And each t is slightly depressed below the normal type-level. The bar of the t is in the same line as the ceriph of the i in ' tion,' instead of being slightly above it, as it ought to be. There's the same defect in your copy."

178

After further scrutiny, he added :

" The d in ' Friday ' and the d in ' Morpledene '
are both slightly depressed, and a shade off the
vertical—same in your copy as in the telegram."

He turned away from the documents, took
up Osborn's book, and hunted for a particular
passage.

" Here you are," he said, after a moment or two.
" This is what Osborn says about it. ' We must first
determine how often, or rather how seldom, each
feature will be found separately, and then, by a
mathematical formula, as fixed as the multiplication
table, we determine how often coincidences of all the
features may be expected. This formula, given by
Professor Simon Newcomb, is as follows : " The
probability of occurrence of all the events is equal
to the continued product of the probabilities of all
the separate events." If one thing will occur once in
twenty times and another once in twenty, the probability of the two occurring in conjunction is repre-
sented by the fraction which is the product of one-
twentieth and one twentieth, or one four-hundredth.'
Now, further on, he reckons the chance of the same
defect occurring in two machines to be about one in
five hundred or so. In these two documents, there are
four characteristics in common ; so if you take it
that out of 500 machines only two would have the
dirt in the a and so forth, you get the probable coincidence of the four characteristics as about—let's see
—one chance in 62,500,000,000. Even if you assume
that one in every fifty machines has got the defect in

the t, and that one in every fifty has the peculiarity of the d, and so forth, still the chance of all four characteristics coinciding in any given machine is only one chance in 6,250,000. And, quite obviously, there aren't six and a quarter million machines of this particular make in the country. In other words, so far as Osborn goes, it's practically outside the bounds of probability that these two documents can have been written on different machines."

"That seems plain enough," Ross admitted. "At any rate, some of the members of a jury would understand it, and the rest would swallow it on the strength of it being all right, but too deep for them. I've no doubts myself. Obviously the two documents came from the same machine."

Iverson nodded his agreement with this, and idly picked up the original telegram form.

"I suppose this explains why I saw Dr. Selby-Onslow at the station that morning," he commented. "A hoax, was it?"

"So far as one can see, it was," said the Superintendent cautiously. "They really ought to have some means of checking posted telegrams; the system lends itself a bit too easily to practical joking, apparently."

"No finger-prints on the envelope, or anything of that sort?" the lawyer inquired.

"There may have been, for all I know," Ross admitted. "But, as the envelope went straight into the waste-paper basket, I don't think they'll help us much at this date."

"But you've got hold of the typewriter, apparently?"

"So it seems," Ross agreed, without offering to amplify his statement.

Suddenly he looked the lawyer straight in the face.

"You didn't tell me quite all you might have done, the other evening, Mr. Iverson."

The solicitor seemed in no way perturbed by this accusation.

"I'm not quite sure what you mean, exactly," he confessed. "I don't think I held back anything that could be of any value to you. What is it?"

"You didn't mention the fact that Mr. Preston was preparing to bring an action for divorce against his wife and that Dr. Selby-Onslow would be named as co-respondent."

Iverson's face betrayed more than a little surprise.

"Now, how the deuce did you ferret *that* out, I wonder?" he ejaculated. Then, after a moment's thought, he added : "Oh, I see now. You've been questioning that girl Poole, the maid at Hillcrest? I might have guessed that."

Superintendent Ross was not going to be put off in this way.

"That was hardly playing the game, Mr. Iverson, if you'll excuse my putting it bluntly. You kept your thumb on that bit of information ; and, what's more, you spent part of your time trying to persuade me that Mrs. Preston couldn't be mixed up in the affair in any way."

Iverson refused to be brow-beaten.

" As I told you, I'm perfectly convinced that Mrs. Preston had no hand in the murder. That's my honest belief, without the slightest mental reservation of any kind, I may say. That being so, it would have been merely starting you off on a wild-goose chase if I had mentioned the projected divorce case to you the other night. At once you'd have drawn wrong inferences and wasted a lot of time in digging up things that have nothing whatever to do with Preston's death."

" That was for me to settle," Ross said stiffly.

Iverson took no notice of the Superintendent's tone.

" Well, since the cat's out of the bag now," he suggested, " I'll give you any information you want on the subject ; but I warn you seriously, remember, that you're barking up the wrong tree."

As though to show that he was ready for a prolonged examination, he moved over to his chair and sat down, motioning the Superintendent to follow his example.

" When did you first hear about this projected divorce suit ? " Ross demanded.

Iverson considered for a moment or two.

" On 12th November, I believe," the lawyer answered at once. " Preston came to see me that morning at my office and told me he was pretty sure of his ground in the matter. We talked it over for a while, and he suggested that this girl Poole probaby knew a good deal about what had been going on at Hillcrest. He was one of these people, you know, who

want to have everything cut and dried ; and it seems
he thought if we got the girl to ourselves, we could
drag something out of her. In fact, he'd made up his
mind to send her to my office on some excuse or
other the next day, so that between us we could put
the screw on her and get at the truth, if she knew
anything definite. I suggested that he could interview
her alone first ; but he insisted on following his preconceived plan. He wanted a witness to her statement, so that she couldn't go back on it, once we'd
got it out of her."

Iverson reached over and picked up the cigar-box.

" Try one," he suggested ; and, when his offer was
refused, he lighted a cigar himself.

" Well, it was no business of mine to object. He was
my client, and I followed his instructions. As it turned
out, he needn't have worried himself so much, for
there was no trouble at all in making the creature
talk. Once she understood what he wanted, she gave
him full measure, and considerably more than he'd
anticipated, I suspect."

Iverson leaned back in his chair and laughed
cynically.

" It was as good as a play ; it was, really," he
continued. " Here was this venomous little hussy,
simply burning to tell all she knew—and perhaps
rather more than that, unless I was mistaken. Once
she found she'd got an interested audience, she
talked on and on, just one ugly detail after another :
what she'd suspected, what she'd overheard, what
she'd seen, what she'd tried to see through the keyhole

or the window—everything came out with a rush, once we'd got her started. It was a perfect revelation of character : the lengths to which a spiteful little slut will go in order to discredit a girl she envies. For that was at the back of the whole affair, quite clearly. She hated both Mrs. Preston and Miss Winslow because they had more money, finer clothes, and, generally, a better standard ; and she took an impish delight in painting the whole thing in the crudest colours. She'd be very coy, when she remembered the pose ; and then she'd forget herself and her language grew—well, shall we say ' painfully direct ' ?

" And Preston's position wasn't altogether enviable, you know. He'd asked for it, of course ; and he certainly got it. Every crude detail, every nasty bit of surmise, all her notions of ' what probably happened, only I couldn't be sure.' The whole affair simply made him squirm—physically, I mean. Well, that was his look-out. I didn't ask to be dragged into it quite so fully as all that ; but he would have his own way.

" And, of course, he made a mess of it in the end. Anyone could see at a glance that this jade expected to be paid for her trouble ; it stuck out all over her. But Preston was too mean to see it. He ought to have given her something to keep her mouth shut— a retaining-fee on the quiet. *I* couldn't be expected to bribe a witness, naturally ; but, if he'd had any sense in his head, he'd have made it worth the little beast's while.

184

" He didn't. And naturally she transferred a fair share of venom to him in consequence, and looked round to see what harm she could do next. I didn't ask any questions, but, when Miss Winslow dropped a very plain hint to me next day, it was clear enough that Poole had given Preston away to the other side ; though I don't suppose she made much of a song about the part she herself had actually played in the business."

He reflected for a moment or two before continuing.

" I expect you yourself sometimes get into positions where your personal affairs cut athwart your professional doings. It's very awkward at times. In this projected divorce suit of Preston's it was especially awkward ; for I was Preston's solicitor, and Miss Winslow's trustee, and Dr. Selby-Onslow's patient, all rolled into one ! I'd have been acting for Preston against my own doctor, with a girl whose trustee I was, giving evidence on the other side. You can guess that, even with the best intentions, one couldn't expect to get through that situation with all one's private relationships intact."

Superintendent Ross showed his sympathy by a faint smile.

" It sounds a bit like the crew of the *Nancy* brig," he confessed. " You must have been puzzled at times as to what exact capacity you were acting in at any given moment. By the way, I didn't know you were a patient of Dr. Selby-Onslow's. When did you see him last ? "

185

" That morning at the train," Iverson replied.

" But you didn't speak to him then," the Super-intendent pointed out. " I mean, had you any talk with him after this divorce affair came on the carpet ? "

" Yes, I went to his house one afternoon to see him about a relaxed throat that was bothering me. That was on "—he pulled a diary from his pocket and consulted it—" on Thursday, 15th November."

" That was the day after Miss Winslow had let you see she knew about this projected divorce suit ? "

Iverson made a gesture of confirmation.

" Yes, she spoke to me about it on the 14th, the day after Preston had the maid up giving her evidence."

" Dr. Selby-Onslow's got a good practice, I believe ? "

" About the best fashionable practice in Horston, I should think," the lawyer assented, with a faint tinge of envy in his tone. " I can't think how a man in his position would take the risk of getting mixed up with a woman among his patients."

Superintendent Ross had no objection to letting people tell him things which he knew already, since there was always a chance of a fresh detail coming to light.

" What would have been Dr. Selby-Onslow's position if Preston had won his case ? " he asked innocently.

Iverson threw up his hands in a gesture which suggested the complete ruin of the doctor.

" He'd have had the devil to pay, and the damages in the suit would have been the least of it," he said seriously. " It would have been the end of him. Look at him just now—at the top of the tree, making a big income and spending practically every penny of it. If he'd lost this action, the General Medical Council would have stepped in at once and struck him off the Medical Register. He could have gone on practising, of course ; but how many people would go to a man who'd just been taken off the Register ? Not these fashionable patients of his, that's certain. And he couldn't sue for fees, if people chose to disregard his bills. What's more, if a patient happened to die under his treatment, he'd be liable to a manslaughter charge.   The law protects a qualified man to some extent ; but, once a practitioner's off the Register, there's no protection for him. No, you can take it that, if Preston had won his action, Dr. Selby-Onslow would have disappeared ; he'd have been driven out of his livelihood—and that would have been complete crash in his case. It's no joke to have the General Medical Council down on you in this country."

Superintendent Ross nodded, as though this were news to him. Actually, the lawyer had told him nothing that he did not already know. He paused for a moment, as though considering the implications of Iverson's summary ; then he put a direct question.

" How much truth do you really think there was in the whole story ? "

" I don't know," the lawyer replied cautiously.

" All one can say is that it would have looked pretty black if it had come into court. There was no documentary evidence. That little jade Poole had spent part of her time prying into all Mrs. Preston's private belongings, opening her writing-case with a key that fitted, and so forth ; but she hadn't succeeded in coming upon a single scrap of writing that would support Preston's case. I'm pretty sure there was none to be had, for Poole's one of these women who get a certain amount of sexual amusement in prying into dirty corners ; and, if there had been anything to be found, she'd have got hold of it, to judge by her account."

The Superintendent rubbed his chin thoughtfully.

" I suppose there was no doubt that Preston really meant business in this affair ? I mean, he would have seen the thing through, once he'd started ? "

Iverson's cynical smile made his opinion quite clear before he spoke in reply.

" If I were a married man—which heaven forbid ! —I'm pretty sure that parts of Poole's story would have roused me too far to allow me to cool down again, even after reflection. Besides, Preston was one of those people who map out a course far ahead and stick to it like grim death afterwards—a matter of foresight, he'd have called it. Actually, it was pure obstinacy, a kind of silly doggedness which some weak fellows pride themselves on, because it looks like strength of character, in their own opinion. Besides, he was really badly shaken by the whole affair ; I could see that. He may have suspected things were going wrong ; but it's different when you're faced with an apparent certainty in an affair of that sort. No matter how you steel yourself, it's always a horrible wound to your pride."

He halted for a moment or two, as though not very sure of his ground.

" Did you ever consider suicide as a possibility in the case ? " he demanded at last.

Ross shook his head.

" There was no pistol in the carriage," he said definitely. " A man can't tuck himself under the seat of a railway carriage, shoot himself to death, and then pitch the weapon out of the window."

" No," the lawyer admitted. " If you put it that way, it's impossible. But, with a little pre-arrangement, it might be managed, I think."

He reflected for a moment or two, evidently putting his case together.

" I happened to ask a few questions when I went to identify the body," he said. " I gathered that some of the wounds were made by a fairly harmless weapon—something firing a reduced charge, for instance—whilst two others were really deadly affairs. Now I'm only giving you this as an hypothesis which *might* fit, remember ; I'm not saying that it's how things did really happen. But suppose that Preston wanted to commit suicide and to do as much damage as he could to other people by making it look like murder. Suppose he provided himself with a couple of pistols, one with reduced charges in the cartridges, the other with ordinary cartridges. Imagine that he

189

tied both pistols to his attaché-case with long strings and let the case hang out of the carriage window. Then he gets under the seat and shoots himself once or twice, harmlessly, with the reduced-charge cartridges ; and finally he uses the lethal pistol and kills himself. In the final convulsion, his hands open ; the weight of the attaché-case pulls the pistols away from him ; the case itself falls out of the window, dragging the weapons with it. That leaves no pistols in the carriage and the body under the seat, doesn't it ? "

Superintendent Ross smiled, but he shook his head.

" I'm afraid it won't work," he pointed out. " Some of the shooting was done before he got under the seat at all."

" The harmless shots," Iverson suggested, and Ross mentally admitted that this fitted the evidence.

" But that would leave the attaché-case and pistols on the line," the Superintendent objected.

" Until someone picked them up, certainly. Have you got either the attaché-case or the pistols yet ? "

" We've got the case," Ross admitted grudgingly.

" Well, I don't pretend my hypothesis is right. In fact, it's not really my own idea ; I read something like it somewhere or other. But you'll admit that it's a plausible alternative to murder."

Superintendent Ross's expression had more than a tinge of scepticism in it.

" It sounds a bit far-fetched," he said, " and you haven't produced any motive for all this hanky-panky you assume on Preston's part. Even allowing that Preston knew Dr. Selby-Onslow was next door to him and might be involved in a murder charge, it doesn't ring true, you know. Preston had a far simpler weapon ready against the doctor—the divorce suit."

Iverson waved his hand as though admitting all that.

."I'm no psychologist," he said placidly. "But remember one thing. That jade Poole, with her evidence, gave Preston the chance of seeing, for once in a while, exactly how he looked to other people, with all his fads and fancies and routine and so forth. Most of us would open our eyes a bit if we saw exactly what the rest of the world thinks of us. Something of a shock, I suspect, in a good many cases ; and a specially rude shock for a self-satisfied creature like Preston, I should think."

He dismissed the whole matter with another gesture.

" Now, since you're here, what about this car of mine ? I want to know if there's any chance of my getting it back ; for, if not, then the sooner I think about buying a new one, the better."

" I think we may have some news for you soon," Ross said hopefully. " We're piecing together some things that may lead up to it."

CHAPTER XIII

THE CAR SNATCHERS

With the lawyer's reminder fresh in his memory, Superintendent Ross sent for Inspector Mornington as soon as he returned to his office.

" Anything to report about that car stolen from Iverson ? " he demanded, when the Inspector appeared.

" I'd rather take things in their order, if it's all the same to you," Mornington suggested. " You kept me pretty busy with all the affairs you told me to look into.; and I'd like to get the lot off my chest at one go, now I've the chance."

" Fire away, then," Ross invited, settling himself in his chair, since he saw from his subordinate's face that there would be a good deal to tell.

" First of all, another marked note's turned up. It's a ten-bob one, X10 177972. Reported by the Esperanza Street branch of the County and Central Bank. Traced back through a tradesman to Maddox. He doesn't deny that it may have passed through his hands."

" That doesn't add anything much to the case," said Ross, though not in a discouraging tone.

Mornington agreed at once.

" Merely nailing things down as firm as possible,"

he explained. " Second, I went down to Morpledene and put Maddox's aunt through it. Her story tallies with the one he gave us, so far as his visit to her's concerned. She feeds at a quarter past one, usually ; and Maddox turned up just after she'd cleared away her dinner-dishes. ' Somewhere about two o'clock' was her estimate of the time he came to her house.

" Third, I got hold of the surface-man who was walking on the line between Seven Sisters and Hammersleigh. He left Seven Sisters a while after the 10.35 went through. That's as near as I could screw him down to, in time. But that tallies with what Maddox told us about seeing him. The surface-man didn't see Maddox on the embankment. The fog was pretty thick, according to him. That again tallies with Maddox's story.

" Fourth, the bit of the line where Maddox said he found the attaché-case in the bushes is exactly as he described it. That shows he must have been there at some time or other.

" Fifth, I found the attaché-case itself in the place where he said he hid it finally. I've got it here. It's a bit sodden. But the place where Preston's card was gummed inside the lid is plain enough. That identifies it, apart from Maddox's story."

The Inspector paused, as though to give Ross time to collate this information.

" That corroborates Maddox's story completely, so far as it goes," he pointed out. " But it's got no bearing on whether he murdered Preston or not. All it does is to confirm his tale of his movements *after* the murder, obviously."

"Obviously," Superintendent Ross repeated. "He's no better off, except that his tale holds water wherever you've tested it."

"Sixth," Mornington went on, "I made inquiries about the cutting of Dr. Whitacre's telephone wire. It seems it must have been done in the dusk, or shortly after that. So the Exchange people make out, at least. He actually discovered it about seven o'clock in the evening, when he went to ring someone up. His house is about three hundred yards away from the nearest line of telephone poles, and his wire goes down on poles of its own over the intervening space. Without a ladder to reach the lowest foot-rests, you can't get at the wire unless you swarm up the pole itself. The wire was cut about half-way between two poles and some ten feet of wire had been snipped out. My notion is that someone threw a rope or a cord over the wire about that point and pulled on the wire till it snapped. Then he cut ten feet off one of the broken ends and decamped. I can't see how it was done any other way. Dr. Whitacre seemed very peevish about the affair. I asked him if he had suspicions in the matter. It appears a ne'er-do-well in the neighbourhood owes him a grudge. There's no proof of any sort."

"Net result, then," the Superintendent commented, "is simply this : It was done after dark, when no one could see what was going on. It was a case of malice aforethought, since the fellow must have brought a rope and a pair of wire nippers with him. And there's no evidence to show who did it."

" That's correct," Mornington confirmed, not in the least perturbed by the paucity of his results.

" Well, let it go at that," Ross said, brushing the matter aside. He had evidence, unknown to Mornington, which carried him a stage farther than the Inspector had gone ; but the matter was one which could wait until further facts came to hand.

" Seventh," Mornington resumed his drab recital of ascertained points, " I went to Oxenden Grange, where Iverson's car was stolen. It's a biggish house —fourteen chimneys, say three reception and eight bedrooms—but it's only got about an acre of ground round it. Garage, couple of tennis courts, small winter garden leading off one of the rooms. Approach from the road, only about a hundred yards from the gate to the front door. Grounds a bit wild at present."

" I understand," Ross interrupted. " ' Company's gas and water ; baths (hot and cold) ; electricity available ; modern drainage.' You can skip that part."

" I'm just telling you what I saw," the Inspector protested, in a faintly aggrieved tone. " You sent me to look at the place. I went and looked at it. Now I'm making a report on it."

" All right," said Ross soothingly. " I see it perfectly in my mind's eye. It's a ' Picturesque Modern House ' or a ' Delightful Freehold Residence ' or a

' Choice Residential Property.' I read about 'em in the newspaper advertisement columns."

" Everything was locked up," Mornington explained. " I can only tell you what I saw of the place from the outside. When I'd seen all that, I went off and interviewed Tenbury, the man Iverson had up at Oxenden Grange that morning over the alterations. Tenbury's a builder and contractor in Hammersleigh. I asked him if he knew anything about the circumstances.

" Tenbury's story's quite clear and tallies with what we got from Iverson. His appointment with Iverson was for noon on 23rd November ; and, when he drove up in his car, he found Iverson had just arrived a minute or two before him and had just got the big gates at the entrance to the Grange unlocked and swung back to let his own car in. Tenbury pulled up his car behind Iverson's ; and then Iverson came over and they began to discuss these improvements that the proprietor wanted. One of them was a rustic summerhouse that was to be erected ; and, when this came to be discussed, they wanted to see the ground ; so they left their cars and walked over to the spot where the thing was to be put up. It's about half-way to the house and a bit off the drive. After that, they went on to the house and looked round the inside, discussing more changes that the proprietor wanted. And when they came out again it was about one o'clock. They walked down to the gate. When they got to it, Tenbury's car was standing there, just as

they'd left it ; but Iverson's car was gone. Tenbury
says his car was a shabby one, whilst Iverson's was
a nearly split-new Rover saloon. So the thieves
naturally took the better of the two."

" Thieves ? " asked Ross, stressing the plural.

" Thieves," Mornington repeated. " I'm coming to
that later. Tenbury says Iverson was pretty wild
when he found his car was gone. He used a string
of what Tenbury called ' quite illegal language.'
Tenbury's a bit of a dry stick. I gather Iverson was
more than a bit upset to find his car stolen. That's
natural enough ; I'd feel much the same myself, I
think. Tenbury gave him a lift in his own car back
to Hammersleigh station and Iverson took the train
home. That finishes Tenbury's account of the theft."

" You said ' thieves,' " Ross reminded him. " How
do you know there was more than one ? "

" Because I've got them both," Mornington
retorted triumphantly.

" Go on talking," said the Superintendent. " This
is the sort of story I like."

But his tone conveyed his real appreciation of
Mornington's efficiency.

" The car itself turned up in the hands of an old
gentleman in the next county. He's a beginner. The
first time he had the car out, after buying it, he
managed to smash a connecting-rod somehow. So
he sent it to a garage for repairs and wrote to the
Rover people, giving them the engine number and
wanting a new connecting-rod for nothing. The
Rover people had never sent out an engine with that

number. There was a figure too many in it. Then the
garage people spotted that the remaining figures
were those of the engine-number of the missing
Iverson car. After that, it was simple enough. I
needn't go into it, because I've got one of the men
here. He's a miserable rat of a fellow, and wants to
squeak to save his own skin at the other chap's
expense, if he can. I haven't taken his statement yet.
It'll save time if I have him in now ; so that you can
hear what he's got to say for himself. His name's
Lawson. The other man's name's Wilkes. Wilkes
runs a cheap garage-and-repair shop in Kempsford ;
and Lawson's his handy-man. My impression is that
it isn't the first time they've gone in for car-snatching;
but they've never been nailed before."

" Bring him in, then," Ross directed. " We may
get something out of him, though it's not likely to
help him when the case comes on."

Mornington went out and in a few minutes
returned, ushering in the car thief. Lawson was
quite devoid of any striking personal characteristics, apart from the lines on his hands ingrained
with black, which would have suggested " mech-
anic " at first sight. Superintendent Ross
remembered Maddox's statement about the big
closed car which had passed him on the road with
" two fellows on board that looked like—well, like
anybody else." Lawson certainly fitted this extremely
indeterminate description. The Superintendent
allowed the captive a few seconds before paying any
attention to him ; and this treatment, as he expected,

produced an increase in Lawson's nervousness. After letting him shuffle restlessly on his feet for a moment or two longer, Ross turned round.

" You want to make a statement ? "

" Yes," Lawson protested eagerly. " I want to tell you just how it happened, an' then perhaps you'll make things a bit easier for me when I come up before the beak."

" Nobody promised anything of the sort," said Ross sternly. " Tell us what you want, and it'll be no worse for you. It's a clear case. That's all I've got to say on that point."

Lawson seemed taken aback by this plain statement. However, after a moment or two of reflection, he seemed to imagine that it was merely official bluff and that he still had something to gain by betraying his associate.

" Well, it was this way," he began, under the stony stare of Mornington, who was taking down his statement. " Wilkes, he keeps a garage in Kempsford, in Tranton Road ; an' he an' I do the car-cleaning an' repairs between us. He owns the place an' he pays me by the week ; I've nothing to do with the management, see ? I'm just a paid hand, like."

He glanced at the two officials as though striving to see if they appreciated the fact that he was merely a subordinate in the affairs of the garage. Neither of them showed the slightest interest, which seemed to damp him a little.

" Wilkes, he does a bit o' trading in second-hand cars, now an' again ; pickin' up a crock an' doctorin' it till the wheels go round an' then sellin' it at a bit of a profit. He's got a sort of a connection in that kind o' line, though I never had nothin' to do with that end o' his business, I can swear to that, if you ask me to, for I never touched it. Wilkes, he ran that end o' the business entirely.

" Now, about this car that there's the trouble over, I'll tell you just how it all happened, an' you'll see how I was let in, quite without meanin' anythin' more than just a bit o' fun at the time."

He glanced hopefully up to see how this was received, but did not appear to be much encouraged by the expressions on the faces of Mornington and Ross.

" It happened this way," he went on, after a pause. " Wilkes, he'd bought a crock—an old broken-down Singer, it was, about pre-war, I should think—an' we'd done a job on it an' made it fit to go, if you didn't push it too much ; an' he'd sold it to a man over in Seven Sisters. So that morning——"

" 23rd November," interjected the accurate Mornington.

" 23rd November, as you say," Lawson continued. " Wilkes, he says, ' We'll take this thing over an' deliver it this morning. The boy can mind the shop for an hour or two.' I had a notion he was afraid something might go wrong with the thing, for we hadn't had time to try it on the road, really. So I says : ' Right oh ! '" an' I got out of my overalls an' off we went. We got rid of the thing to the man at Seven Sisters all right ; but there was a bit o' hagglin' at the last moment, and, what with that an' other things, we just missed the train at Seven Sisters. Wilkes, he was in good form ; he must ha' turned a good penny or two o' profit over the crock, for he was in high spirits an' a bit above himself once he's got the money. So, as we'd missed the train, we dropped into a pub an' had a drink ; an' then we started to tramp back to Hammersleigh to fill in the time until the next train come along.

" A bit along the road we come to a big house, an' at the gate of it there was two cars standin' empty and nobody in sight."

" I wish witnesses would give definite times in their statements," Ross interrupted, speaking ostensibly to Mornington, so as to avoid questioning Lawson directly. " They never seem to think of it."

Lawson took the hint.

" That would be gettin' on for about one o'clock," he explained. " Bein' in the motor line ourselves, you understand, we naturally walks up to the cars an' has a squint at 'em, just as a matter o' curiosity. One of 'em was pretty well used, but t'other was a big blue-painted saloon Rover, near brand-new. We noses around it for a minute or so ; an' then Wilkes, he turns to me with a grin on his mug, an' says he : ' I wonder just how one o' them Rovers runs.' An' then he winks, an' says he : ' What about a bit of a joy-ride up the road ? ' An' with that he opens the door an' hops into the drivin'-seat ; an', before I thinks what I was doin', I jumps in too, alongside him.

"I thought we'd be nabbed, sure, before we got away ; for Wilkes, he ran the self-starter about five times before he got the engine goin'. 'She must ha' been near stone-cold,' says he, when she started up at last. An', with that, he lets in the clutch, an' off we went up the road in the Hammersleigh direction. I thought he was just havin' a bit o' fun ; but by an' by he tells me as he means for to keep the car. Says I : 'Don't you do it, Tom.' Says he : 'You leave it to me ; there's no risk. I've done it afore this an' they never catched me yet.' So I says nothin' more ; an' by and by he turns the car off down a sort o' field-track an' into a wood—a fairly lonely place where it didn't look as if anybody'd be goin' at that time o' the year. 'If anyone sees it standin' there,' says Wilkes, 'they'll think the owner's some-where near by, an' they'll leave it alone. We'll come back for it after dark to-night. An', mind,' says he, 'if anybody asks you, we haven't seen no car. You stick to that,' he says.

"So we went back for it that night, an' took it to a shed Wilkes has in Trump Street, where he keeps old stores an' things ; an' then Wilkes, he set about an' faked it a bit. He repainted it, an' he etched extra figures on to the engine number an' the chassis number, an' he altered all the fittin's that could be shifted. An' then, one day, he took it away ; an' I've never seen it since, an' he never told me what he did with it or where it went to. An' that's all I know about it, the very last word."

"You've charged him with stealing this car ? " the

Superintendent asked Mornington. " Then you'd better read over to him what you've taken down, and he can sign it."

When this formality had been completed, Ross turned again to the prisoner.

" You've been charged with this theft, and I can't ask you any questions about it, according to the rules. I'm not going to. But I can ask you about other things ; there's no bar to that. You understand the position ? "

Lawson nodded to show his comprehension, and Ross continued.

" According to you, Wilkes said that he'd done this kind of thing before. Have you any knowledge of anything of the sort, anything that would support his statement ? "

Lawson consulted his memory for a moment or two.

" There was some things in that shed in Trump Street that didn't seem like as if they was Wilkes's."

" Such as ? "

" Well, once I saw a pair o' number-plates that didn't come off of any car we had in the garage. Another time, I noticed a typewriter ; it disappeared again almost at once, an' I never knew Wilkes to do any typing. An' once I saw a pile o' clothes in a corner under a bit o' sacking. Then another time, in the evenin', I happened to go round to the store, an' Wilkes was busy repaintin' a bicycle in a fresh colour. That's about all I can remember."

" These things didn't strike you as curious ? "

203

"Well, what if they did? They was no business o' mine, was they? Wilkes, he didn't go for to encourage questions about his affairs."

Superintendent Ross reflected for a moment or two.

"I can't ask you any questions," he pointed out again, "but I'm going to tell you that it might be as well to make things clearer at one point. You didn't give any details about what happened when you and Wilkes brought the car to the Trump Street shed that night."

"Because there was no details to give," Lawson protested. "When we got the car into the shed, Wilkes was at the wheel. I'd got out for to open the shed door an' let the car in. An' Wilkes, he turns round to me and says he: 'You'd better cut off home, Jimmy. I'll look after things.' So off I went. I never laid a finger on the car after that. All the fakin' of her was done by Wilkes, an' that's the truth. The most you can say against me was that I was sittin' in the front seat while Wilkes was drivin'. I never touched the car; I never had no hand in the fakin' business; an' I had nothin' at all to do with the sellin' part. My hands is quite clean, so far as all that goes."

"H'm! Want to add that to your statement?"

"If it's goin' to do me any good, then certainly."

"I can't give you my opinion. Sign it or not, just as you wish."

After a careful inspection of the faces of the two officials, Lawson decided to sign the addendum; and then Mornington took him away. When the

Inspector had disposed of his prisoner, he came back to Ross's room.

" What do you think of your friend ? " the Superintendent inquired.

" A damned liar with the wind up badly," Mornington said bluntly.

" I'm not going to quarrel with your definition," Ross admitted. " If he thinks he's helped himself much by all that, I've got to differ from him. Now, what about the rest of that report of yours ? "

" There's just one more point. That ram of Chepstow's isn't dead yet ; but it's on its very last legs, so the vet. says. I guess the autopsy's near due. I've arranged about it."

" All right, then," said Ross, though his tone suggested that Chepstow's ram was taking a secondary place in his thoughts at the moment. " Now, I've got some more work for you to do. First of all, I want to know if any of the bank officials was absent from duty in the Garfield Street branch on the morning of 23rd November. Then I want the same information about the employees in Preston's Hammersleigh factory and in his office in the city here. That won't take you long. And, finally, I want every pawnbroker in the district questioned. It's essential to find out if Wilkes has pawned any clothes since the day of the murder. Try the old-clothes dealers as well. It's a very long shot, but it's worth trying out as far as we can go. Get on to that as quick as you can, and do it thoroughly, will you ? "

" And I suppose I'd better keep a look-out for

anything else that Wilkes has been pawning, when I'm at it ? "

" Yes. But clothes are what I'm really after. You can go through his house for pawn-tickets, to start with ; and, of course, if there are any clothes there, you'd better collect them too."

The Superintendent paused for a moment, then added :

" Wilkes doesn't want to unburden his soul about the theft of the car, by any chance ? "

Mornington shook his head.

" Wilkes is a tough," he volunteered concisely as he left the room.

When his subordinate had closed the door behind him, the Superintendent remained for a few moments with knitted brows, conning over the bearings of the fresh evidence which they had just obtained. Then he took out his notebook and sketched in it a fresh diagram.

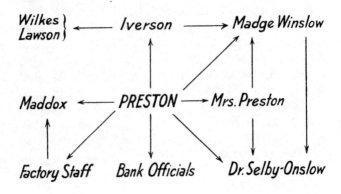

For a time, Ross stared at the scheme, tracing out step by step the relationships which it displayed. At last he dropped the point of his pencil on one item in the diagram.

" That's where the blame lies," he reflected impatiently. " I'm fairly sure of that. But the bother is to prove it beyond dispute. Conjectures are no good in a hanging case. The jury want something fair and square in the way of proof ; and, although we could put up a pretty story for them, it wouldn't be clinching. Unless we can get hold of a suit of clothes and connect it with Wilkes, there's a hole in the case."

Superintendent Ross closed his notebook and returned it to his pocket with a gesture of vexation. To feel sure that he is right, and yet to be unable to prove it, is an annoying state for any man ; and the Superintendent was very human.

CHAPTER XIV

THE TWO TICKETS

Inspector Mornington pulled a list from his pocket and consulted it before beginning his report.

" I've raked through every likely place where Wilkes might have pawned stuff," he explained, " and I've looked up the old-clothes dealers as well. I don't claim to have got everything. But what I've got, the dealers are prepared to swear is stuff handed over to them by someone who answers Wilkes's general description. Here's a list of the articles. A typewriter. A suit of clothes. A photographic camera. A silver cigarette-case. A leather suit-case. Some assorted motor tools. I have them all here, if you want to look them over."

Superintendent Ross seemed satisfied with his subordinate's results.

" Let's have a look at the suit," he suggested, " and the typewriter as well. We can't do anything with the motor tools ; though perhaps Iverson might be able to identify some of them as stolen along with his car. That can wait."

When the typewriter and the suit of clothes were forthcoming, the Superintendent appeared to become more alert. Leaving the typewriter aside for the moment, he picked up the jacket and examined the fabric carefully.

" Cloth's too good for ready-made," he suggested, holding it up for Mornington to see. " No tailor's name on the hanger-tape. Let's see . . ."

He turned the right-hand breast-pocket inside out and made a careful inspection of the lining.

" There's been a tailor's tab sewn in here at one time," he pointed out, " but it's been cut away. You can see one or two ends of thread showing on the lining. There, and there."

Mornington followed the Superintendent's finger and agreed with the inference.

" Of course, Wilkes would cut that out before he attempted to get rid of the thing," he commented. " Usually the owner's name's written on these tabs by the tailor. It might have been awkward for Wilkes if it had been looked at."

" Nothing in the pockets, I suppose ? " the Superintendent questioned.

" I haven't gone through them yet," Mornington explained. " I thought you'd prefer to see them just as they came in. But, from the feel of the clothes, there doesn't seem to be much left in the pockets."

Superintendent Ross began methodically to search through the pockets of the jacket, but discovered nothing. Just as he was about to put the garment down, he suddenly remembered the ticket-pocket, which he had overlooked. As he put his fingers into it, Mornington saw his face light up.

" Here's something ! "

And he withdrew his hand and held it up, revealing two railway tickets between the fingers.

" Ah ! " said Mornington, with satisfaction, as he recognised the bits of pasteboard. " Wilkes was a bit of a fool to overlook these, wasn't he ? "

Superintendent Ross put down the coat and scrutinised the two railway tickets.

" They're both first-class return halves," he reported. " One's for the journey from Horston to Hammersleigh ; and the other's for the journey from Seven Sisters to Hammersleigh. And the date on both of them is 16th November. Now, that's interesting, if you like ! "

He reflected for a moment or two in silence, staring absent-mindedly at the tickets in his hand. Mornington did not disturb him, but, when the Superintendent appeared to have reached the end of his train of thought, the Inspector threw out a fresh piece of information.

" I just wanted to check Lawson's statement as far as possible," he pointed out, " so I went down and questioned the man they sold the car to, the day of the murder. Lawson told us they haggled so long that it was too late for them to catch the train. That may be so ; but the purchaser thinks they might easily have caught it all right, if they'd hurried a bit. It's only his impression, though, and he wouldn't swear to it. Still, there it is."

" Just as well to have everything checked," the Superintendent agreed. " Let's see. They'd have had time to walk back from Hammersleigh and steal Iverson's car even if they'd taken the train, I believe."

" I walked over the ground, just to see," the Inspector confirmed. " They could have come on by the train from Seven Sisters, got out at Hammersleigh, and then walked over to Oxenden Grange in time to snap up Iverson's car, just as Lawson admitted they did."

" Yes, but, if they'd done that, they'd have had to give up their tickets—and quite obviously they didn't give up these tickets. Besides, you checked all the ticket-surrenders at Hammersleigh yourself, didn't you ? "

" Some people have the knack of travelling without giving up their ticket," said Mornington glumly. " And, of course, return halves like these were out of the calculation, if they weren't handed over at the Hammersleigh barrier. There was no way of including them in the scheme at all, in that case. They're the weak link in the chain."

Superintendent Ross returned to his abstracted study of the two rectangular pasteboard slips which he still held in his hand. Suddenly his eyes became alert. He fished a triple-lens magnifier from his pocket and scrutinised the tickets through it, one after the other.

" Did you inquire at Seven Sisters Station if anyone remembered Wilkes and Lawson getting aboard the 10.35 ? " he demanded.

Mornington shook his head.

" I'd gone into that fully at the very start of the case," he pointed out. " The station people's memories were fresher then, and they didn't mention Wilkes and Lawson. There wasn't any point in going back and heckling them again, when the scent's as cold as it is now."

Ross seemed less dissatisfied with this than Mornington had feared.

" Well, it doesn't make much odds," he commented. " Now, just have a look at these two tickets " —he held them up—" and tell me if anything strikes you about them."

" They're both snipped with a ticket-checker's clipper," Mornington pronounced rather grudgingly. " It's been a plain clipper that leaves a triangular snip in the ticket. That's the kind used by the men at the barriers all along the line, I noticed when I was going into the ticket question. But I don't see where all this leads to. There's no proof, even, that these tickets were snipped on the day of the murder at all. That's just a chance."

" Here, take the glass," Ross ordered. " Now have a good look at the place where the snip-mark is on each ticket. See anything rummy about the marks ? "

Mornington subjected both tickets to a most careful examination. Then, with a look of astonishment on his face, he turned to the Superintendent.

" These things weren't snipped with a clipper at all. Is that what you mean ? Instead of a bit having been punched out, clean, there's been a bit cut out with scissors. And in each case one of the cuts over-shoots the apex of the triangle by a trifle. Somebody's gone to the bother of forging a clip on an unclipped ticket. Well, I'm damned ! That's a new stunt to me. Usually the notion is to get in through the barrier *without* having your ticket clipped, so's to be able to use it over again if you get away with it."

" Well, we'll leave it alone for the present," the Superintendent said, as though dismissing the matter from his thoughts. "We haven't finished with these clothes yet. Anything in the pockets of the waistcoat or the trousers ? "

Mornington picked up the two garments and went through the pockets.

" Nothing here," he reported.

" Where do you carry your matches ? " the Superintendent asked, with apparent irrelevance.

" In my left-hand jacket pocket," Mornington said, producing a cardboard box as he spoke.

" So do I," Ross informed him. " It seems a likely place. Just turn the left-hand jacket pocket inside out, will you ? Have a look at the lining."

Mornington picked up the jacket and did as he was directed.

" Not much here," he reported, examining the fold of the lining. " Wait a bit ! There's a small brown stain on the lining itself—on what would be the outer side of the pocket when the jacket was on. Is that what you expected ? "

" I didn't expect it, but I hoped there might be something of the sort," Ross said, with hardly suppressed satisfaction. " No use jumping to conclusions, of course. It may not amount to anything. But we'll have that bit of cloth tested for blood."

Mornington pondered for some moments with a puzzled look on his face. At last his expression changed.

" I see it," he said slowly. " That burnt paper in the carriage put you on to it ? "

" Yes, there was just the chance that some blood was left on the fellow's hands—just a trace or two—when he felt in his pocket to get out the matches to burn the paper. I didn't really expect to find a stain ; it was just a long shot that happened to come off. And, of course, there's no guarantee that it's really a bloodstain. We'll need to wait for the expert's opinion on that, before we build too much on it."

Mornington inspected the stain once more and then put down the jacket.

" Now let's have a look at that typewriter," Ross suggested.

He lifted it on to the table, noting as he did so that it was of the same make as Dr. Selby-Onslow's machine. Then he inserted a sheet of paper and sat down before the instrument.

" H'm ! How did it run ? *Please come for urgent consultation Friday morning. Shall meet* 10.35 *train with my car at Morpledene Station. Whitacre.*"

He rattled off the duplicate of the bogus telegram, drew the sheet from the machine, and scanned the printing.

" This isn't the machine that wrote the fake

214

message," he announced, almost at once. " The fake telegram had defects in its d's and t's, for one thing ; and there's nothing of the sort here. No, this type-writer isn't going to help us much. It's just an accident that Wilkes happened to steal a typewriter of that make. There's nothing in it."

Mornington received this with an air of resigna-tion. Then, seeing that Ross seemed to have come to the end of his investigation of the stolen property, the Inspector drew out a battered piece of metal.

" This is the bullet that killed Chepstow's ram," he explained. " It died, finally, and I went down to see the bullet taken out of its innards. It's a bullet of the same calibre as the one that killed Preston—the one that landed in his brain."

Ross took the distorted object and turned it over in his fingers without saying anything. Suddenly Mornington appeared to see a fresh light on the case.

" 'Strewth ! I never thought of that ! " he ex-claimed, in a tone of vexation. " That ram was shot on the 16th of November. And that's the date on these two tickets we found just now."

" Of course ! " said the Superintendent, rather impatiently. " What do you suppose I've been bothering over that ram for ? It was as plain as anything could be that the ram was shot by accident from the window of a passing train. Nothing else would fit the facts. And it didn't need the brains of a Sherlock Holmes or a Thorndyke to see what was behind that, either. I managed it myself without straining myself much. It was a preliminary canter

215

over the course—a rehearsal of the big show that was planned for the 23rd of November. It was meant to make sure that a shot could be fired in the carriage without attracting attention next door. The ram happened to get in the way of the bullet. That was as plain as daylight. But we had to get the bullet and see its calibre before we could call it more than a guess. That's the bother about this damned case— proof ! There's no great trouble in guessing who's mixed up in the business—that's dead easy. But the infernal thing is to scrape up enough evidence to bring it home clearly enough to convince a jury. You know that."

Superintendent Ross's unwonted loquacity gave the Inspector a gauge of how much his superior was irritated by the lack of clinching evidence ; but he was not called upon to offer any opinion, for the Superintendent swung round on him with a fresh set of instructions.

" You can take away that typewriter. Leave the suit of clothes. And now I want you to get on to something fresh as quick as you can. Go to Maddox and ask him if the train stopped after he saw the attaché-case thrown out—I mean stopped in the fog before it got to Hammersleigh. You can tell him that this has nothing to do with his own case ; and nothing he says will be used against him in court. It's a different case altogether, tell him. And coax an answer out of him at any cost, if he'll give you one. Don't let him see what answer you expect, of course. I want the plain truth, without any leading

questions. And then get on to the railway people—
get the guard of the train, if you can—and find out
just what stops the 10.35 made between Seven
Sisters and Hammersleigh that morning. I know it
made one, because the express I was in stopped just
alongside the 10.35. But I want full information, if
we can get it, and as quick as you like. It's high time
we saw the end of this affair."

It was an hour or two before Mornington returned
with the required evidence.

" I've seen Maddox at the gaol," he reported. He
remembers one stop the train made, between the
place where the attaché-case was thrown out and
Hammersleigh. It was just short of Hammersleigh. Then I got hold of the guard who was on the
10.35 that morning. I had to wait till his train came
in. He was on duty when I got to the station. He says
he remembers a stop just beyond Seven Sisters and
another stop just before Hammersleigh—about half
a mile or so. He described the place. I can identify
it if you want that, because the guard said they
stopped at a signal. The fog was very thick there, he
remembers. A man was setting fog-signals at that
point, and the guard had a few words with him while
the train halted. I've got that man's name if you
want it."

" No, I think that'll be enough," Ross decided.
" We can always get hold of the fellow later on if we
need him. By the way, have you found out about the
bank people and the employees at the factory, for
me ? "

" No one was off duty at the bank on the 23rd. And none of the factory people were away from their work that day, either."

" I expected as much," Ross admitted. " But it's just as well to be absolutely sure in things like that."

CHAPTER XV

THE KEYSTONE

On the following morning, as soon as Iverson's office opened, Superintendent Ross telephoned to inquire if the solicitor had arrived.

" Not in yet ? " he said, on getting from the clerk the negative answer which he expected. " Well, when is he likely to come in ? When does he usually turn up in the morning ? I'm Superintendent Ross."

" He ought to be here in a quarter of an hour, or so," the clerk assured him. " Do you want to make an appointment ? "

" No, no," said Ross hastily, " I'll take my chance of seeing him if I come in. I'm pretty busy this morning, and I can't say when I may be free."

Had the clerk seen the Superintendent's next move, he might have been surprised. Ross waited just long enough to allow the lawyer to leave his house ; and then, with a brown-paper parcel under his arm, he set out for 83 Warlingham Road.

" Mr. Iverson at home ? " he demanded, when the maid opened the door.

" He's just gone into town a few minutes ago."

Superintendent Ross feigned vexation at this news.

" Missed him, have I ? That's a nuisance."

He paused, as though in reflection.

"You'd find him at his office now," the maid suggested.

"Unfortunately I'm in a hurry and haven't time to go to his office."

"You might telephone from here, if you like."

The Superintendent appeared for a moment to accept this solution, then he seemed to change his mind.

"I think I'd better leave a note," he decided. "Can you give me some writing-paper?"

As he went into the hall, in answer to her gesture of invitation, the Superintendent put down his brown-paper parcel and, taking off his overcoat, hung it on the hatstand beside one of Iverson's. The maid led him into the lawyer's study; and Ross, sitting down at the desk, wrote a short letter, which he then sealed up in an envelope and handed to the maid.

When he emerged again into the hall, he stepped over to the hatstand and took down a coat; but at that moment he seemed to change his mind again.

"After all, I don't think we need bother about that letter," he said, holding out his hand for it. "I think I can just manage to find time to go and see Mr. Iverson at his office."

The maid returned the envelope to him, and he began to struggle into the overcoat.

"Hullo!" he said, in apparent surprise. "I must have taken down the wrong coat."

He glanced at the tab inside the collar.

"Silly mistake, that," he said apologetically, as he

hung up Iverson's overcoat and took down his own from the peg.

Then, picking up his brown-paper parcel, he left the house. He had spent a certain amount of time in getting the information he wanted ; but, after all, one can hardly go to a man's house and blurt out a demand for the name of his tailor.

The Superintendent's next port of call was at the address he had read on the tab of Iverson's overcoat. There he demanded an interview with one of the partners and disclosed his official position.

" We need your help, if you can give us it," he explained, opening his brown-paper parcel. " We've come across some stolen property lately, and we want to get it identified, if possible. Would you mind looking at this suit and seeing if you can tell whether you made it or not ? "

The tailor picked up the jacket and searched for the identification tabs.

" Our name's not on it," he pointed out. " How did you come to think of us ? "

Superintendent Ross put on a mysterious expression.

" We have our own methods," he said, in a tone which suggested extraordinary sources of information.

" I recognise the cloth, certainly," the tailor admitted, as he examined it. " We had some of this grey-brown stuff last year. We didn't get much of it in, so perhaps I could track down the customers who had suits made from it."

" And the measurements of the suit may let you put your hand on the customer who got this particular suit from you," the Superintendent suggested.

The tailor went off to consult his books. After a time he returned with an expression on his face that showed his search had been successful.

" It was easier than I expected," he explained. " That suit was made for Mr. Iverson, of 83 Warlingham Road, last year—in October."

" You could identify it positively if we needed that ? "

" Oh, yes. The cutter is quite sure about it. He remembers it well enough."

" Thanks for your trouble," Ross said, taking his leave. " Of course, you'll say nothing about this to anyone. We don't want any information to leak out until we've got the case put together, you understand ? Thanks."

As he came out of the tailor's shop, he glanced at his watch, and then hurried off to the station just in time to catch a train to Hammersleigh. From Hammersleigh Station, he made his way to the office of Tenbury, the contractor in charge of the projected alterations at Oxenden Grange. From him he learned that the work had not yet been begun. The Grange was still locked up. But Tenbury had a set of keys which the Superintendent succeeded in borrowing, after a little persuasion.

A taxi took him to the gates of the Grange, and there, telling the driver to wait, he got out and let himself into the grounds with a key. The house itself seemed to have no interest for him ; and he walked round it to the garage, which he opened cautiously.

Once inside, he examined the floor, and, with a half-suppressed exclamation of satisfaction, he noted a few drops of oil on the concrete, just in the position where they might have dripped from a standing car. They were obviously not fresh ; but, equally clearly, they were not months old.

Superintendent Ross made a note in his pocket-book and then set himself to a minute examination of the floor of the garage in search of wheel-marks. Only one set of wheel-tracks was visible, very faint indeed ; and Ross had to spend a considerable amount of time before he could be quite certain of the make of the tyres. A reference to his notebook proved that this make of tyre was the one specified in the description of Iverson's stolen car.

" It all fits together," he commented to himself as he locked up the garage again and returned to his taxi. " There's just one point more ; and, if that tallies, then we've got enough to convince any jury."

He returned to Hammersleigh ; handed over the keys to the contractor with a warning that on no account must the garage be tampered with in the meantime ; and then took the next train back to Horston.

As he settled himself comfortably in his seat, he reflected that the last time he had made the journey

was on the afternoon of the day on which Preston
had been murdered ; and it was with a certain satisfaction that he contrasted the state of the case then
with the present position. Then, beyond Preston's
name, he knew practically nothing. Now he had all
the threads in his hands.

As a craftsman, it gave Superintendent Ross more
pleasure to defeat a skilful criminal than to track
down a mere blunderer ; and in the Preston case he
felt the satisfaction which comes to a chess-player as
he says : " Mate in three moves " to a worthy
opponent. Surveying the case in retrospect, he admitted to himself quite frankly that luck had stood
him in good stead at one point : the discovery of the
two railway tickets. Apart from them, he could claim
that the required evidence had been collected with
a definite policy in view ; and, after all, the tickets
had fallen neatly into place in the already forged
chain of proof. He had been ready for them when
they turned up. The whole affair was practically
settled now. Three more facts, all easily ascertain-
able, and he could send the prosecutor into court
with a case which would convince any jury.

At the Horston terminus he went straight from the
train to a public telephone-box and rang up Inspector Mornington, to whom he gave some instructions.

" Report to me as soon as you've put it through,"
he concluded. " I'm going straight on now to Dr.
Selby-Onslow's house."

Leaving the station, he hailed a taxi and drove to
Prince's Square. There, he was fortunate enough to

find Dr. Selby-Onslow at home ; and by pleading urgency he was able to gain an immediate interview.

As the doctor came into the room, it was evident that he had no liking for this unexpected visit.

" Well, what do you want now ? " he demanded, with more than a tinge of hostility in his voice.

Superintendent Ross wasted no time in preliminaries.

" You keep a case-book, I suppose, doctor ? I'd like you to look up some entries in it."

The request evidently took Dr. Selby-Onslow by surprise ; but he stifled his astonishment with fair success.

" It's against medical etiquette to tell you anything about my patients' affairs," he objected.

" I'm not asking anything about your patients' healths," the Superintendent explained. " I know you can't say anything about matters of that sort. All I want is to know when a certain patient called on you. I could get that from your nurse, so there's no medical etiquette involved ; but I'd rather trust your notes than her memory. That's why I come to you first."

Dr. Selby-Onslow seemed still surprised at the turn which the interview was taking. However, being apparently satisfied on the point of etiquette, he gave a nod of assent and waited sphinx-like for the Superintendent to proceed.

" I believe that, about the middle of November, Mr. Iverson the lawyer paid you a visit ? " Ross said interrogatively.

Dr. Selby-Onslow nodded again : crossed the room to his desk ; and pulled from a drawer a large loose-leaf volume. He turned over the leaves of this for a moment or two, and then found the page he wanted.

" Yes," he said, " Mr. Iverson came here during my consulting hours on Thursday, 15th November."

" Now," Superintendent Ross pursued, " I'd like to know just exactly what happened in the course of that visit of his. This is your consulting-room, isn't it ? Was he shown in here, or into your waiting-room first of all ? "

" How do I know ? " Dr. Selby-Onslow retorted, in his customary way of asking a fresh question instead of answering the one put to him. " I don't receive my patients on the doorstep and show them in myself."

" Perhaps your nurse, who opens the door to patients, might know ? "

" Possibly," said the doctor ungraciously. " Better ask her. I can't tell you."

" Do you mind ringing for her ? "

Dr. Selby-Onslow stepped over and rang the bell. His mask counterfeited total indifference fairly well : but it was clear to Ross that he was both puzzled and inquisitive.

" Superintendent Ross wants to ask you some questions," he explained, when the nurse appeared. " Do you want to see her alone ? " he added to Ross.

The Superintendent shook his head.

" I can ask my questions just as well in your presence," he said.

The doctor moved over to a chair, seated himself, put his finger-tips together, and seemed to isolate himself in a brown study ; but Ross noted that, behind the mask, he was following the proceedings with close attention.

" Now," said the Superintendent, turning to the nurse with a reassuring smile, " I wonder if you can remember Mr. Iverson the lawyer. You know him by sight, perhaps ? "

" Oh, yes," she replied at once. " I know him quite well."

" Then perhaps you could recall the last time he came here ? "

The girl considered for a moment or two.

" He hasn't been here for a while," she replied at last.

" Surely you could come nearer it than that," Ross suggested encouragingly. " Was it this week ? Or last week ? Or earlier than that ? "

At length he succeeded in coaxing the girl to think carefully ; and her final statement coincided with that of the doctor.

" The 15th of November ? " Ross pursued. " That's capital. Now try to remember just what happened when he came here that day. You opened the door to him ? He came during the doctor's consulting hours, perhaps ? "

" Yes. Now I remember about it. He came in without an appointment, and I told him that several patients were waiting. He didn't seem very pleased at that ; and he seemed in two minds about going away again, instead of waiting his turn. Then he sort of made up his mind about it, and asked if there was a room where he could write a letter or two while he was waiting—the doctor's study would do, he said. So I showed him in there, apart from the rest of the patients ; and he asked for some note-paper and envelopes. Then I left him there until his turn came ; and then I showed him into the consulting-room."

" He was writing letters when you came back to show him in ? What was he writing with, do you remember ? "

" A fountain-pen. He'd written two or three letters, for I saw him put the envelopes into his pocket when I came to call him."

" Ah ! Now that's very good. That's very good indeed," the Superintendent said, inspecting the nurse benignantly. " And you won't forget any of these points, will you ? You'll keep them well in mind ? Splendid ! "

He turned to the doctor.

" Do you mind if we go into your study ? We shan't be disturbing anyone if we look in for a moment ? Thanks."

He ushered the nurse across the hall and into the study, while Dr. Selby-Onslow followed them, as though uncertain what was coming next.

" Now just look round," Ross suggested to the girl. " Things here are much the same as they were that day, I suppose ? Some papers on the desk, the type-writer there, the chairs much as they are now ? "

" Just the same," she assured him.

" Ah, that's good. Now, I think that's really all I have to ask you. Thanks for telling me these things."

And, with that, he skilfully shepherded the nurse out of the room and closed the door. When he turned to the doctor, all the surface benignity had gone from his expression. That sort of thing was good enough for women ; it would hardly help him with Dr. Selby-Onslow.

" When I was here before," he began, " you happened to mention that you'd lost a pair of reading-spectacles not long ago. Can you remember the exact date when they disappeared ? "

Dr. Selby-Onslow shook his head.

" No."

He thought for a moment or two.

" I daresay I could find out, though, if you need the information," he supplemented. " I remember ordering a fresh pair from Irlam & Holmes the next day. I'll ring them up and ask the date, if you like. They'll have a note in their books, most likely."

" I'll ring up myself, if you don't mind showing me the telephone," Ross suggested, as though merely saving the doctor trouble.

" It's in my consulting-room," Dr. Selby-Onslow explained. " Come this way."

Superintendent Ross got into touch with the firm of opticians, while the doctor, sitting down and assuming his favourite attitude, again feigned to relapse into a brown study.

" Sixteenth ? They were ordered on the 16th

229

November, you say ? Thanks." The Superintendent concluded his telephone conversation and turned round to the doctor.

" I take it, then, that you lost that pair of reading-spectacles on the 15th ? "

" That is so, if the new ones were ordered on the 16th. May I ask what all this is about ? I don't quite see the point of these inquiries."

As Ross had good reason to know, the doctor was still in ignorance of the fact that a spectacle-lens had been found in Preston's compartment ; but the Superintendent saw no reason for divulging this information.

" I shan't trouble you much further," he said, evading a direct reply. " Just another point or two. Cast your mind back to the time you were getting into the 10.35 on the morning of the murder. Did you see anyone you recognised on the platform ? "

Dr. Selby-Onslow considered for a moment or two before answering.

" I saw Iverson—just caught a glimpse of him going out at the gate in the barrier as I came up."

" Can you picture that clearly ? "

" More or less," the doctor qualified cautiously.

" What sort of clothes had he on, for instance ? "

Dr. Selby-Onslow closed his eyes, apparently racking his memory.

" An ordinary dark overcoat, I remember . . . and a grey felt hat . . . and, I think, dark trousers—brownish, if anything. But I couldn't swear to all that."

" Like the ones I'm wearing at this moment ? "

The doctor shook his head decidedly.

" No, not in the least that shade."

The Superintendent seemed nonplussed. Then an idea appeared to strike him, and he loosened the string of his brown-paper parcel.

" Which would you say was nearest the tint ? " he asked. " My suit or this one here ? "

Dr. Selby-Onslow examined both fabrics carefully in turn.

" That one, I should say," he decided at last, pointing to the stolen suit. " But I wouldn't swear to the exact colour. It's just a vague impression I had."

" I daresay I can get some other people to help," Ross confided, thinking of the ticket-collector at the station barrier.

Dr. Selby-Onslow had resumed his mask-like expression.

" I don't quite see where these inquiries are leading," he pointed out. " This is the Preston murder case, I suppose ? "

Before the Superintendent had time to reply, their ears were caught by a prolonged ringing of an electric bell ; a visitor was admitted at the front door ; and in a few moments Mornington was ushered into the consulting-room. A glance at his face showed Ross that something had gone wrong.

" He's slipped through my fingers," he announced curtly, making no attempt to excuse himself.

Superintendent Ross repressed a gesture of vexation.

" What happened ? " he demanded, keeping any suggestion of blame out of his tone.

" He went to his office as usual this morning. Then he was rung up from his house. So I learned from the clerk who took the call. He didn't hear the message itself. After that, Iverson went to his safe and took out a number of packages. He put them in his pockets. Then he left the office, leaving word that he would be back soon after lunch. That was about midday. I've traced him to a restaurant. He had lunch there. After that, he ordered a large packet of sandwiches to be made up, and he took it away with him when he left. After that, the trail's lost. He disappeared, so far as we're concerned."

Superintendent Ross rubbed his chin for a moment or two as though considering this report before making any comment on it.

" A curse on all officious maid-servants," he said at last, whimsically. " I wonder what possessed that girl to give the show away. H'm ! Perhaps he'd left instructions with her to let him know if the police called on him. That's likely enough. He had most of his affairs cut and dried, ready for emergencies."

He reflected again in silence for a short time, while Mornington and Dr. Selby-Onslow waited for him to speak. The doctor's sphinx-like expression had relaxed a little. Evidently he understood that he was no longer under suspicion ; and he could not repress his relief at the turn of events.

" Ready for emergencies," Superintendent Ross echoed himself. " That means he's got his get-away all planned out in advance. Useless for him to think of the railway . . . "

" I got his description handed to the booking-clerks within ten minutes of finding we'd lost the trail," Mornington explained. " Nobody answering to anything like it has taken a ticket to-day."

" No, he won't try the railway," Ross continued. " He's got a fair notion that we're pretty efficient on that side of things. He won't risk it. But he can't hang about the streets. Either he's in a picture-house or else he's dived into some digs he's taken long ago— pretending to be a commercial traveller, most likely, to account for not sleeping in them often. He'll have a fresh suit of clothes stored there, ready to change his appearance as far as possible. You'd better put out an S.O.S. on the wireless : describe him as someone who's missing and may have lost his memory. Give a wrong name, of course. His landlady may have a wireless ; it's always a chance."

" He can't hang about in digs for long," Dr. Selby-Onslow pointed out.

" I don't expect him to," Ross said impatiently. " Horston's too hot to hold him. He'll get off to-night, if he can, even if he has to walk on his ten toes."

" But where ? " persisted the doctor.

" How do I know ? " the Superintendent snapped, with more than a tinge of irritation in his voice. " He's got the initiative, as they used to say in the War. We've got to conform to his movements, as soon as we can find out what they are."

He failed to repress a gesture of annoyance.

" I couldn't have him watched, for fear of frightening him into a bolt before I had my case ready. All I could do was to pretend to swallow all the bits of evidence he served up to me against other people—you, among them. I thought I'd got him convinced that I had no suspicions of him."

" So he was making out a case against me, was he ? " Dr. Selby-Onslow said, in a voice which even the teachings of *Æquanimitas* could hardly keep steady. " I didn't know that."

" Oh, yes, you were to be the scapegoat," the Superintendent said indifferently, as though his mind were fixed on much more important matters.

Dr. Selby-Onslow was of the type which grows pale when enraged. The blood receded from his face as he heard the Superintendent's confirmation. For a few moments he stood silent, as though digesting the intelligence.

" I begin to see a few things now," he said, at last slowly. " That wire, for instance . . . "

Ross paid no attention to him, and the doctor's comment was broken off.

" I'm interested in hearing what success you have," he went on grimly, after a pause. " Quite natural, I think. May I come down to-night and hear if you've any news ? "

" Oh, if you like," Ross conceded. " But most likely you won't find me there. This looks like being a busy evening for some of us."

" Well, I'll take my chance," said the doctor.

" And now, if you like, I'll run you down town in my car. It'll save you time."

He rang the bell, ordered the car, and gave instructions that he could see no more patients that day.

" This beggar means to hang on to us if he can," the Superintendent reflected morosely. " He seems to think he's got a claim to a front seat at the show. Not much ! "

A fresh idea seemed to cross his mind.

" Is your car fast ? " he demanded in a different tone.

" It'll do seventy-five without touching its limit," the doctor returned, with the air of a man stating a plain fact. " Do you want the loan of it ? You can have it for the asking—so long as I drive it."

" That seems fair enough," Superintendent Ross answered after a moment's reflection. " Perhaps we'll take your offer later in the evening. I'll let you know."

CHAPTER XVI

THE CHINK IN THE ARMOUR

When Dr. Selby-Onslow offered the use of his car to the police, his motive was not altogether dictated by public spirit. The discovery that Iverson intended, if possible, to make him the scapegoat in the Preston case had roused feelings which even the teachings of *Æquanimitas* were powerless to repress ; and the plain truth was that he had a lively desire to be in at the death and to witness the final defeat of the man who had done his best to ruin him. Through the evening, he waited impatiently for a message from Ross; and, at eleven o'clock, tiring of inaction, he took out his car and drove down to interview the Superintendent in the hope of extracting some fresh news.

Ross received him without enthusiasm. He was worried, and had little desire to be cross-questioned by the doctor.

"There's nothing fresh," he said concisely, in answer to Dr. Selby-Onslow's inquiries. "We haven't got on his track yet."

In spite of the obvious desire to be rid of him, the doctor sat down.

"I've nothing better to do," he explained. "I'll wait here for a short time, on the chance of something turning up. My car's outside."

Ross was about to frame a formula of polite dismissal when the telephone bell rang. The Superintendent picked up the receiver, listened without comment to the message, and then gave a few curt directions over the wire. When he turned round, the doctor saw that there had been an unpleasant surprise.

" There's been another murder," Ross said tersely.

" Iverson again ? "

" How should I know ? " Ross asked irritably. " A man's been shot at Berry's Corner on the Kempsford road. There's blood on the road ; and the body was dragged through a gate and put in behind the hedge. A young fellow and his girl, looking for a quiet spot to spoon in, stumbled on it. That's all I know."

" Iverson's get-away ? " the doctor suggested. " Perhaps he landed on someone who knew him, and took the quickest way of silencing a witness. I remember the *Spectator* once said that the one chink in the armour of civilisation was the assumption that murder won't be committed. Iverson found the chink once ; he may have got his knife through it a second time."

" I'm going down to see things," the Superintendent said. " After that, it'll be time enough to theorise."

" My car's at the door," the doctor pointed out.

" Very well, we'll take it," Ross acquiesced.

The roads were clear at that time of night ; and

in a very short time they reached the scene of the tragedy. A policeman was on guard ; and with him was a young man, the finder of the body.

" Tell your story, and be quick about it," Ross ordered, as soon as he found he had the witness before him.

The narrative which he extracted was simple to the verge of baldness, though the nervousness of the teller led to some waste of time. He and the girl had been walking along the road, looking for a quiet spot to sit down in. They had seen the gate and had turned into the field by the roadside. After walking a few yards along the back of the hedge, they had found a place that suited them, and the man had taken a newspaper from his pocket to spread over the moist grass and keep them dry when they sat down. While he was busy with this, the girl had gone a few yards farther to make sure there was no one about to disturb them ; and she had come upon the body, lying close under the hedge. She had screamed; and they had both run out on to the road in search of help. A police patrol happened to come along and they had gasped out their story. The girl had been sent home, and the man had been kept. He and the patrol had gone to the nearest house and tele- phoned to the police-station. Then they had come back to the body to await assistance.

Superintendent Ross listened in silence ; then, pulling a flash-lamp from his pocket, he ordered the policeman to show him the bloodstains on the road. They were plain enough, a large patch and a smaller

one, showing plainly enough on the sticky surface
on the near side of the highway on the road out from
the city.

" Did you hear a shot as you came up ? " he
demanded, turning to the witness.

" After we found the body, I sort of recollected
I'd heard something like a bang—but it might have
been a motor back-firing. It didn't strike me at the
time, only afterwards when we found the body ;
because there was a motor standing just about here
as we came round the corner, yonder, and it drove
off before we came up."

" Away from town, you mean ? It didn't pass
you ? "

" No. It was a saloon car, that's all I saw of it ;
and I only saw that because I could make out its
outline against the glare of its headlights on the road
in front as it was standing. I didn't pay any attention
to it, for what's a car on the road ? I didn't see its
number or anything like that—too far off, even if
I'd wanted to ; and, besides, I'd never have thought
of making a note of it. It was just a car that had
stopped, I thought."

The Superintendent turned to the policeman.

" You were coming along towards town ? Then the
car must have passed you on the road. About what
time was that ? "

" About twenty-five minutes ago, I should think.
Between that and half an hour. It was a saloon car,
as this man says."

" You didn't see the number ? "

The constable shook his head. He had no orders to stop cars, he pointed out ; and the motor had gone past him too quickly for him to see the number. In fact, he hadn't turned round to look at it, since there was nothing to excite his suspicions.

" Where's this place you telephoned from ? " Ross demanded.

The constable indicated a big house close at hand.

" This looks like the ambulance," the Superintendent said, as a pair of headlights gleamed in the misty air between them and the city. " You can stand by and tell them what's what. Say I've gone on. Now, doctor, we'll get on to the 'phone, if you'll drive me up there."

The household were all wide awake when they arrived, having been put on the alert by the earlier visit from the constable. The Superintendent went to the telephone and gave detailed instructions. When he came back to the car, he hesitated for a moment.

" Care to see it through now ? " he asked the figure at the wheel.

" Of course. Get in. Where next ? " the doctor answered at once. " You're out to chase him, I suppose ? Well, I can drive as fast as you care to. There's plenty of petrol in the tank, and, unless he's got a racer, I'll guarantee to give him a run for his money."

Superintendent Ross gave a sigh of relief, and busied himself with some arrangement on the roof above Dr. Selby-Onslow's head.

" You needn't hurry too much at the start," he

pointed out. " We've got to get our information as we go along. Stop if a police patrol waves to you. I've fixed my flashlight on the top of the saloon, so that they can recognise this car as it comes up to them."

He got into the seat beside the doctor, and the car moved off.

" Whether it's Iverson or not, this murderer has between half an hour and forty minutes start of us," the Superintendent calculated. " He won't want to drive too fast, for fear of attracting attention. Say thirty miles an hour. That puts him some twenty miles away from here, probably, by this time."

" Somewhere round about that," the doctor confirmed. " If we do forty, including slowing down here and there for information, we could pick him up in three hours."

" Yes, if we knew exactly where to look for him," Ross remarked drily. " It's not so easy to locate a man at a moment's notice in a thousand square miles of country, with the available area growing as he goes forward. Here's what I've done."

He seemed to go over his plan of campaign in his mind before outlining it to the doctor.

" The coast's over yonder," he said, with a gesture to the right. " A motor won't help him there ; and I've got to take the risk of his having a boat ready somewhere. I don't think it's likely. That reduces his possible hiding-area by about half. All the railway-stations are watched already ; every booking-clerk and ticket-collector has his description, for we

241

put that through to them as soon as he slipped between our fingers. His best hope would be to reach
one of the biggest towns and conceal himself there
temporarily. But he's no luggage with him. To go
to an hotel would be to ask for trouble. Railways
and hotels, then, are off the map."

The doctor nodded in agreement with this reasoning.

" That stolen car is his weak point and his strong
card all in one," the Superintendent went on. " It
makes him free of a wide area ; but it's also the best
identification-ticket from our point of view. If he
sticks to it, he's labelled ; if he leaves it behind and
takes to Shanks's mare, then he can't go far, and
the car's sure to be spotted. Then he'll be located
in quite a small area. If he leaves it near a big town,
it's sure to be picked up almost at once. His best
chance would be to make for open country as far
off as possible ; scupper the car in some out-of-the-
way spot ; and then go on as a man on a walking-
tour who's sent his luggage in advance and hasn't
made up on it."

" That sounds logical enough," the doctor admitted, " but there are a lot of assumptions in it."

" It's all assumptions together. But one must have
some basis for a working scheme. Now our best
chance is to get on his track and run him down at
once. The telephone wires all up and down the
country are buzzing with orders just now. We're
going to fling out the full force we can gather on all
the roads and question every car that passes. One

242

can always ask for a driving-licence as an excuse for stopping them. Any car that refuses to stop will have its number and description taken ; and that information will be sent along the road ahead. In that way, we ought to be able to draw a circle round him and know roughly within ten miles of the spot where he is."

" You see a flaw in that scheme," the doctor commented. " Your tone gives you away."

" There is a flaw," the Superintendent admitted frankly, " and it's a flaw I don't like thinking about. What's to hinder him changing cars by doing what he did already. It's evident that he signalled that poor devil to stop, and, as soon as the man got out and came over to see what was wrong, Iverson shot him dead. Suppose he stops his car, pretends to be in trouble, signals a fresh driver to stop, and treats him the same way ? That would give him a second car, and all our identification would be wasted. That's what's worrying me. Here ! Pull up ! There's a patrol signalling to us."

The doctor brought the car to a standstill and a constable came up towards them.

" I'm Superintendent Ross. Got any message for me ? "

" He's past Kempsford," the man said breathlessly. " I was to tell you that a constable stopped him and asked for his licence just beyond High Catton. The man in the car felt in his pocket, as if he was hunting for the licence ; but he pulled out a revolver instead and shot the constable down as he stood, and then drove on, just as if the poor chap had been a dog."

" Killed ? "

" Shot in the brain, sir, almost at arm's length as he stood at the side of the car. They don't think he'll recover consciousness before he dies."

The Superintendent made an inarticulate sound of sympathy.

" Drive on, doctor," he ordered. " We'll stop at Kempsford for news."

When Dr. Selby-Onslow let the car out again, Ross found the driving fast enough to suit even his eagerness for haste. The doctor seemed to know every inch of the road ; and he had not been making an idle boast when he praised the speed of his car. Almost before the Superintendent expected it, they ran into Kempsford and drew up before the police station. As Ross ran up the steps, Campden came out of his room into the hall.

" You've thrown out these patrols on the roads, I suppose ? " Ross demanded.

" We've got a screen of them all round the area where the swine's car must be ; and behind them we're calling up others in the farther districts. Every available man's on the roads now ; and we've re-cruited a fair number of unofficial helpers as well. I've done as you suggested : all cars trying to enter the patrolled area are being turned back and sent round-about ; and every driver's been warned not to stop for any car in distress, even if he's signalled to do so. By this time, that car must be almost the only one inside the ring of the patrols. Of course, I've sent out several cars to chase him."

Superintendent Ross smiled grimly.

" I've got a car outside that'll probably manage to give your fellows a few miles start and a good run for their money. I mean to take the brute myself, if it's possible. By the way, lend me a pistol, will you ? I came away in such a hurry that I haven't got one with me."

Campden opened a drawer and handed over a heavy revolver together with a packet of cartridges.

" We'll have to do something drastic," Ross said decisively. " I want him kept on the main roads, if possible. That gives us a fair chance of running him down, instead of having to dodge about through all the lanes in the county. Could your patrols lay down broken glass at the entrances to side-roads just ahead of him—all round the circle of the patrol ? If he runs into that, it'll scupper his tyres, and then we have him. If he spots it the first time, it'll make him chary of going into any side-road, for he might find glass on the fairway a mile down the road, for all he knows, and have to waste time in coming back to the high road again. Fix that at any cost, as quick as you can."

" That'll take some doing," Campden commented. " But I'll see about it. Anything else ? "

" Give me a couple of spare flash-lamp batteries for my roof-light. Tell your patrols to signal me their whereabouts, but not to stop me at any cost. I'll

pull up if I want news. There's the 'phone, Campden.
Just see if there's anything on the wire before I clear
out."

In a few moments Campden returned with fresh
news.

"They seem to have located him temporarily,
just beyond Levendale," he reported. "That's about
thirty miles out from here on the Fenminster road.
His car's a dark blue Austin saloon, numbered JX
6365. He was travelling fairly fast, but nothing out
of the common."

Superintendent Ross considered for a moment or
two.

"You'd better get the side-roads blocked first,"
he decided. "Then, once we've got him hemmed
in and kept to the main road, you'd better lay down
a heavy lot of broken glass right across his main track
and stop him, once for all. Another thing, Campden,
don't let any patrol try to tackle him. They'd simply
get shot for their pains. Once we get him pinned
down, it'll be time to think of taking him. I hope
to see to that end of the business myself, if I can get
to the spot in time."

He hurried out to the waiting car and gave Dr.
Selby-Onslow the gist of what he had heard.

"You can drive for all you're worth," he ended.
"You're not likely to meet anything on the road
now."

Once they were clear of the Kempsford streets,
there was no reason to complain of lost time. Like
a huge projectile, the car hurtled through the night,

its headlights opening up fresh vistas in the darkness. As he lay back in his seat, the Superintendent's eye sought the faintly lit dial of the speedometer and saw the needle quivering round 70, with an occasional twitch upward towards the 80 mark. For night driving, it was far above the safety limit ; but Ross felt complete confidence in the doctor's skill.

Suddenly, ahead of them, shone the twin cones of another car travelling in the same direction as themselves. Dr. Selby-Onslow's horn roared, and in a few seconds they had shot past the first of the police cars which were on the track of the fugitive.

The Superintendent, staring down the long vista of the headlights' beams, cast his mind ahead of them. Away there in the darkness, he hoped, the great loose screen of patrols was spread out over the country, a vast net of observation around Iverson's flying car. And by this time the avenues of escape would be closing one by one, as the broken glass came down on the side-roads. In his mind's eye, Ross could see this second network coming into existence, blocking exit after exit from the trap.

In Superintendent Ross's experience, man-hunting was mainly a matter of collecting trifles of information which eventually could be fitted into place in the framework of a jig-saw puzzle. This night's work was something fresh, and he enjoyed it to the full. The exhilaration of the speed, the nervous tension born of the risks, the old hunting instinct, all combined to lift him out of his normal mood, as he listened to the swift thrum of the engine at his feet.

247

A roar from the horn, a faint swerve, a glimpse of a second car packed with uniformed men, and once more they were alone in the night, flying headlong on the track of the murderer.

Dr. Selby-Onslow, his eyes on the road ahead, made a suggestion.

"There's an A.A. box a couple of miles farther on. You might telephone from there and find out if we're still on the right road."

The Superintendent agreed ; and, when the car pulled up, the doctor handed him his key. In a couple of minutes, Ross came back and stepped into the car again.

"He's only a mile or two ahead now," was his news. "That car he picked up is no great shakes for speed. If you hustle a bit we'll run him down very soon."

On into the darkness they raced again, both infected by the spirit of recklessness engendered by this rush at high speed. Once a police patrol, by the roadside, signalled to them ; but the Superintendent ignored everything except the quarry in front. The glass was down on the roads now ; and there was no escape for the fugitive over by-ways. It could only be a question of seconds, Ross calculated, as he glanced at the dial of the speedometer.

"There he is ! "

Ahead of them, the twin cones of headlight beams showed faintly in the night air above the intervening hedges, not more than a mile away. Dr. Selby-Onslow pressed down his accelerator to the full, and the car slightly increased the speed of its rush. Superintendent Ross, revolver in hand, leaned forward with his eyes fixed upon the rapidly brightening beams of the quarry's headlights.

" Hullo ! He's slowing down. . . . He's stopped. . . . Look out ! Don't let's run into a trap ! "

The doctor swung the car round a turn in the road and brought it smoothly to a standstill. They had come on to a long straight stretch ; and the beams of their powerful headlights lit up the highway like moonlight. A hundred yards away, clearly visible in the glare, the hunted car was standing ; and from the driving-seat a figure descended in frantic haste.

" His tank's run dry," the Superintendent exclaimed, as he guessed the state of affairs. " We've got him pinned down now."

The figure turned as he spoke ; there was a flash of light ; and a bullet sang over their heads into the darkness.

" It's all right," said Dr. Selby-Onslow collectedly. " He can't see us to take aim, even if he could do anything with a revolver at that distance. He's just firing into the glare of my headlights on the chance of winging us."

A second shot whistled out of the night and smashed the windscreen in front of them, embedding itself with a thud in the back cushions of the car. No damage was done by the flying glass. In the glare of their lights they could see Iverson feverishly busy with the spare tin of petrol on the footboard of the stolen car. Revolver in hand, the Superintendent jumped down into the road.

" Wait a bit," the doctor said, checking him as he was about to hurry off. " I've got an idea. If you'll go and snipe him—put a shot through the car's tank first of all to disable it—and drive him to take cover *in* that car, not behind it, I think I can guarantee to hand him over to you without either of us being as much as scratched."

" How ? " demanded the Superintendent, surprised.

" No time to explain. Hurry up or he may escape yet. Keep him busy and drive him inside his saloon for cover. That's your part of the affair."

Ross nodded his acceptance of the directions and hastened off down the road, keeping slightly to one side. He knew that in that position he would be invisible to Iverson, since the murderer's eyes would be dazzled by the doctor's headlights. So long as he did not come directly between the lamps and the fugitive, he would be as good as invisible. At twenty yards' range he opened fire. Though he made no boast of it, the Superintendent was a good pistol-shot ; and his first bullet went clean through the spare petrol-tin, knocking it out of Iverson's hands just at the moment when he was carrying it round to refill his car tank. The murderer's revolver exploded in reply ; but, dazzled by the doctor's headlights, Iverson was firing almost at random, and the shot did not come within ten yards of Ross.

With the advantage of clear vision on his side, the

Superintendent very soon forced his antagonist to take refuge inside the saloon, from the cover of which Iverson could compete on more even terms with the marksman on the road. Ross lay down, offering a poor target, and contented himself with an occasional shot to keep Iverson engaged.

There was no sign of any action on Dr. Selby-Onslow's part. A glance backward showed the Superintendent that nothing could be perceived in the glare of the big car's headlights ; and he began to wonder what plan the doctor had in his mind to cope with the situation. Just at that moment, the great projectors began to move down the road ; and Ross, carefully calculating his tactics so as not to expose himself in the changing glare, slipped to one side, out of the way of the approaching car.

Swifter and swifter the lights bore down on him, whilst Iverson, awake to a fresh danger, turned his revolver on the new and monstrous assailant. As the car swung past Ross, he caught a glimpse of the doctor sheltering behind a rough breast-work of seat cushions and steering direct for Iverson's refuge. Then, in an instant, Selby-Onslow's car was wrapped in flame, and the Superintendent saw the driver jump for safety while the blazing wreck rushed forward like a gigantic torch. A moment later, the two cars collided with a crash. There was a tinkle of splintered glass ; and over the ruin the flames blazed up like a beacon into the night sky.

Superintendent Ross, throwing caution to the winds, darted down the road towards the bonfire.

The doctor, at whatever cost to himself, had delivered
Iverson into the hands of the hunters. Scorched,
blinded, and choked, he could be in no state to put
up a fight. And, as the Superintendent dashed up to
the wreckage, out of the furnace there struggled a
figure, with clothes afire, which staggered gropingly
towards safety.

Ross pounced on the helpless creature, beat out
the flames, and then, before Iverson had recovered
from the shock, fixed a pair of handcuffs on his wrists.

" Go and sit down by the roadside," he ordered ;
and then ran off to help the doctor.

Dr. Selby-Onslow was sitting on the road,
watching the scene by the light of the blazing
wreckage.

" It's nothing," he assured the anxious Superintendent. " I sprained my ankle in the jump, that's
all. No bones broken, so far as I can find. I see you've
got him. Is he badly damaged ? "

" Quite fit to be hanged," Ross said callously.
" I was more worried about you, lest you'd come to
smash when you jumped for it. Pity to see a fine car
like that in a blaze, though. We owe you more than
a little, in this business."

Dr. Selby-Onslow seemed to look at the matter
from a different viewpoint.

" What's a car, after all ? " he said. " I can buy
another to-morrow. If we'd waited for your re-
inforcements, he'd have shot one or two people
before we got him under. A car's cheaper than a
life, I suppose."

The Superintendent, having no possible quarrel with this mode of thinking, acquiesced with a gesture and changed the subject, since Dr. Selby-Onslow quite evidently desired no special thanks.

" You managed to engineer a grand firework display," he commented.

" I had a couple of open tins of petrol on the roof ; and a lot of the stuff sprinkled over the outside of the car. Just as I jumped off, I put a match to the open tank of my car. When the collision came, the two tins shot off on to the top of Iverson's car, and the petrol got splashed about and then caught fire. No wonder the swine found it too hot a corner for him. Is he much burned ? "

" A good bit, but nothing dangerous, I think."

The doctor stared across at the bowed figure by the roadside.

" I guess I've squared the account with him," he commented at last.

The author of *Æquanimitas* would have found the tone of voice hardly in keeping with his principles.

CHAPTER XVII

THE PIECES OF THE PUZZLE

" So you saw Iverson before they hanged him,
I heard ? "

As he spoke, Dr. Selby-Onslow pushed a box of
cigars across to the Superintendent and made a gesture of invitation towards the whisky-decanter. They
were in the doctor's study ; but the atmosphere of this
meeting was markedly different from that of their
earlier encounters.

" He asked me to visit him in the condemned
cell," Ross confirmed, as he cut the cigar he had
selected. " He was just the same, as cool as ever."

" Changed surroundings, though."

" Oh, it isn't in the least like a prison-cell, you
know," the Superintendent explained. " It's just
a sort of rather cosy sitting-room : easy chairs, books,
nice carpet, bright fire burning. Except for the two
warders on guard night and day, you'd never associate it with prison. And, of course, he was wearing
one of his own suits—no convict uniform in his case.
To tell you the truth, I felt far more embarrassed than
he appeared to be. But he managed to put me at my
ease. He wanted me to understand that he bore no
malice. Humanity's a rum contrivance, really."

The Superintendent lighted his cigar and stared at the fire for a moment or two.

"The funny thing is that I believed him," he continued. "He didn't talk any stuff about forgiving me for having brought him to the gallows ; he just took it for granted that I'd been doing the job I was paid for and that there was nothing personal in the matter at all. A very detached outlook, altogether. Then he explained he'd been adding a codicil to this will."

"Left you a legacy ? " asked the doctor, sardonically.

"The joke's on you," said the Superintendent. "He did. He's left me his criminology library."

"Well, I'm damned ! "

"That's as it may be," said Ross, echoing the doctor's sardonic tone, "but a fact's a fact. He wanted, it seems, to prove that he really bore no ill-will ; and he thought that would be a rather nice way of showing it. So it was. He knew I envied him that collection of his."

"So you shook hands and parted on the best of terms ? "

"He wanted something first."

"What was that, if one may ask ? "

"Exactly what you wanted when you asked me here to-night. He wanted to know how I'd put two and two together. Oh, one can't help having a certain respect for that side of him, even if one doesn't admire him on the whole by any means. It was a piece of pure intellectual curiosity on his part; he wanted to hear what slips he'd made."

The doctor picked up the tongs and adjusted a whistling coal on the fire.

" It's funny that the Preston murder hardly came into his trial, after all."

" Well," the Superintendent pointed out, " we had a clear case over the murder of the constable. We could prove that up to the hilt, with no chance of confusing the jury. There was no point in using the Preston case, where the evidence was far more intricate."

" That is so," admitted Dr. Selby-Onslow, putting down the tongs. " And you gave him a sketch, did you ? Then, if you don't mind, I'd like to hear the outline of it myself. You poked your finger into my affairs. Turn and turn about's fair play."

The Superintendent acknowledged the justice of this with a gesture of his hand.

" Theoretically, these things are confidential," he said, " but this case is finished, once for all ; and, besides, we owe you something for sacrificing that car of yours and probably saving a life or two by doing it. I'll tell you the story."

He leaned forward and stared absently at the fire for a few seconds, as though putting his thoughts into order.

" You're a doctor," he. began, rather unexpectedly, " and, by my way of looking at it, every doctor's a detective. You're tracking down disease, just as we're hunting down criminals. You look for symptoms and use them to guide you to the origin of your patient's trouble. You don't, perhaps, get them all at once ; but one or two at the start may set you on the right track, and then you begin searching for others, and so on, until at last you get from uncertainty to certainty It's the same with us in our line ; only what you call symptoms we call clues, and what a medical man would term diagnosis is what we call getting up a case. The method's the same, if the names are different. And that's why I expect you'll appreciate that we, in the police, don't always get straight on the track immediately. We have to worry through a lot of confusing symptoms and settle which are the important ones, before we can get to the root of the trouble—just like you, at times, I expect."

Dr. Selby-Onslow gave a judicial nod to show his acceptance of the parallelism.

" I was at Kempsford Junction when Preston's body was examined," the Superintendent continued. " It was a clear case of murder. The first rum symptom I struck was the fact that a shot from an automatic pistol, obviously fired in the carriage, hadn't had enough vim in it to penetrate the upholstery of the carriage. Then we found that Preston had been shot at with bullets of two calibres—small automatic pistol bullets and heavy revolver bullets."

Ross then outlined the facts with regard to the wounds which had been elicited at the station.

" This was a determined murder," he continued. " Now, I couldn't imagine a pair of determined murderers, one of whom took care to arm himself with a

257

pistol that would hardly shoot a dent in a pat of butter. But I could imagine, easily enough, a single murderer faking evidence to suggest that two men had taken part in the crime, because that would make it more difficult to get to the bottom of the business. Therefore, from that symptom I inferred that it was a single-handed job. And, further, since no man has a pistol loaded like that in his pocket by mere accident, it was a carefully premeditated job.

" Preston's ticket was for Hammersleigh, so it was reasonable to assume that he probably was shot before the train reached that station. The distances between the stations are short ; and, if it was a premeditated affair, then the murderer would pick out the bit of the train route that gave him most time for his dirty work. That, to my mind, limited the thing down, with fair probability, to one or two strips of line, including the stretch between Seven Sisters and Hammersleigh.

" Now, by a bit of luck, I'd just heard that very morning of a prize ram having been shot, most mysteriously, between Seven Sisters and Hammersleigh, just at the time when the 10.35 train passes over that section. That affair took place on the 16th November—exactly a week before the murder, almost to the very minute. Well, what about it ? What was to hinder this murderer travelling by the same train on the same day of the week—so that the conditions were as near as possible identical—and seeing beforehand if he could squib off his pistol without being heard in the next compartment. And naturally he'd shoot out of the window, because a bullet aimed inside the carriage would be apt to leave unfortunate traces."

" I've no quarrel with the reasoning," Dr. Selby-Onslow admitted.

" It was all pure hypothesis," the Superintendent hastened to make clear, " just as I guess some of your preliminary hunt for the seat of a disease is based on hypothesis. It's the only road open, when one knows next to nothing. In any case, it's safer to over-estimate an opponent than it is to under-estimate him. So I assumed on the face of things that I'd a pretty cool and cautious criminal to deal with.

" That made me a bit careful of accepting some things at their face value. There was a bit of a spectacle lens on the floor of the compartment. It might be one of three things. It might have belonged to Preston ; or it might have belonged to the murderer ; or it might have been planted by the murderer to incriminate a third party. It turned out not to be Preston's. Therefore it was either the murderer's or was planted by the murderer to throw suspicion on a third person."

" It was mine, I suppose ? " Dr. Selby-Onslow interjected.

" I'm coming to it by and by," said the Superintendent, holding up his hand to deprecate further inquiry at the moment. " It fits in better later on. It was apparently part of a pair of reading-glasses, so far as I could find out at the time. That's all I knew about it, except that it was a cylindro-spherical lens such as an astigmatic person might use.

" Finally, there was a bad fog on the line that morning. Now, obviously, if this affair had been planned and rehearsed so carefully, the fog was an accidental complication which couldn't have entered into the murderer's original plans. His initial scheme didn't require a fog. But, if there *was* a fog, it was just on the cards that the murderer might see his way to profit by it and diverge from his original plot. It might look like a gift from the gods, too good to waste ; and he might have dropped his cut-and-dried arrangements to take advantage of it. That had to be kept in mind."

Superintendent Ross knocked the ash off his cigar with an air of regret before pursuing his story.

" I suppose, doctor," he went on, " that you might have a patient coming to you and reeling off a lot of symptoms which made it look like a case of *angina pectoris*, while all the time it was just indigestion and nothing more ? I knew a fellow once who imagined he'd heart-disease on the strength of that. A good laugh we had at him, when the truth came out, after all the sympathy we'd wasted on him. Well, the Preston case played the same game on me ; it began to trot out a lot of clues that looked like *angina* and turned out to be nothing important after all. I'm not going to deny that I got a very bad impression from Miss Winslow, and especially that woman Poole."

" I've settled with the woman Poole," Dr. Selby-Onslow said grimly. " We discovered the sort of thing she'd been spreading abroad, and we put a stop to it—pretty sharply. There wasn't a word of truth in it. She was a pathological case, that creature. She got some obscure satisfaction out of her lies, something a bit inkier than mere spleen, you understand ? "

The Superintendent hastened to get off the thin ice.

" Apart from all the misleading stuff, I did get three points of importance at that juncture," he went on, without giving the doctor a chance of amplifying his statements. " The first was about Preston's slavery to routine ; and, of course, that made it clear how the murderer could reckon so firmly on a fixed plan, drawn up a week ahead at least. But that implied that the murderer was someone who knew Preston fairly well—well enough to bank on the routine as part of his scheme. Unfortunately, that was rather a wash-out as a clue, for everybody seemed to know about his methods : the household, the people at the bank, all his employees here and at Hammersleigh. Still, it was always something.

" Then there was the missing money point. Every week he took down the factory wages on Friday morning by the 10.35 train. We found no trace of any such sum on the body or in the railway carriage. Obviously, since he was an absolute slave to routine, he must have had that money with him when he left Horston ; and it disappeared *en route*. Now many a man will commit a cold-blooded murder for far less cash than the sum Preston had with him. And, whether the murder was done for the sake of the cash or not, the murderer had evidently got rid of the money somehow or other. If we could get on to the money, it was bound to lead us somewhere in the murderer's direction at least."

Dr. Selby-Onslow, sunk back in his chair in his favourite attitude, examined his joined finger-tips in the pause which the Superintendent made in his narrative at this point.

" You certainly hadn't got very far at that stage," he commented.

" I'd been at work for exactly six hours, including the time I spent on the railway, coming in from Kempsford Junction," the Superintendent retorted. " I don't profess to work by divination, you know. And my clues aren't all collected together in the carcase of a patient, as yours are. I've got to hunt for them over a widish stretch of country at times."

" I didn't mean to be sarcastic," the doctor assured him, in a slightly less superior tone. " I was merely stating what seemed obvious."

" The last point of the three," Ross went on, ignoring the explanation, " wasn't of much apparent value at the time. I learned that Preston was one of two trustees for the estate of Miss Winslow ; and the remaining trustee was Iverson. That put me on to Iverson, naturally, as a man who might give me some pointers about Preston's personal affairs ; and I went off to see him at once.

" What I learned about Iverson you could put in a nutshell. He had an excellent library on crime ;

he'd had his car stolen from Oxenden Grange that morning ; he'd been down there by a previous appointment to see a contractor about some alterations, an appointment which he'd fixed himself; and he'd seen Preston in the railway carriage before the train started. He confirmed the statement that he was a joint-trustee with Preston. Later, he told me that he had witnessed Preston's will, so obviously he couldn't profit by any legacy from Preston.

"What I noticed about Iverson's talk was that he seemed very ready with theories about how the murder came about, very ready indeed, considering that he'd only got the news of it, presumably, from me at the beginning of our interview. Of course, he might have had a fertile mind. . . . And he had the Dickman case and the Barrême case—both of 'em train murders—on the tip of his tongue. Not very surprising, perhaps, since he was an amateur criminologist ; but it just happened to strike me at the moment.

"Then he threw out, quite casually, a hint that Preston's sight was quite normal and that he had a fad about not reading in the train. Curious that he should have volunteered that, for no one had said a word to him about the broken lens we found in the carriage. It might have been coincidence, of course. None of these points meant anything, if you took it by itself ; it was when you put them all together and added up the total that he seemed to be—well, a bit lucky in his subjects.

"His next line was to implicate you, doctor. He

did it most artistically—let me drag it out of him, pretending to be reluctant about it and throwing all sorts of cold water on the mere notion that you had anything to do with the business. *But*, he managed to suggest that you'd got into the train somewhere close to Preston ; and he was careful to insinuate that your attaché-case was big enough to hold Preston's one. He meant to make sure that you got into the limelight and that we'd turn our attention to you as soon as possible."

Dr. Selby-Onslow shifted in his chair as though even in retrospect these machinations vexed him.

" And I suppose you took his hint ? That accounts for your descent on me, shortly afterwards."

" I took the hint," the Superintendent agreed. " Why not ? *You* don't ignore the eruption in the case of smallpox, merely because it's unpleasant, do you ? Why should I ignore evidence because there seems to be animus behind it ? It may be sound in spite of the animus. But, as a matter of fact, some things cropped up before I went to see you.

" First there was the bank information, from which I learned that Preston had a packet of marked notes with him, in addition to the normal cash for the factory wages. Naturally we took steps to get these marked notes reported, if they turned up in circulation.

" Then there was the whole railway side of the case. One of my men—you saw him, Mornington— took that over and managed to identify fifty-two passengers on the 10.35. He also proved that fifty-two tickets had been surrendered up the line at various stations. That meant that, if the murderer had surrendered a ticket, he must be among these fifty-two individuals. But, unfortunately, there was that fog on the line ; and the murderer might have left the train under cover of it, in which case he would not have given up his ticket. But, as Mornington accounted for all the tickets sold that morning before the 10.35 left, the murderer didn't buy a ticket before getting into the train. And yet, since this was a carefully prearranged crime, it was evident that the murderer must have had a ticket of some sort. He couldn't afford to draw attention to himself by being caught ticketless. Ergo, he would provide himself beforehand with the half of a return ticket from some station up the line, a return half which would be available on any day and would leave no trace of its purchase in connection with the crime."

" That seems sound enough," Dr. Selby-Onslow admitted. " I'd no idea you went into things so thoroughly as all that."

" The next stage was the visit I paid you. Out of it, if you remember, I got the information about the forged telegram and the cutting of Dr. Whitacre's telephone wire. I also got a copy of the telegram typed on your machine ; and I broke your reading-glasses."

" You did," said Dr. Selby-Onslow, " and for the life of me I couldn't see why. It looked like gratuitous clumsiness."

" I got the prescription for them from your spectacle-maker by that means ; and one of your glasses was identical with the broken lens found in Preston's carriage."

Dr. Selby-Onslow was unprepared for this.

" How the devil could it be ? " he demanded.

" You'll see in due course. But what struck me as curious was that it was a lens from *reading*-glasses. You wear a different pair of spectacles for normal work. If you were the murderer, and these glasses had been broken in a struggle in the carriage, how did you come to be wearing reading-glasses when your normal glasses would suit the business so much better ? It looked a bit queer.

" As to the typewriter, I compared my own copy of the decoy telegram with the typewritten original which I got from Morpledene post office—the thing that was sent to them by post and which they tele-graphed on to you first thing in the morning—and I found they'd both been typed on your machine. The characteristics were identical in the two.

" Now, either you had typed the decoy yourself, or else it had been typed by someone who had access to your machine. That was plain. If you were the murderer, you might have typed it yourself, not knowing how easily the work of a particular machine can be identified. But you certainly wouldn't voluntarily have dropped a bit of your reading-glasses in the carriage. Question arose : Was there anyone else who had access to your glasses and to your typewriter ? And, you remember, you told me that you'd lost your reading-glasses not so long before. That didn't clear you ; for you might have broken your glasses in the carriage and tried to cover up the business by saying you'd lost them. Still, it made me think a bit.

" Then some of the marked notes began to crop up ; and we laid our hands on a poor devil—a late employee of Preston's—who'd stolen them. He'd been on the 10.35 and saw Preston's attaché-case thrown out of the window between Seven Sisters and Hammersleigh ; and he walked back from Hammersleigh and picked up the case at the side of the rails. That pinned down the murder to the place I'd been betting on. Further, this poor devil was able to tell me that the fog was thick enough there to hide a man easily enough. So, obviously, the murderer might have left the train without attracting notice. And the train stopped shortly before it came to Hammersleigh station. After that, it was plain enough that the murderer wasn't necessarily among the fifty-two passengers identified by Mornington. He might have got on to the train with a return half of a ticket which would frank him through if a ticket-inspector came along ; and he might have got off in the mist without having to surrender any ticket at all."

" In fact, a fresh factor coming in and disturbing all the bits of the jigsaw puzzle you'd just succeeded in fitting together so neatly—the identification of the passengers, the tickets purchased and surrendered, and so forth ? "

" Precisely. I had to reconsider the whole business and take into account a person who, before that, we ' knew ' wasn't on the train. Question was : if there was such a person, who was the most likely man ? What was the motive, if all the identified people on the train were ruled out ? And then I couldn't help remembering that Preston's death left Iverson as sole trustee for Miss Winslow and gave him complete control of her money until she was twenty-five. That *might* be a motive. It was worth following up, anyhow.

" Then another thing struck me. All the places of importance in the case lay near together. There was Oxenden Grange, where Iverson had been to meet the contractor that morning ; there was the point on the line where the murder was committed ; there was the spot where the attaché-case was flung out of the window into a clump of bushes ; there was Whitacre's house, where the telephone line had been cut ; there was Hammersleigh station, near which this hypothetical murderer must have got off the train. On a motoring map, you could cover the lot of them with a half-crown, almost. That seemed suggestive, somehow, though at the time I couldn't be sure it amounted to much.

" I went off to pay a second visit to Iverson, posing as a simple soul—a bit out of my depth—and asking for his help in the matter of the typing of the decoy telegram. He reacted better than I'd hoped. I suppose he thought I'd fairly played into his hands by going to him for advice ; and he gave me the help I asked for. *But*, I noticed, he was able to turn at once to the very page in one of his books which dealt with forged typewriting—no hesitation of any sort, no considering where he'd find the best account of the matter. No, he just opened the book at the right place, read me a bit, and then turned back to another reference three hundred pages away, without a hitch. I think it's a fair inference that he'd been studying that very point himself not long before. Now nothing had leaked out in public about your decoy telegram, so he couldn't have been looking up the matter out of curiosity, with his attention attracted to it by some newspaper account. So it looked as if he'd had his own reasons for familiarising himself with the problem of forged typewriting not long before. No proof, of course, but another bit fitting in with what I had already ; that's all it amounted to.

" Then he asked a question which pointed in the same direction. He wanted to know if I'd got the envelope that the decoy telegram had been enclosed in when it was posted. He wanted to know definitely if that risk was eliminated, you see ? Probably he used gloves when he handled that envelope ; but there was always the chance he might have left some traces, and it was a relief to him to hear positively that the thing had been lost and couldn't be traced back to him by any means. Just another straw, you see ?

" After that, he began to direct my attention to you again, playing the same game as before. If he'd

269

brought out the matter of Preston's divorce action at our first interview, it might have looked too plain that he was turning the searchlight in your direction. He was cleverer than that. He knew that creature Poole would babble the thing out to us, so he sat tight and waited till I asked him point-blank about it. That gave the impression that I'd had to drag it out of him against his will, and heightened the effect of the evidence. But, once he started, he was quite free with the information—told me all about it in detail, and explained most carefully what a hole you'd be in if Preston won a divorce action with you as co-respondent. In fact, he made it seem quite worth your while to put Preston out of the way before the case got under way."

"I'm not so sure about that," said Dr. Selby-Onslow drily. "The woman Poole might have been glib enough with her lies to satisfy a man who wanted to believe her; but she wouldn't have stood cross-examination for ten minutes in the witness-box. It was a pack of lies from start to finish."

The Superintendent had no desire to discuss this side of the matter; it was no affair of his.

"Well, to get on with my story," he continued, "Iverson painted a pretty black picture, but he was careful not to accuse you in the most indirect way. In fact, as a counterpiece, he set up an absurd—purposely absurd, I think—sketch of how the whole affair might have been a case of suicide. Deadly moderation was his cue, you see?

" But, in elaborating his tale, he made just one slip, though I don't suppose he knew he was doing it. He volunteered that he was a patient of yours. And that was the thing I particularly wanted to know just then. Quite casually, I asked him when he'd seen you, and he admitted he'd been at your house on 15th November. The obvious question was : Had he then got access to your typewriter and your reading-glasses ? If so, then things looked as if they would fit together fairly neatly. Dr. Whitacre's telephone wire, you remember, was cut on the evening of the 22nd, and it was the first overt move in the game that culminated in the Preston murder. That move implied that the murderer had already had access to your typewriter and had in his pocket the decoy telegram, which he must have typed in your study. If he had not, there was no point in cutting the wire.

" But before I could take up that line of inquiry, some fresh evidence dropped in from a new quarter. We got hold of Tenbury, the contractor for the alterations at Oxenden Grange ; and he testified that, when he drove up to the gate of the house at noon on the day of the murder, he found Iverson's car already there, and Iverson had just opened the big gates to let the cars through. They left the two cars standing there, and went up to the house on foot. Meanwhile, two fellows came along and lifted Iverson's car.

" We caught these chaps, and one of them squealed without too much persuasion. He described exactly how they'd driven off in Iverson's car, and he told us, just in passing and with no stress on the point, that they'd had difficulty in getting Iverson's car to start. The engine was stone-cold."

Dr. Selby-Onslow's eyebrows lifted.

" Stone-cold ? " he demanded.

" Stone-cold was the word he used. Well . . . could any engine be stone-cold immediately after having been driven for twenty miles or more ? Not without a special intervention of Providence. But it *was* stone-cold. Therefore it hadn't been driven twenty miles out from Horston that morning. And therefore Iverson's story of his doings had a hole in it fit to sink a battleship. That car had never been in Horston that morning at all ; and Iverson had come from Horston to Oxenden Grange by some other means. It stared one in the face. At that point, I knew who had murdered Preston. I'd guessed it before, but now I was certain. But I was still without definite proof that would satisfy a jury.

" Now at that point I tried to put myself in Iverson's place, bearing in mind that this affair had been carefully planned in advance. He'd fixed his appointment with Tenbury at Oxenden Grange for noon—obviously to provide an excuse for being in the Hammersleigh neighbourhood just after the murder, in case he was recognised by anyone. Well, if I had just committed a murder, the first thing I'd think about would be changing my clothes in case a splash of blood had got on to them without my noticing it. So it seemed to me likely, though not proved by any means, that Iverson would want to change into a fresh suit before meeting Tenbury, so as to be on the safe side. Where could he effect that change? Obviously at Oxenden Grange; it was the only place. And, for that, he'd have to arrive before Tenbury turned up at the Grange.

" Normally, the 10.35 got into Hammersleigh at 11.22, which gave him just sufficient time to walk over to the Grange, and get ready for Tenbury's visit. But on the day of the murder the train was held up by fog, which meant that Iverson was behind his time-table. That was why he diverged from his pre-arranged plan and slipped off the train when it stopped at the signal before Hammersleigh. By that means he saved time and had a shorter distance to walk to the Grange.

" Since he came by train, and since Tenbury saw him with his car at the gate of the Grange, it was clear enough that the car must have been left at the Grange —in the garage—overnight. And, further, since Tenbury was going over the Grange, Iverson couldn't leave his clothes lying about there. He'd do his changing in the garage and put the discarded suit into a bag or suit-case in the car, where it wouldn't strike Tenbury as odd, even if he happened to notice the case at all. Then he'd drive his car out of the garage down to the gate, and arrange things so that when the contractor came up, it would look as though Iverson had just arrived from town that moment."

" That's a very neat attempt at an alibi," Dr.
Selby-Onslow commented judicially.

" It was neat enough to take me in—for a time,"
the Superintendent admitted. " It seemed quite all
right. But the car thief's evidence about the engine
being stone-cold killed it at one stroke. Also, I found
fresh oil on the garage floor, showing that a car had
stood there not long before. And, what was more
serious for Iverson, I guessed that the car thieves
must have got away with more than the car itself.
They must have stolen Iverson's clothes as well, if
my notions were correct, for he would stow the suit
away in his car after changing.

" Without details, I may say that we got hold of
that suit of clothes eventually. One of the car thieves
had disposed of it to an old clothes dealer. There
was a small stain on the lining of one of the pockets.
The experts say it's a bloodstain. The suit itself we
got identified by Iverson's tailor. Finally, in the
ticket-pocket of the jacket, I found two first-class
railway tickets : one was a return half for the journey
between Horston and Hammersleigh, the other was
a return half for a journey between Seven Sisters
and Hammersleigh. They'd obviously been over-
looked ; and that fitted in with the notion that Iverson had changed his plans at the last moment and
had forgotten these tickets owing to his divergence
from the pre-arranged scheme. And there was another point about these tickets : each of them had
been nicked with scissors to represent a ticket
snipped by a collector's punch. Finally, each of

these tickets had the date 16th November stamped on it."

" I don't quite follow that bit," Dr. Selby-Onslow admitted."

" I'll put the whole story together in a minute, if you'll just wait," Superintendent Ross assured him. " I want to give you all the evidence first. The final point was given by you and your nurse, the last time I was here. Your evidence made it clear that, when Iverson called as a patient on 15th November, he insisted on being shown in here and not into the usual waiting-room. That gave him undisturbed access to your typewriter ; and he also picked up your reading-glasses—probably an after-thought to strengthen the case against you. To my mind, that clinched the business ; and I ordered his arrest. The rest of the story you know by this time."

" Could you put it all in chronological order ? " the doctor asked. " I'd just like to see if I've got the evidence fitted together properly."

He made a gesture towards the decanter, and Ross recharged his glass.

" To get the start of things," he went on, in answer to the doctor's request, " you have to go back a good way before the murder. We've been through Iverson's books and so forth ; and it's clear that he had been misappropriating some of his clients' money ever since he became sole controller of his firm on the death of his senior partner. Things didn't go right with his affairs, and he dipped deeper and deeper into various accounts, until at last it became a serious matter. Some of these embezzlements were bound to come to light unless he could find enough money to repay his withdrawals.

" Miss Winslow's affairs offered him the chance of staving off disaster. If he could dip into that fortune of hers, he could replace the money he'd embezzled from other clients before any trouble arose. But Preston was his co-trustee for the Winslow estate ; and Preston was, as everyone knew, a stickler for routine and a man with a very careful mind where cash was concerned. Iverson knew quite well that, so long as Preston was alive, the Winslow estate was the last possible thing he could afford to play hanky-panky with. But suppose Preston died, what then ? Miss Winslow doesn't become a trustee till she's twenty-five, and she's only twenty-one or twenty-two at present. For three years, Iverson would be in sole control of the estate and could embezzle to his heart's content. And there was enough there to pay off all his previous thefts. Miss Winslow's only a girl ; he'd ingratiated himself with her ; and he could make himself even better liked by increasing her allowance, which Preston had insisted on cutting down to the lowest limit. After that, it wasn't likely she would take any very direct interest in her financial affairs as a whole. He was pretty safe.

" My impression is that for a time he funked the business, simply because the risk seemed too big. Preston had no open enemy. The factory wages were the only things that seemed likely to serve as a blind. And, in that case, the murder would have to be done on the journey between Horston and Hammersleigh. Iverson had thought it over, and looked up the Barrême and Dickman cases as guides to procedure —as he betrayed in one of his interviews with me. But my impression is that he wanted a better red herring than the money before he would take the chance.   •

" Then, out of the blue, came Preston with his plans for a divorce suit, with you as co-respondent. Here was a second red herring positively thrust into his hands, ready-made. A successful divorce suit would have broken you, doctor. It looked like a perfectly sound motive for murder. So obviously the thing was to cast you for the part of stalking-horse and pile up evidence against you. And, if you cleared yourself there was always the factory cash as a second choice to bemuse the police with."

Superintendent Ross picked up his glass and sipped his whisky and soda appreciatively.

" Iverson must have worked tremendously hard in that week," he went on. " He had to plan everything swiftly and carry it into execution immediately, before Preston got completely out of hand over the divorce case ; for the essence of the affair was to make it seem that you had murdered Preston to avoid even a whisper of such a thing getting abroad. Once it was public property, you see ? you'd never have dared to murder Preston—a bit too obvious. And Iverson wanted a plausible case against you. So he had to hurry. Here's a time-table of his doings which will give you some notion of the affair "

Superintendent Ross felt in his pocket and produced a slip of paper, which he passed across to the doctor.

Monday, 12th Nov. : Divorce case broached by Preston.

Tuesday, 13th Nov. : Poole gives her evidence to Preston and Iverson.

Wednesday, 14th Nov. : Miss Winslow lets Iverson know that she has heard of project, and so he is sure that Dr. Selby-Onslow also has heard of it.

Thursday, 15th Nov. : Iverson visits Dr. Selby-Onslow as a patient and secures reading-glasses as well as writing the decoy telegram on the doctor's machine.

Friday, 16th Nov. : Iverson carries out rehearsal of the murder, travelling on the 10.35 and accidentally shooting the ram. At Hammersleigh, on the way back, he buys the two tickets.

Saturday, 17th Nov. : Iverson arranges his meeting with Tenbury at Oxenden Grange.

Thursday, 22nd Nov. : Iverson goes out in his car, cuts Dr. Whitacre's telephone wire, posts the decoy telegram, and leaves his car in the garage at Oxenden Grange, returning home by rail.

Friday, 23rd Nov. : Murder of Preston.

Dr. Selby-Onslow read carefully through the schedule point by point before making any comment.

" If he thought all that out between the 12th and the 14th, he must have done some quick planning," he said, at last. " Of course, most of it was directed towards manœuvring me on to the 10.35 train that morning. Rather neatly contrived, one has to admit it. And, another thing. I notice that he planned the whole business so that he wasn't committed in any way up to the very moment when he fired his first shot. If anything unforeseen interfered with his plans, at any stage in his game, he could simply stop short and there was nothing to incriminate him. One must give him good marks for ingenuity, whatever one thinks of his moral character."

He paused for a moment, and then added :

"But this leaves out the main point. How did he get on to the train at all ? "

" That was obvious enough," the Superintendent explained. "If it hadn't been for his alibi with the car and Tenbury at Oxenden Grange, the thing would have been transparent, once we began to consider him at all in the light of a possible criminal. I saw in a moment how he could have managed it. But, seeing a thing like that's no use; we've got to convince a jury. That was what held me up."

" Well, how did he manage it ? "

" Dead simple. He came to the station with his two return halves of tickets in his pocket. He took a platform ticket and went up the train to speak to Preston. Five minutes before the train started, he left the platform by the same gate as he came on to it, taking good care to attract the ticket-examiner's attention as he did so, and thus provide a witness who'd swear that he passed out through the barrier.

Then he hurried out of the front entrance to the station ; took off his overcoat ; hid his soft felt hat in it as he carried it over his arm ; put on a soft cloth cap he'd had in his pocket ; and walked down King Street to Campbell Street, and so to the low-level entrance to the station, at the front end of the platform. He passed the low-level barrier with a second platform ticket. Then he joined Preston in his carriage, and that was that. If a ticket-inspector dropped on him on any part of the journey up to Seven Sisters, he had his ticket to Hammersleigh in his pocket, faked to represent a ticket which had been clipped at the barrier. After the murder, he planned to give up the other ticket at Hammersleigh—the ticket from Seven Sisters—so as to confuse his trail if we took to investigating the sale and collection of tickets, as we did in practice. But, when the fog came down, he probably jumped at the chance of getting clear away without leaving any ticket at all, as well as saving some time by getting out near Oxenden Grange, since the train was late."

The doctor seemed rather sceptical at this part of the narrative.

"You seem very sure of your ground there," he remarked.

"It's Iverson's own account of his doings," the Superintendent countered, with a hardly suppressed grin. "I asked him about it, and that's what he told me."

"It seems to me he took a devil of a risk," Dr. Selby-Onslow commented.

" So does every murderer," Superintendent Ross declared bluntly. "Besides, it wasn't so big a risk as you'd think. While he was standing at the window of Preston's carriage, he'd taken a careful look round to make sure that no friend of his was on the platform. Once you were in your compartment, you weren't likely to see him through those frost-covered windows. The only other person likely to give evidence against him was the low-level ticket-examiner whom he passed when he came to the platform a second time. But ticket-examiners are there to look at tickets, not at the people who present them. Besides, he'd altered his appearance in its most salient points, even if the man did look at him in passing. And he took care to pass the man along with two other people who were going up to the train. The risk was very small, really. As it happened, the ticket-examiner on the low-level entrance was a stupid sort of man who could give us no help when we questioned him. And Iverson had another bit of luck as well. Miss Winslow might have recognised him. But she came on to the platform while he was walking round by King Street ; and she was in a hurry to see you and get away again before Preston spotted her ; so by the time Iverson appeared at the front end of the platform she'd finished her errand to you and had gone away again,"

He picked up his glass again, suggesting by the gesture that he had finished his story. But, when he had taken a drink, a fresh thought seemed to strike him, and he swung round to face his host.

" What I couldn't make out about him," he said slowly, " was why he went out of his way to assert that Mrs. Preston had nothing whatever to do with the affair. His game was to mix up as many suspects in the business as possible. Why did he take pains to clear her ? For I could see quite plainly that he meant what he said on that point. One couldn't mistake the ring of it."

Dr. Selby-Onslow sat up in his chair.

" You're by way of being a student of human nature," he said, with a tingle of irony in his tone. " It shouldn't be beyond you to fit another bit on to the puzzle. Iverson was a bit in love with Mrs. Preston. She wouldn't have anything to do with him ; but she managed to keep him friendly in spite of that. Naturally that made him observant where she was concerned ; and he saw well enough that she liked me better than himself. So you can add personal jealousy to your motives when you come to his plans for making me his scapegoat. I suppose he thought that, if I were out of the way permanently, he might still have a chance of getting hold of her for himself. A case of literally killing two birds with one stone, you might say. And I think that may enlighten you as to why I was so ready to smash up my car in order to ensure that we got him."